THE OUTRIDER

C. R. JAHN

ISBN 978-1-62646-697-5

Published by BookLocker.com, Inc., Bradenton, Florida.

Printed in the United States of America on acid-free paper.

BookLocker.com, Inc.
2013

First Edition

AUTHOR'S NOTE

This will be unlike anything you've ever read.

Supposedly, my book belongs in some subgenre of dark urban fantasy, but there are no vampires or elves here, no paranormal romance, and certainly no whimsy. Indeed, the core theme seems to be bleakness and despair, with a plot involving demonic possession on a mass scale, targeting Denver's street people, transforming them into a covert paramilitary force in preparation for some unknown objective. Perhaps it would be best to think of it as magickal realism with a hard edge, similar to noir. I anticipate poor reviews simply due to the tone and subject matter.

The concept of "perfect possession," as elucidated by Malachi Martin in *Hostage to the Devil*, resonated with me, as it rang true with my own personal observations of functional psychopaths who seemed to be either psychically gifted or exceptionally lucky. Sara Gran's fictional depiction of the demonic in *Come Closer* also proved a strong influence, as well as Thomas Ligotti's dreamlike tales of an inescapable supernatural malevolence.

I spoke with a number of clairvoyants about their experiences interacting with the demonic, and one commonality was the illusion of dramatic facial change, like a ghostly mask appearing over the face of the possessed. Hundreds of personal accounts, both modern and centuries old, speak of several distinct demonic races, and describe the physical and mental effects of having such an entity focus its attention on you. The way I've chosen to depict the demonic in this fictional work stays fairly true to that research, although of course I have indulged in a number of artistic liberties.

The mysterious and seemingly contradictory nature of the demonic is confusing. By extension, many aspects of this story may also seem confusing. The protagonist only sees part of the puzzle, as the spirits he interacts with choose to keep much concealed as they use him as a pawn towards their own ends. As a result, a great deal remains unexplained, which could at times be interpreted as "plot holes," although upon a second reading it may make more sense.

Many of the characters are composites based upon individuals I've met, but none are modeled entirely on any one person. Most of the addresses and businesses are actual places here in Denver. *Max's* does not exist (although there is a *Conoco* a few blocks away from where it should be) and the Temple's address is a vacant lot, so don't bother looking for either.

Angelo's was a family run pizzeria which indeed made the best pizza in Denver, but sadly they recently sold to a young entrepreneur who destroyed the wood fired pizza oven in an effort to "modernize" and quality suffered accordingly. *Smiley's Discount Laundromat* on Colfax also closed their doors while the story was being writ. I elected not to change either location in the final draft, as both feature prominently herein.

Demonology is an interesting subject, especially when you take a non-denominational cross-cultural approach. I've studied it for over thirty years and make no pretense of understanding it, because it's complex and multifaceted. Names, ranks, and correspondences seem largely subjective, if not irrelevant, but are included for artistic purposes as well as clarity. This book, in its entirety, is a work of fiction, and certainly not intended as any sort of theological or metaphysical treatise.

C. R. Jahn
Denver, Colorado
October, 2013.

Acknowledgements

Gratitude and respect to Cayora Rue and Halie Koehler. I would never have finished this project without your perseverance and support. Thank you.

PART ONE

"Doesn't have arms, but it knows how to use them. Doesn't have a face, but it knows where to find one."

– Thomas Ligotti, "The Shadow at the Bottom of the World"

I follow the path through the woods until it opens into a clearing. It is the greenest grass I've ever seen. Vibrant, healthy, pure. Pulled free of brambles and deadfall, nary a shrub to be seen. Manicured short, like a park or a campground. I know I've been here before, but it has been a long time. I don't know where I am but it feels like home. *This is where I belong.*

The dog comes for me then, charging. 200 pounds of sinew and fangs. It leaps and hits my chest hard and we go down. He loves me. I hold him tight as he covers my face in kisses, tears streaming freely. He has been dead for over three years now and was my truest friend. The only one I could ever trust completely. I get back to my feet to face the dead man and the dog chases after a pair of happy puppies frolicking on the grass.

My Da is smiling. His glasses are gone, he looks about forty years old, maybe thirty-five, and there isn't a cigarette in his hand. He seems at peace. I do not recognize the woman beside him, but they belong together and it is right. My Grandfather looks about fifty and has trimmed down a bit. He smiles and scratches his spaniel behind the ears. That dog was evil incarnate and hated everyone but him and Gram, but seems perfectly calm and sane now.

My Da takes a sip of his beer. The woman hands me one. It is cold and fresh and tastes of wheat and dandelions. The brown glass bottle has no label and never did.

"There'll always be a place for you," he says.

BRAP! BRAP! BRAP! BRAP! BRAP! BRAP!

The scene dissolves and I hit the snooze button. I drift back to random images bereft of Significance. The alarm sounds again. I stand, threadbare sheet falling away, once white, now grey and sour with old sweat.

My eyes focus and take in the dingy studio apartment: the torn mattress on the linoleum floor, the thrift store bookshelf stacked with thirdhand paperbacks, the red plastic bucket in the corner. I walk to the bucket, reaching inside, pushing aside the spray cleaner, paper towels, and trash bags to grasp the tool hidden beneath. The gateway. The key.

I thumb the hammer partway and spin the cylinder once before locking it back to full cock and reversing my grip. The steel emits a familiar tang as it rests against my tongue that I find comforting, soothing...I close my eyes and visualize green grass and puppies.

clack!

It appears I have stuff to do today. I toss the pitted Bulldog .44 back in the bucket and trudge into the kitchen to switch on the coffeemaker and fire up the kettle for instant oatmeal.

* * *

I work at *Max's Petrol*, the last full service gas station in Denver. No self-serve, no mechanic, no plastic. It's been largely unchanged since the Forties and remains an anachronism.

Although its location at 8th and Washington puts it near the center of Capitol Hill, the hipsters stay clear. We don't sell flavored iced tea or organic cigarettes, and we're not noted for our customer service, as reflected by the dozens of one star reviews on Yelp.

Half the lights are burned out and the once white building looks like someone wiped their ass with it...I don't think it's ever been hosed down, let alone power washed, and the original paint is grimy enough to be indistinguishable from the patches of concrete stripped bare by the Colorado sun. The flat roof has a layer of rotting leaves a foot deep. I'm guessing...no-one's ever gone up there to check, but there's a lot. A small shrub has even taken root in the humus.

Business is slow. I spend most of the day in the office trying to stick a few dull and blunted throwing stars in a pizza box nailed to the wall. It would be easier if they weren't bent from years of rebounding off cinderblocks and asphalt.

I hear the straight pipes from blocks away. There are nearly fifty clubs in the greater Denver area and they're all different, so you never know what to expect until you see the patch. When they roll up to the pumps I recognize the colors...Regulators.

The Regulators are a local unaffiliated one percent club rocking that old school 1970s dirtbag look: unshaven, unwashed, grime caked denim cut offs, usually loaded on booze or weed. Their patch looks like a child's art project, one they got a C minus on, and sorta resembles a pair of crossed sixguns and a bottle of whiskey...a winning combination indeed.

There are five of them, astride battered ratbikes covered with flat black *Krylon*, peeling stickers, and road burn...ballpeen hammers strapped to triple trees with bungee cords. They ignore me and help themselves to the fuel. I note that a couple of them have lit cigarettes.

"Hey," one of them slurs, "Gimme a Red Bull and a pack of Camel Filters."

"You do not want to fuck with me today," I warn him. He freezes, then turns towards me slowly, eyes hidden behind black dime store shades. He grins, turning to his brothers for support.

"He says he doesn't want us to fuck him." They laugh. I see the flash of metal as he rushes me, arm swinging downward...*kerambit*.

I spin on my heel, sidestepping the slash of the small hooked blade, flipping *balisong* as I pull it across his belly to unzip his guts, but twisting my grip at the last moment to connect with the flat rather than the edge. The point tears a rent in his T-shirt and a few small dark spots slowly spread.

"You motherfucker! You cut me! Fuck!" He pulls up his shirt...it's just a scratch. His brothers laugh again. He folds the blade of the cheap flea market knife, clipping it back inside his front pocket.

"Don't be a pussy," Tattooface advises him. Vulture approaches and offers me a hit off his joint, which I accept to be polite. It tastes like burning plastic and sears my throat. I start hacking convulsively, which they find hilarious.

"What the fuck? Are you shitheads smoking lawn furniture now?" I pass it back.

"Naw, we rolled a few Black Diamonds up in this. It makes the ride more interesting."

"What's that?"

"Dunno. Sumpthin' new." He hits it again and passes it back. I look down at the joint dubiously.

"This isn't that bath salts shit, is it? I can't be freaking out at work and chewing people's faces off."

"Naw, it ain't like that at all...this stuff is good...it gives you all this *energy* and you see trails and hear music and shit."

"Really? What kind of music?"

"Polka," Vulture mutters, hanging his head in shame.

"I just hear, like, factory noises...buzzing and clanking and shit," Tattooface says. Billy is still pissed off about his shirt, but takes the joint, hits it, and passes it on before disappearing into the office. He comes out a few minutes later with a *Red Bull* and his smokes.

"Checks ain't here yet?"

"No, Max said they'll be here by six."

"Bank will be closed by then."

"You're not supposed to cash it 'til tomorrow."

"Fuck!" He holds up the stuff in his hands. "Add this to our gas tab."

"Alright." They fire up their bikes and roar up 8th in tight formation, likely heading for one of the pubs on South Broadway.

Medical marijuana is a major industry here in Denver and there are hundreds of strains readily available, many of which I've sampled. While I'm certainly no connoisseur, I'm familiar with *sativas*, *indicas*, hybrids, and every type of hash, as well as crap like *salvia* and *datura*. I know how different herbs make you feel. This isn't a weed buzz I'm feeling. Not a weed buzz at all...more like 'shrooms, but different.

My field of vision expands and everything seems sharper, magnified. I become aware of a ball of tension right behind my forehead, swollen, pulsating, squirming...something is definitely moving inside my brain, twitching, fluttering, awakening. My gut clenches as the world shifts and everything snaps grey. Icewater shoots through my spine and I close my eyes...when I open them again I'm seeing everything through a black and white filter. I shake my head and blink...colors are gone.

The thing in my head unravels like a knot and the tension drains. Colors return, flare, brighter, richer, more complex. Suddenly, my vision blurs, chest tightening, heart fibrillating...I can't believe this shit, I'm having an allergic reaction and going into anaphylactic shock!

I stagger to the office, ripping the first aid kit off the wall, dumping it, popping open a plastic bottle and chewing several aspirin, washing the bitter paste down with half a cup of forgotten coffee, following them with a couple Benadryl and focusing on my breathing exercises. After a few minutes, things come back into focus and my heart rate stabilizes...probably just another anxiety attack.

I dump the tepid coffee and pour myself a fresh cup. This is from my own private stash of Sumatran that I hide up in the dropped ceiling. Half a pound costs more than I make in tips all week, and those other screwups are happy with whatever is on sale at Wally World in the big tin can. There's a 5 pound can of *Maxwell House* sitting beside the coffeemaker, but that poison sears my bowels and gives me the shits...I can't drink it.

I tear open a few packs of raw sugar and stir it in before retrieving my pint of *Horizon* Organic Half & Half from the back of the cooler, behind the bottles of expired *Strawberry Quik* that no one ever buys. It is essential to have at least one positive experience each day, and lately for me that's been limited to good coffee. I chug it quickly and immediately feel better.

The remainder of my shift is a dreamlike blur. Boots sink into asphalt as if it were foam rubber, customers' voices seem muffled and distant, and I see shadows darting in the corner of my eye...but it feels real nice, fuzzy around the edges, the way Demerol makes you stop giving a fuck entirely.

I'm extra careful making change, as not giving a fuck has its limits. Eventually I realize that I should've cut the lights and turned off the pumps fifteen minutes ago, so I do that, jot down the readings, bag the receipts, and leave the morning shift's till in the cash drawer. I punch out, set the alarm, and lock up. It's a long strange walk home.

* * *

I have difficulty getting to sleep. I feel agitated, tense. Every time I close my eyes it feels like someone is shining a powerful flashlight in my face...I swing up my arms, eyes snapping open, flashing back to the night those cops beat me in the park, but there is nothing but darkness...yet something in the darkness is shifting, churning, fulminating.

I finally drift off to sleep and wake with a start, wind knocked out of me...I swear I must've dropped onto the mattress after floating motionless a foot above it. I keep my eyes clenched shut, waiting for the patterns to emerge, geometrically shifting like a kaleidoscopic lotus Mandela, but all I'm getting are angry red sparks, then I'm falling through a tunnel, down through the levels, into the sewers and past them, further than I've ever been.

I am walking through the endless subbasement of a housing project, pipes overhead, but there are public restrooms down here too, and a huge institutional kitchen. The walls and ceiling are peeling, rotted, deteriorated; everything covered in spongy layers of thick ochre mold, with an occasional spray of chalky pink or green. I wade through a putrid miasma of fermentation and decay, air no doubt filled with parasitic spores. I Will my shield to full strength, aura solidifying into flexible plate armor with breathing filters, before continuing.

I thought I'd been to the foulest levels of the low Astral before, but I'd never seen anything like this. I walk for miles, expecting the attack to come at every turn, but it never does. Nothing has lived down here for a very long time...even the earwigs and centipedes seem to have fled. There are no doors, no stairs, not even a ladder; nor are there light fixtures, just a dim phosphorescence emanating from the thick carpet of mold. There are no sounds, even my footfalls are silent. I have never felt so completely and utterly alone.

I awake soaked in sweat, shivering, ill, throat hoarse from dryness. I stagger to the kitchen and get the medicine from the freezer...a fifth of *Absolut*, murky with a dollop of pureed ghost peppers. I give it a couple of shakes before twisting off the frosted cap and tilting it back, feeling the Fire & Ice pour down my gullet, pooling in my empty stomach. Eyes snap wide, gut rebels, limbs cramp, the carcass practically goes into seizure. I take full control.

I light a burner on the stove and get the sage wand smouldering, blowing on embers hard until the apartment is filled with smoke, fumigating Astral and Ether...then I lift the oversharpened *Chicago Cutlery* chef knife from the drawer and start scraping at the usual attachment points.

Something is trying to take root. Something is trying to pull me to a place I've never been, and I think it was a combination of luck and panic that kept me from getting pulled further, possibly trapped, leaving my body in coma. I have no doubt there are worse Hells than the Endless Basement of Mold, and it felt like someone threw me a lifeline at the last possible moment before I was dragged to my final destination. I take another slug of the peppered vodka. I know what I need to do.

I type up a quick text to the Goddess and glance at the clock. 4:44. It is Tuesday, it will be slow. I type: *10:00?* and hit send, then fall palms first to the linoleum floor for my first set of fifty pushups.

* * *

I hold her close, one hand dampened by sweat beading in the hollow at the base of her spine, fingers of my other hand entwined in her hair. She smells of lavender. We are one, within the same shell, a free flow of energies, thoughts, and other contaminants. We filter our lives through each other: pain, regret, sorrow, rage. I press myself deep and hold, feeling the star blazing into nothingness, gazing into her empty hungry eyes.

"At this moment, you are everything to me...I wish you could love me." She convulses, clenches, every part of her squeezing me tight as she's racked with tremors.

"At this moment, I *do* love you," she pants softly in my ear. We kiss, and it is beautiful and pure and real and True. I gaze into her eyes again, and this time I actually see a person...the girl she once was, what might have been, what can never be...and a single glistening tear. We kiss again, and I hold her tenderly and whisper in her ear.

"I would die for you."

"I know you would...that is so fucking hot." She starts riding me hard, pumping, like a machine. I want her to relax and slow down.

"Tell me you love me...even if it isn't true."

"I love you." The emptiness returns. I want to look in her eyes but she's looking at the clock. She pumps faster, flushing, sweating, constricting...I push her back, putting her legs up, stretching them back, giving her long even strokes as she loses control and cums hard.

"Oh, shit...I love you so much, Jake." It sounds like she means it this time...but it's always fleeting. I empty myself into her, a chalice overflowing, and kiss her sweetly, exhausted, drained. We lay together for a long while, unspeaking.

"It's always so special with you. You've always been incredibly sweet to me. You're the only guy I rawdog anymore, and I only bill you for a half, no matter how long you stay...you're the closest thing I've got to a boyfriend right now and that's the truth." I try to ignore the bullshit coming out of her mouth, holding tightly to the illusion of our love. We kiss again. Now I look at the clock.

"It's nearly one thirty...you feel like goin' for a ride, maybe getting some Chinese?"

"Can't. I got a regular scheduled for three and he's a real big tipper. You need to go, love. See you next month?"

"Probably. Yeah. I'll call you. Here's something to help with bills and something for your head," I hand her a Franklin and a gram of hash. "I need to take off." I feel bitter, my blood sugar has crashed and I need some air. I see myself out.

* * *

I fire up the bike and pop the clutch, bald rear tire spinning, smoking, screaming. The bobbed Honda goes sideways out of the parking lot. I clench the tape wrapped dragbars and push the old 750 hard, swooping across lanes at double the posted limit as I burn down Evans.

Yellow changes to Red and the front wheel lifts as I downshift and punch it, missing a *Metro Taxi* by mere inches as I veer through the traffic crossing the intersection. I hear brakes screeching and the dull crunch of bumper hitting bumper, but that's a block behind me now, no longer my problem.

By the time I reach Federal I've slowed to a normal speed. I head North, towards *El Padrino*. A steak burrito and a couple double Jack & Cokes is what I need...and maybe some flan.

* * *

A few hours later I pull into *Max's*, half drunk and smoking a joint. I am so past giving a fuck at this point, but I'd promised Billy I'd cover for him from 6 to close so he could do a club thing. The kickstand on the flat black CB750 snapped off when I hopped the curb and nearly dumped it after dinner, so I roll alongside the building and lean it against the wall. I should probably roll it inside but I'm not feeling up to that level of exertion right now. Billy glares at me.

"I was startin' to think you weren't gonna show."

"It's ten minutes 'til 6." The wind has knocked the cherry from the joint...I fumble with my *Bic* and relight it. It tastes stale.

"You are fuckin' polluted. Are you too fucked up to work?" He takes the joint from me, burning the remainder to ashes with a single toke before popping the tarry roach in his mouth and swallowing it.

"I'm only pumping gas, not driving the ambulance." He cocks his head, regarding me strangely. I don't know why I said that. I never talk about that. It's been a couple years since I'd driven the bus. They took that away once I was locked down. You get your name in the paper for the wrong reason and everyone turns their back on you. Now I'm in the trash bin with the rest of the animals.

"Are you alright, Brother?" I look at him and he seems genuinely concerned. I sober quickly, touched and humbled.

"It's cool. Just had a bit too good of a time. I've got this...you go do your thing." He nods, satisfied.

"Right on." He walks into the office to punch out and I follow, looking for my timecard. By the time I find it I hear him firing up his battered Pan-Shovel and taking off down 8th. I climb up on the desk, sliding aside a ceiling tile to secure my dwindling stash of *Dazbog* Sumatran, and prepare a fresh pot of strong coffee.

* * *

Around 8:30 Matt shows up. I don't think Matt has had a shower since he was admitted to *Denver Health* after being hit by that car last Winter. I smell the stench of rancid grease and unwiped asshole from thirty paces away. It serves as a force field of sorts, keeping the usual predators at bay. Besides, Matt is over six feet of crazy and seldom has more than a pocketful of change and a flask of *Wild Irish Rose* to his name...that, and the slender folding fish knife he's fond of waving about when he's in his cups and the moon is full.

Everyone on the street knows not to mess with Matt, as he's been barred for life from all the shelters, eats roadkill grilled over an open fire, and has slept under a bridge next to the Platte for the past five years with no apparent ill effects. Most of the street crazies on Colfax are just playing a role, in hope of gaining sympathy or instilling fear, but Matt is crazy for real. He also is unfailingly polite and always has cash, so I like him better than most of our regular customers.

"Hello, Jake! How are you today?" I look at his smiling face, blue eyes shining brightly. This raggedy guy with his matted red hair, long beard encrusted with remainders of several meals, and mudstained trenchcoat he'd been sleeping in. Like I'm gonna tell the troll under the bridge that my life sucks and I've had a rotten day. I got laid this morning, had a steak burrito, and rode my motorcycle hard for hours. Thank you, Matt, for reminding me that my hopeless existence really isn't that bad in comparison to yours.

"Things are going okay now that I've gained a clearer perspective. You want your usual?"

"Indeed." I go to the cooler and get him a bottle of *Arizona Green Tea*. Unlike the other street rats, Matt never buys cigarettes, energy drinks, or candy. Just green tea from us and

Sriracha hot sauce from the market on 6th, to hide the taste of whatever spoiled discards he scavenges from the dumpsters around Capitol Hill. That's probably why he seems so much healthier than most of them. An urban mountain man with the constitution of a billy goat.

He meticulously counts out a dollar and thirty-five cents in dimes and nickels. He has something against pennies. Whenever he gets pennies for change he invariably dumps them in the take a penny dish, saying, "Someone might need those." Today, however, he has exact change. He reaches into his grimy trenchcoat, producing a paper wrapped *McDonalds* burger.

"You hungry? I got a few extra cheeseburgers if you want one."

"I already ate, but thanks."

"You sure you don't want it for later?"

"No, I'm good." He nods and stuffs it back in his pocket before zipping the tea deep in his backpack. It's a metal framed mountaineering pack that probably retailed at well over two hundred bucks. The yuppies are always donating brand new backpacks and parkas to the dozens of local outreach programs, which is one of the many reasons homeless are bussing here from all over the country. Denver's official policy of "Hug-A-Bum" guarantees that everyone will get food, clothing, and medical care...as long as they are actually on the street. If you're working two part-time minimum wage jobs, and can barely afford canned ravioli after paying rent, they could give two shits about you.

When I had my first heart attack a few months back, I needed to wait a month to see a cardiologist, and he refused to do any tests beyond blood pressure and EKG because I didn't have insurance...but if I was some homeless on Public Assistance you'd bet I'd get a full series of tests, several scripts, and regular follow up visits. But I digress.

Denver apparently has become the homeless Mecca of the United States, and they have overrun Capitol Hill and Downtown like vermin...which is probably why so many shelters and soup kitchens have been firebombed lately. It's not "declining property values" and "public nuisance" offenses; people are pissed off about the smash and grabs, burglaries, and strongarm robberies that occur all day, every day, but are never reported in the *Denver Post*.

The arsonists' identities remain a mystery. They're blaming it on "skinheads," but the skinheads were run out of Denver over a decade ago and haven't made a comeback. Most of the working class has since relocated to Aurora and Lakewood, as Capitol Hill was gentrified and rents doubled, so now those same buildings are filled with petulant emaciated hipsters incapable of violence, let alone vigilantism...hell, most are probably incapable of a single pushup.

"I hear tell that a new shelter is opening up. A big one up near Commerce City. It's supposed to be open all day long for job training and stuff, and I hear tell that once you're in, you're in...none of this wait in line for five hours bullshit every night to see if they pick your number for a cot. If I get my shit together maybe I won't get kicked out of this one."

"Well, you're gonna need to get some clean clothes from the Sally and take a shower if you want to impress those folks. You can use the hose out back anytime you want, and I can give you a towel and some soap when you're ready."

"That's okay, I can just use the sink in the bathroom."

"You wash your balls in my bathroom and this'll be another place you're banned for life from. Besides, the hose is a lot better. Rinsing off is the only way you'll get clean."

"Thanks, Jake! I really appreciate this! You have a great night!" And then he spins and lumbers off, arms swinging at his side, letting everyone know HE owns that sidewalk. His stench remains. I prop open the door and get the *Lysol* from the bathroom.

* * *

Once again, I find myself in the Hell of Endless Doors. It has been a recurring dream I've had hundreds of times from as far back as I can remember. Often it starts outdoors, on a suburban sidewalk or a gravel path through a park. Then I find myself drawn to a massive structure, typically a hotel, but sometimes a school. As usual, there are very few people here, and they have little apparent interest in me, keeping to themselves.

I start walking down a wide hallway with tall ceilings. I pass ornately carved double doors that open into ballrooms, banquet halls, and auditoriums, all empty. I continue exploring, the hallways becoming narrower, the doors smaller, presumably leading to apartments or offices, all unoccupied, most stripped of furnishings. Invariably, the doors are unlocked. Occasionally there is a stairwell, an elevator, a ladder, or a ramp...usually only leading downwards...deeper.

Soon, wood paneling and carpets become institutional pastel paint and concrete floors, the rooms now windowless cubes, and it's obvious no-one has been on this level for a very long time...it's an abandoned wing and I am utterly alone.

Eventually, the floor, walls, and ceiling become bare stone, the doors rough hewn boards with wrought iron fittings. Everything is surprisingly clean. I am unafraid, even though I'm completely lost. I'm searching for something, or someone, but haven't the vaguest idea of what or who...I'll know when I find it, but in hundreds of attempts I've rarely come close. As usual, the dream seems to last for days.

I awake drained and confused, calves tight as if I'd walked for miles, mouth parched. The alarm is about to sound so I switch it off, then rise from the mattress and stagger into the kitchen to switch on the coffeemaker.

* * *

The day starts off uneventful. It's dead until the noontime rush, then tapers off until three when shifts change, and remains busy until seven...then it is dead again. The usual pattern.

Billy had stashed a few joints in the usual place so I light one up. Plastic. They're laced with that Black Diamond shit that bends my head and gives me bad dreams. Acrid black smoke rises from the cherry, reeking of industrial accident. Word on the street is it's some sort of long lasting synthetic DMT. I feel the tarlike residue gumming up my lungs with every inhalation, but it doesn't make me cough this time.

My lips and tongue go numb...that can't be good. Pain shoots down my left arm and my legs go weak. I chew up a few aspirin and pinch out the joint, leaving it in the ashtray for now. I won't be finishing that tonight. Two hits fucked me up last time, I think I had four or five just now. It should be okay. After all, there is a fresh pot of coffee brewing and two slices of garlic pizza left...

* * *

At first I thought the office was on fire due to the smoke...but it was only the ceiling dissolving into mist, swirling, churning...then a rent tears through from the Other Side and glistening eyes the size of basketballs spill out. I throw up my arms to protect my face but nothing hits me. When I look again, the ceiling tiles are back in focus.

I relax and look out the window...still no customers, which I'm grateful for. I hear whirring, like the sound of a ceiling fan slightly off balance, and look up. The swirling white mist is back. I decide it's time to step outside for a clove.

After an hour, I've managed to convince myself that the shadowman lurking behind the empty shelves at the far end of the office is not real...or at least he's finally left the building. A critter that looks like a grey dust bunny but moves faster than any mouse hops over my boot and zips along the baseboard. A black bumblebee slowly flies across the room, disappearing into the wall, and I clearly hear the buzz, even feel the air vibrate as it passes my ear.

I'm not entirely certain these hallucinations aren't actually "real" on a different plane of consciousness. It almost seems as if I'm able to peer between dimensions, spotting fauna of the Ether which regularly pass us by unnoticed. Several times I spot flames, but it's nothing more substantial than a brief flurry of red and orange sparks, spinning in a column before dissipating. That column of red sparks is something I've seen before, in dreams. It only manifests in dark corners, well away from the lighted pumps.

I see the customers differently now. It's as if their false masks are stripped away, allowing me to view their True selves, their hidden thoughts, suppressed traumas, secret vices.

That sweet old woman in the blue Cadillac with the Jesus fish on the trunk always smiles, says, "God bless you," and tips a dollar. Now I see she's filled with hatred: raw, unfocused, directed at everyone, including me. She does those things because she feels obligated to...and she resents it.

She thinks the fact I work at a gas station is proof of my wickedness, because God rewards good people who work hard with success. Her conviction on this point is strong. She gives me a dollar only after having me check her oil and squeegee her windows. Sometime she asks to have her tire pressure checked too.

Her new car that she hardly drives never needs oil, and those tires never need air, and I often see her pulling into the car wash down the block right after she has me clean her windows. It is a game to her. She needs to make me *earn* that dollar. I now realize I have a duty to piss in that squeegee bucket every night. Perhaps I'll need to start carrying a license plate screw in my pocket as well.

Another regular customer pulls in, driving the familiar Dodge stationwagon with fake wood panel decals peeling off and glass Mardi Gras beads dangling from the rearview. As always, his wife sits beside him with their daughters in the back. They're all smiling, laughing, holding their *McDonalds* pseudo-milkshakes that taste nothing like ice cream but give you brain freeze and barely creep through the straw no matter how hard you suck. Their laughter rings hollow, weary.

I gaze into his watery eyes, taking in the creepy smile, awkward movements, furtive glances. Yes, his daughters know all about sucking. He thinks of them as property, and knows they'll never tell. His wife, with her thinning hair and sunken cheeks, will never tell either, nor will she protest or seek any sort of "help." She doesn't even think of it as abnormal. After all, her Dad did the same to her and her sisters, as did her brothers. Her cousin took her away from them for good, and between his two jobs and the EBT card they're practically respectable now, as far as she's concerned.

I take all this in with a cursory glance, seeing so much that had never registered before. I'm sickened and enraged, compelled to grab a handful of that bleached blonde mullet and yank his head out the window so I can saw his throat open with my knife. *My knife*...I look down and see it already in my hand, unopened.

He's babbling inanely about some popular television show I've never watched and hasn't noticed. Discretely, I slip it back in my pocket and take his seven crumpled dollars before pumping two gallons of the cheap stuff. I neglect to clean the windshield and he doesn't seem to notice that either.

The next customer is dressed like a stripper on her way to one of the classier clubs Downtown, like *Diamond Cabaret*. She's driving a new Jeep Wrangler with the top and doors off, and her fancy shoes probably cost more than a week's pay for me. She has a small wooden bowl clenched between her naked thighs that she'd been hitting while driving, but doesn't offer me a toke.

I gaze into those green eyes and see the intelligence, the Graduate degree, and the fact that she'd realized she can earn more in a few hours on stage than by working 9 to 5 at the office all week long, at least while she's still young. She doesn't tip, but flashes a genuine smile and talks to me almost like a friend before paying for her gas with a crisp folded twenty, exact change, and slowly driving off. I was so distracted I forgot to get the money in advance.

Now there's this asshole. Black Lincoln Town Car, blocking access to the second pump and with his gas cap on the wrong side. White guy, mid-30s, hair slicked back, dressed like an undertaker, texting furiously on his touchscreen phone. Scandinavian Black Metal blares discordantly from his speakers...I think it might be *Mayhem*.

A generic red Cavalier pulls up on the other side. It's driven by a nondescript pudgy office drone clad in the industry standard, white poly-blend dress shirt. He frowns at the music, frowning deeper when I tell him we don't have a credit card machine or an ATM. He hands me a roll of quarters, whining that it is his laundry money. Fuck you, the laundry has an ATM and a change machine, and we need quarters. I pump his ten dollars and he leaves. I turn back to the Black Metal undertaker, who has finished his text.

I get a clear look at him now, since he's staring directly at me. His skin seems unnaturally pale, nearly translucent, with a thin sheen of oil, eyes far too dark...a sharp stabbing pain strikes immediately behind my left eye, like a migraine, but I've never had one before.

I break eye contact as I circle around the pumps, and the pain subsides to a dull ache. Leaning against the trunk for support, steel sags beneath my weight as if it were gelatin, and I spasmodically jerk away out of fear that I might somehow be absorbed, amoeba-like, by this sinister black car, trapped and horribly digested in its trunk. I reassure myself it's only the drugs and everything will be fine as long as I stay cool. I look up and he's out of the car.

"You want gas?" I ask. Not necessarily a stupid question, as he has Nebraska plates and might only want directions or the key to the john. His entire body shifts to the side as he cocks his head, one arm jerking skywards as if pulled by an alcoholic puppeteer.

"Yoo want gassss?" he mimics, a shrill falsetto. The toothy grimace on his doughy face stretches obscenely, improbably, impossibly wide, all the way to his earlobes as his eyes fill with ink...then he snaps back to semi-normalcy for a moment...a Midwestern traveling salesman on the road for weeks, staying at fleabag motels and wearing a fresh off the rack suit from *JCPenney*. I blink and shake my head.

"If you want gas, your gas cap is on the wrong side. You'll need to turn it around." Suddenly, he's a mannequin with a fresh coat of flat white paint, smouldering black pits for eyes, and a wide maw crookedly filled with hundreds of thin needle teeth.

"You're on the wrong side! Yoo need to turn it around!" The shrieks actually seem gleeful. I'm tripping balls, and this guy is

obviously out of his mind. No cameras, no panic button, here by myself. Overhead lights flicker and dim, or maybe that's a hallucination too...the angles of the gas pumps are all wrong, distorted, non-Euclidean. I cannot deal with this bullshit tonight. We close at 10, and it's nearly quarter of...I don't even need to throw him out, we may as well close right now.

"Dude...we're closed. The *Conoco* at Colfax and Colorado is only a mile away and they're open all night. You have a good day." Overhead lights are out for real...probably the breaker tripped again. The office lights remain on, providing a soft glow from the windows. The stereo fades in volume until it shuts off...I give the car a second glance, but no-one else is inside. Instantly, he's standing in front of me, and there's no way he could've moved that fast. He smells of almonds.

"Come closer..." I spring about five feet back and pull the gun, a pocket sized Jennings with a bumper chrome finish that flashes like a signal mirror.

"YOU KNOW WHAT *THIS* IS, MOTHERFUCKER?" I yell. He smiles that impossible Stretch Armstrong smile and slips something out of his sleeve...a sleek Italian stiletto that snaps open a 6" blade, making it over a foot long overall. I rack a round into the chamber and point it at his chest.

"YOU NEED TO GET YOUR CREEPY CLOWN ASS THE FUCK OUTTA MY GAS STATION *RIGHT* NOW!"

"Ooooooooo..." he mocks, lifting the knife over his head, twirling it playfully, slowly closing the distance even though his legs aren't moving, gliding over the asphalt as though his Oxfords are on casters. The slender blade is double edged, but from my experience with stilettos they tend to be only slightly sharper than the average tent stake...and he's holding it wrong.

I'm on parole and ain't even supposed to be in the same room as a gun, so even though I'm clearly justified I decide not to shoot him dead. I fire a warning shot...into the top of his foot.

BRRAAAPPP!!!

Six shell casings tinkle to the ground. One of the design flaws of the early J-22s is that if the breech face gets peened, or the sear spring weakens, or the firing pin channel gets gunked up, they have a tendency to slamfire and go full auto. Mine happens to have all of the aforementioned problems, so two and three round bursts happen fairly regular, but rarely a full mag dump.

So I'm now facing a knife wielding maniac with an empty gun...and from the look of things I even missed his foot. The slide doesn't lock back on these zinc nightmares, so I decide to bluff. I point it at his face.

"The next one is going right in your forehead." He frowns, lowering the knife. Metal suddenly blasts from his car again, startling both of us. I sprint to the office, locking the door behind me. When I turn around, I see the Town Car pulling onto 8th with no headlights.

My heart is pounding out of my chest and I feel like I'm about to puke. I roll the chair over to the window and sit down. I don't hear any sirens. We're far enough from the *ShotSpotter* sensors that they may not have been able to triangulate my position. I go to the breaker box. Sure enough, the breakers for the outside lights have tripped. I flip them back on and cut power to the pumps. I need to collect that brass before taking the readings...but first I need to stash the deuce-deuce up in the ceiling tiles in case the cops are on their way.

I only find four of the nickle plated casings and rush through the readings. I count out the till, make the drop, punch out, kill the lights, set the alarm, and lock the door behind me. I walk over to the bike and listen...nothing. I glance up Washington and down 8th...no Town Car anywhere to be seen. I kick the old Honda to life and go home.

* * *

I awaken disoriented and drained. I feel like I might be coming down with the flu. I have no recollection of any dreams at all. I recall getting in bed, closing my eyes, and lying there with my eyes closed for roughly ten minutes, *trying* to get to sleep, then opening them to glance at the clock and seeing daylight. The clock says 9:27. Eight hours have literally passed in the blink of an eye. That's never happened to me before. I am deeply disturbed by this, and still exhausted...I feel as if I haven't slept at all.

Luckily, I don't need to be at the gas station until three. I stagger into the kitchen and crack open a bottle of *Deep Rock* spring water, washing down a handful of *Echinacea* capsules and a multivitamin. I don't bother to walk to the bathroom...I just take a long piss in the empty sink, run the faucet, and stagger back to the mattress where I collapse. Everything goes black...

* * *

There is a little man standing in the room examining my paperbacks. Well, not a man, but a distinctly humanoid figure, less than two feet tall and bright yellow, with somewhat reptilian features. He notices I'm awake and staring at him. I'd left the Jennings at work, and the Charter Arms with one bullet is in the bucket across the room...I don't even have a bent throwing star handy.

"Why, hello! How are you today?" he exclaims. I don't quite know how to respond to that.

"What's up?"

"How marvelous! What an intelligent and perceptive individual you are! I have come to offer you a proposal."

"And what might that be?"

"You are clearly a seeker of Truth. I can teach you a great many things. You shall be respected by all. I can even reveal how to clear your name so you may attain the success you so rightfully deserve."

"Alright. But what do you expect from me in return?"

"Why, absolutely nothing! This shall be my gift to you...all you need do is agree to be my friend. Would you like to be my friend, Jacob?" A lifetime of social conditioning compels me to agree out of politeness, but the moment I open my mouth to speak, a black blur streaks across the room and slams into him.

The little man's eyes bug out of his head, mouth gaping in a silent scream, as the giant Rottweiler chomps down on his torso, viciously shaking him like a stuffed doll. I now realize this devious creature was attempting to trick me into agreeing to a binding contract. I decide to let Otto use him as a chew toy for a while longer before finally barking the command, ***"GIVE!"*** compelling my dead dog to drop him to the floor.

He sits up, dazed. There is no blood, but indentations from Rottweiler fangs sank deep into his yellow flesh like punctures through Plasticine. I elect to go with the *Adirondack Hill Folk Rite of Banishment,* since it is quick, informal, and fits my mood:

"You need to get the fuck outta my house and don't come back." The air around him shimmers and he vanishes.

BRAP! BRAP! BRAP! BRAP! BRAP! BRAP!

It is 1:30. At least I got four good hours of sleep. I switch off the alarm and start the coffeemaker.

* * *

Fubucky is a gangly bucktoothed motherfucker with a scraggly goatee and tightly curled hair that hasn't been trimmed in months, giving him the appearance of a demented Poodle with mange. He rarely speaks...I think he's probably autistic or some shit...but he always shows up early, and his count is never off by more than a few bucks here and there, so he's unlikely to get fired anytime soon.

If the cops showed up to ask about gunshots I think he'd probably mention it, but he doesn't, so I assume I'm good to go. Besides, my little .22 doesn't make a lot of noise, and people in this neighborhood tend to mind their own business, because a single interaction with Denver's finest is usually more than enough for most, since they have a shittier attitude than practically any other department in the country, so the hipsters and yuppies are rightfully terrified of them.

I still worry, because a lot of them recently migrated from places like Illinois and Massachusetts for the legal weed, and calling 911 is practically a reflexive compulsion for Yankees. I spot the maroon Crown Vic pulling in and my heart stops for a couple of beats. I casually slide the old Manila Folder out of my pocket, tossing it in the office wastebasket, before walking outside.

The Crown Vic's windows are tinted far darker than the law allows, but the spotlight on the side shows it *is* the law. The window rolls down and I see my parole officer's bigfakesmile under his thick moustache. He makes a point of staring at my belt buckle: a standard open-faced garrison buckle, since the conditions of my parole specifically forbid me from wearing buckles over 4 ounces due to the incident. I haven't weighed the buckle, since I assumed it was fine, and apparently he decides it's fine too.

He glances over at my bike. A small set of baffles is spot welded inside the straight pipes to make it street legal, and due to the non-association clause I'm not stupid enough to have slapped a support sticker on it. He turns back to me.

"Well, I see you're still gainfully employed, so I can check that box on my monthly report. Everything going well here? No problems?"

"This is a nice low stress job for me. I like talking to the customers and being outside." I think that was a good answer. He nods. It looks like he won't even be getting out of the car this time.

"Good, glad to hear that. It's been a year and you've been doing okay, so I think we can probably dispense with the monthly appointments. You just give me a call every month to check in and let me know if anything changes."

"Any particular day or time you want me to call?"

"Just once a month, but make sure you talk to me, personally. Don't just leave a message on voicemail."

"Alright." A lazy cop is a good cop. Besides, after the very first month he realized I wasn't one of the usual scumbags and took it easy on me, not subjecting me to the bullshit patdowns, surprise piss tests, and unannounced home visits that other guys had to deal with. While I know I can never trust him, or any cop, he seems decent enough...on our last appointment a squirrel climbed onto his windowsill, and I saw he'd left a few cashews there. The window rolls up and he drives away. He's never gotten gas here, probably because it's a city vehicle and we don't accept plastic.

I walk back inside as Fubucky is leaving, eyes blank, plugged into his cheap *SanDisk* player. I have no idea what he listens to...Billy said he thought it was audiobooks of some sort. I retrieve *balisong* from the wastebasket and stand up on the desk to retrieve my Jennings and Sumatran from the ceiling.

I pull a ziplock bag and wadded latex glove from my boot, putting on the glove before carefully reloading the mag with 6 CCI Stingers, the only round that reliably cycles. I rack the slide, cocking the striker over an empty chamber so I'll only be pulling against one spring rather than two, and pop in the mag...that's the only safe way to carry one of these. I've heard too many stories of Saturday Night Specials going off in people's pockets to feel comfortable carrying it any other way, especially since these guns have a tendency to discharge if dropped.

Regardless, tucked behind my wallet it provides a sense of comfort, knowing that if some freak tries to kill me while I'm working alone, even though it may not be powerful enough to stop him, he ain't gonna get away clean. The Jennings is accurate enough to hit a paper plate within 10 feet, and those Stingers have enough pop to go through an inch thick pine board.

I still feel a bit off from that shit I smoked last night, but the coffee should help. I splurge and make a full pot.

* * *

It is another slow day. Shortly after the sun goes down, a hearse pulls up to the pumps. I blink and shake my head. Nope, not a hearse, but a battered Volvo 240DL wagon covered with black primer...probably about 10 rattle cans worth, as even the side windows in the back are primed. The flat primer sucks up the light, absorbing it, a rolling shadow.

I walk up from behind, taking in the Texas plate and the old school Industrial stickers: *Skinny Puppy, NIN, Tool.* I approach the driver side and hear *Joy Division* playing at low volume.

The woman looks to be older than my mom. I blink twice and stare at her directly...the wrinkled face with hollow cheeks and sunken eyes is gone, replaced with that of a girl recently out of high school, maybe a college student. That Black Diamond shit is obviously still in my system. I note dyed black hair roughly snipped at collar length with a few facial piercings: "snakebites" double labret rings and a spiked horseshoe piercing the septum. Her brown eyes are flat like the primer.

"Twenty," she says, and hands me two tens. The car barely takes eighteen dollars worth. I hand her back the change.

"Keep it. Where's a place that sells good pizza around here?" I point down Washington Street.

"Go South two blocks. *Angelo's* is my favorite. You can park in the lot for the barbeque place across the street. Whaddaya like on your pizza?"

"Thanks." She doesn't answer my question, doesn't crack a smile, just looks straight ahead and drives off. I watch her taillights disappear before walking inside for another cup of coffee.

* * *

A half hour before closing, the Town Car returns. I rack a round into the Jennings before walking outside, tucking it in front of my wallet rather than behind it. I slowly approach from behind, hearing Classical music blaring rather than Metal...something by *Wagner*. Nebraska plates again, but the tag number is different. Not the same car.

The driver could be Creepy Clown's brother: same style of suit, but the slicked back hair is dirty blond, his face a bit longer and more angular. I glare at him, saying nothing. I break out in a cold sweat, pins and needles all over my clammy skin, suddenly dizzy and weak. He turns shark eyes to me, grinning impossibly wide, cheeks stretching past his head a half foot on either side as black vapor rises from the shoulders of his cheap polyester suit.

"What issss your doggie'ssss name?" Everything blurs out of focus like I'm underwater and I feel this pressure like a 200 pound weight pressing down on me, a roaring in my head as dozens of voices shout words I don't understand, and I know I'm about to pass out for sure. His door swings open.

Without even thinking about it, my arm snaps up and I shoot him in the face, three or four times, almost like someone else is pulling the trigger. The bullets' impact makes doughy flesh ripple and open, but nothing splashes, spills, or even drips. It doesn't seem to faze him a bit as he steps out of the car and faces me, grinning, arms wide, coming closer, ever closer, gliding across the asphalt, gliding *over* it. I put the last two in his throat, and that stops him in his tracks. He raises a hand to his neck and coughs, hacks, gags, finally spitting out a misshapen grey and copper mass that I realize is an expanded Stinger hollowpoint.

I drop the Jennings, flipping *balisong* as I close the distance, burying it up under the sternum as I slam my weight into him, riding him to the ground, jerking the brass double handle around like I'm shifting gears on a sports car. I yank the blade free as I roll to the side, springing to my feet. He doesn't move. I look down at my knife and see there's no blood...it's only damp, as if I'd run it under water to clean it, oily droplets beading.

I wipe both sides on my faded black Levis before flipping it closed, sliding it back in my front pocket. I quickly glance up and down the street, seeing no witnesses staring in slackjawed horror, before bending down to snatch up the Jennings and sprinting into the office. I flip the breakers for the pumps and overhead lights. We're closing early again.

I'm overwhelmed with dozens of thoughts zipping through my mind. I need to lose these weapons, but it can wait until later, they'll go up in the ceiling for now. I need to get that body in the trunk of the Town Car before ditching it somewhere, but I can't leave prints or fibers...maybe I should burn it? I grab a fresh set of latex gloves from the cleaning closet, pulling them on before turning to switch off the neon OPEN sign in the window. The car is gone.

I rush outside, running to the pumps. There's no sign of the car or any trace of the body. One of the local goblins might've jumped in a nice car left running at a gas station and jetted, as that happens from time to time along Colfax, but they wouldn't have touched the body. Hell, if they even noticed a body they would've ran away, not wanting to risk catching any heat. Some of these dirtbags would even dime me to the *Crime Stoppers* hotline, hoping to cash in on a reward. Report a homicide that results in an indictment, you're guaranteed at least a grand if you promise to testify, and a thousand bucks will make the party last all week long. Next to insurance settlements for walking into slow moving traffic, *Crime Stoppers* tips are a solid source of revenue for crackheads and cart pushers.

No, this guy that I repeatedly shot in the face and churned a tunnel through his heart apparently got up, brushed himself off, and drove away, not even leaving a single drop of blood behind. This is bullshit. This did *not* happen. Those weird drugs have damaged my brain. Then I see the shell casings.

This is really bad. Hallucination or not, I just emptied my gun at the same location, same time, two nights in a row. Hopefully, everyone assumed the rapid series of loud pops was some asshole setting off a string of illegal firecrackers.

Maybe I hallucinated the guy from last night too? This is really bad. I'm clearly going insane, having some sort of chemically induced psychotic break, and it's getting worse. I can't trust myself anymore. I need to drop this gun down a sewer grate before I seriously hurt someone and go back to prison. I am losing my mind.

Eventually, I calm down. I close up as usual and ride home.

* * *

I'm 10 years old, in my Cub Scout uniform, back on the hayride. Well, it was *supposed* to be a Halloween hayride, but there was no hay, just a big flatbed trailer pulled behind an old tractor, loaded up with about thirty kids from three different Scout troops, all arguing and picking on one another as the tractor drove up the hill, into the fields, into the dark...

I still don't understand what happened that night. I was hanging over the railing, looking at the ground, wondering what that green light was, shining on the dirt, keeping pace with the trailer. There were lights back there, but they were red and dim. This was like a focused beam.

Look up, the voice in my ear said. I look up and see a green light in the cloudless sky, a shimmering green oval hovering motionless and silent far above us. I ask my friends Joey and Mike if they see it, and they do. Unexpectedly, it blinks out of sight, instantly reappearing in another part of the sky not far away, then it does it again, again, again...I realize it's doing this for my benefit, trying to convey something to me, a combination of advanced concepts incomprehensible to my conscious mind being downloaded directly into my wetware.

This light is intelligent, this light is communicating with me telepathically, this light is somehow teleporting or passing through dimensions, and perhaps most importantly, this light is shining a beam right on me!

I take my eyes off it for a moment to look around, and it's as if time is frozen. Joey and Mike gape wordlessly upwards, and the other thirty Scouts don't even notice it, continuing to slap and pinch each other like stupid monkeys, but everything has gone dead silent, or perhaps I've gone deaf...I can't even hear the tractor's loud unmuffled motor anymore.

I look up again, continuing to watch the light zip about, dancing, for what seems like at least fifteen minutes, until I get tired of watching it...so very tired...then it's gone. It didn't shoot across the sky or do anything dramatic, it didn't even wink out, I guess I probably took my eyes off it right before it disappeared, so I never saw it depart.

I have a vague recollection of yelling at the light, yelling the word, ***"LAND!"*** over and over, hoping it would drop down to Earth and make formal contact like in the movies. Actually, that's the last thing I recall before it vanished.

I feel dazed. Looking around, the other Scouts were leaning all over one another, as if awakening from a drugged stupor, confused, disoriented. I look to the farmer, and he's sagged over the steering wheel as if passed out, but the tractor is still moving slowly forward and he straightens, shakes his head, and continues driving.

Everyone is quiet as we ride back to the parking lot. Something powerful, meaningful, and deeply Significant has just occurred, although I have absolutely no idea what it entailed. It's like my memory has been wiped clean. I smell their fear, feel their panicked energy, and realize everyone else has determined something had gone terribly wrong.

The tractor stops in the parking area and is mobbed by parents. They shout angrily at the farmer. What happened? Did the tractor break down? They were worried! Why is he over an hour late? Is he drunk? The farmer is an old man and practically in tears. *"I don't know,"* he chants over and over, like a mantra.

"Mom, I feel sick," one of the Scouts from another troop says. A lot of them are sick. Someone says it must be carbon monoxide poisoning from the exhaust. Someone else says they'll sue.

I ride home in the back of the car, a metallic blue Chrysler Imperial. My Da is furious. He hates being kept waiting, and was not allowed to drink his beer at a Scout function. He is in a hurry to get home. He blames me. "What happened?" my Ma squawks, "Why were you so late?" I tell her I don't know. I don't mention the light. I'm physically and mentally exhausted. I fall asleep on the way home.

* * *

I wake up gradually, painfully, stiff as if I'd slept wrong. I twist to the side and feel several vertebrae pop, which offers some relief.

I pick up the Bulldog, recently cleaned, oiled, and fully loaded with five fat .44 Special hollowpoints, stowing it out of sight beneath the worn mattress.

The alarm hasn't sounded yet so I switch it off. I turn on the coffeemaker and trudge over to the shower.

* * *

I have the day off, but swing by *Max's* because I know Billy is working. I kill the engine, rolling the bike over and leaning it against the wall. He's pumping gas for a customer so I walk into the office while he's busy and get the Jennings from the ceiling. He walks in as I'm coming out.

"I'm selling the deuce-deuce but don't wanna deal with the retards on Craigslist...you want another gun?"

"How much you want for it?"

"For you, a hundred bucks." He thinks it over for a moment, then nods.

"That's a nice little pistol. Okay." I hand it to him butt first and he racks back the slide, checking to make sure the chamber is clear, before nodding again and tucking it in his boot.

"I like the walnut grips on that. It looks like a James Bond gun." He opens the thick leather trifold and pulls out a few twenties.

"Here's sixty...I'll pay you the rest next week, you know I'm good for it."

"Cool." I'm just glad to be rid of it. I need to straighten out...I haven't been sleeping well and skipped breakfast, and when my blood sugar crashes I degenerate into something dangerously subhuman...especially in traffic. I need to eat food.

I start the bike and head down Washington to 6th, roaring towards Monaco then up to Colfax, turning West. I pull up in front of *Phoenician Kabob*, then remember the kickstand is broken, so I pull into the back alley and lean the bike against the wall. A bowl of hummus and a couple glasses of Arak should fix me up just fine...

* * *

I have protein in my stomach and a nice warm feeling from the booze as I leisurely cruise through Cheesman Park, taking care to abide by the 10 mph limit. It's a lovely day for a ride, and seeing the puppies playing Frisbee makes me smile, but I need to open up the throttle and clear my head.

I apply the brakes and come to a stop as a gaggle of hipster girls wearing mismatched clothes and oversized neon shades blindly stride across the paved road, fully absorbed in whatever they're texting. After they pass, I slowly let out the clutch so my tires don't chirp, as there's always a few cops hiding out waiting to bust folks for anything from unleashed dogs to littering...but after the sun goes down and the park officially closes, they disappear, and Cheesman becomes the place to go for upscale deviants from Cherry Creek seeking Ecstasy, hash, or anonymous gay sex.

I consider all the forgotten corpses buried here, well over five thousand from when it used to be Prospect Hill Cemetery back in the 1890s. The city fathers wanted a nice park and contracted with a local undertaker to exhume the dearly departed, transplanting them a few miles away in Riverside Cemetery for less than two bucks a a body, including labor, transportation, and the cost of a new coffin. The undertaker soon realized he could triple his money by ordering inexpensive child sized coffins and chopping each body into three parts. People from the neighborhood watched them do it for weeks before the press finally confirmed it.

Long story made short: everyone said, "Fuckit," and decided it would be a whole lot easier just to move the tombstones and forget the whole ugly affair ever happened. Thousands of unmarked graves remain, like in the movie *Poltergeist*. Some folks swear the park's haunted, but it doesn't work like that.

After a slow lap around the park, I swing West on Colfax until I can turn up Park Avenue, a long straightaway where the diagonal "streets" and horizontal "avenues" intersect. Triangle Park between Larimer and Lawrence looks like a zombie apocalypse: hundreds of homeless bunched together on the little concrete island, ruined camping gear and discarded clothes strewn all over the sidewalk, spilling onto the street.

One of the Christian motorcycle clubs is there with an improvised catering truck, serving free hot dogs and vegetable soup to anyone who wants some, right across from the gutted shell of the *Denver Rescue Mission*. On the steps of the burned out building, I see two humans sharing hits off a crack pipe and another taking a dump, right out in the open. He tugs up his trousers without wiping and holds out a hand for the pipe.

I'm not sure which I hate more, the zombie horde or the naive do-gooders feeding the animals. Momentarily, I wish I had a couple frags. One of DeNiro's lines as Travis Bickle runs through my head, *"Someday a real rain will come and wash all the scum off the streets."* Not in Denver. The filth here has metastasized, and a few crooked politicians have found some way to profit from it, funneling kickbacks from tax dollars and private donations into their own pockets.

I ride on...

* * *

As usual, I ride with no destination in mind, simply the elusive goal of "no mind," or as the Zen Buddhists say, *mushin.* The bikers call it "moving meditation." It's a Zen thing, one of the few things that clears my mind, calming me, bringing me peace.

If it wasn't for the peace I found in motorcycling and Tantra, I'd definitely be locked down for the duration by now. PTSD and anger issues can do that, especially when you drink whiskey and carry a gun, but I think I'm done carrying guns for awhile, now that I've lost my sanity and am shooting at figments of my imagination. If my parole officer finds out about that shit, I'll be in a rubber room getting Thorazine in my juice and electroconvulsive therapy.

I ride past the Red & White clubhouse on Navajo and the Sons' clubhouse on Brighton, but nothing seems to be going on.

On the way back, I briefly consider stopping at the infamous *Royal Spa* because I'm bored, depressed, and somewhat curious, but cannot justify the expense, and my libido is in the toilet anyway. I push those thoughts away, locking my mind down...I need to keep myself pure for my Goddess, and the Astral contaminants you pick up in a brothel can be far worse than any STD.

I cruise through Park Hill and see the Bloods are having a barbeque. It smells real good. I know a few of them, but it's four in the afternoon and there's nearly a hundred red bandannas swaggering around the yards of several Section 8 properties waving blunts and forties with *Cypress Hill* cranked at full volume, so I decide not to risk putting myself in a situation where I'm surrounded by a mob of drunk 'bangers trying to explain that my Irish ancestors didn't pass through Ellis Island until the 1900s and never owned any fucking slaves. The last time I had that conversation it didn't end well. I keep riding.

I cruise up Smith Road, crossing the tracks at Holly and heading North into Commerce City, turning East at the T on 48th before turning onto 47th Avenue Drive. It's an industrial zone with a lot of tall fences, vacant lots, and cul-de-sacs. A maze of dead ends, with street signs far and few between, many no doubt long uprooted and sold for scrap at one of the "no questions asked 'cause we no habla English" metal recyclers.

You need to slow down up here, as some of the potholes are aggressive enough to not only blow a tire but destroy the rim. If you're in a car and hit one the wrong way you could easily snap an axle, but on a bike it's a lot more serious...you could do a Superman over the handlebars, road rash sanding face and hands raw, bones splintering, and if you don't have medical insurance it will suck even worse.

I keep it at a steady 20 until it turns onto Sand Creek Drive, a paved frontage road between Sand Creek and Route 270. Something to the South blazes, an old factory on fire...but when I turn to look directly the orange flames are gone, nothing but sunlight reflecting off a fresh coat of paint. Fresh paint on the cannery?

I need to take a closer look, so when Sand Creek Drive becomes 56th, I turn South on Dahlia and take a hard left onto 52nd, deep into the industrial park, and there it is, *Happy Beans Cannery*, just South of Sand Creek and the Greenway Trail.

Happy Beans was an abandoned cannery claimed by the Outcasts, a small tribe of hardcore Punkers who'd mostly given up on music, skating, art, and pretty much everything else. There hadn't been electricity or functional plumbing there since the 70s when it closed down after the first fire.

There were never any raves or concerts there, as between the huge mounds of shit in every corner, broken bottles and rusty hypes scattered underfoot, rats big enough to hunt raccoons, and the rotting floorboards that could give way and drop the unwary into the basement, it was downright hazardous.

One of Billy's ex girlfriends lived there for a while before she detoxed from Oxycodone and got herself cleaned up. Now she paints surrealistic oils that are in galleries nationwide, and gets paid more in a week than both of us make in a month. Very cool lady with a lot of talent...and, if the legend is true, an inordinate fondness for German Shepherds.

It looks a lot different now. The broken windows are all boarded up and the whole building has a fresh coat of bright white paint covering the "Welcome To Hell" mural and assorted quasi-Satanic graffiti. They must've powerwashed decades of grime off the walls and given it several coats of thick latex. It practically glows in the scorching Colorado sun. Several overflowing dumpsters and a small fleet of contractor vans sit parked in the lot: plumbers, roofers, electricians, carpenters, painters.

It must've cost well over a million bucks to get the gutted factory presentable for a walk through, with at least another million needed to get it up to code. The furnace, pipes, wiring, and every scrap of metal the tweakers could rip from the walls and ceilings was scavenged years ago, and I recall gaping holes in the roof like the result of meteor strikes.

I'm surprised they didn't level that shithole and start from scratch...it probably would've been cheaper. I take a closer look at the vans, and they all read *Malphas Contracting* with a 402 area code, which is out of state. It pisses me off when people hire out of state labor for big jobs like this...that's almost as bad as hiring illegals. Lots of local non-union contractors need work, and are willing to work dirt cheap...even cheaper if no 1099s are involved.

I wonder how they got the Outcasts to leave? Several multi-agency raids with gas grenades couldn't do it. They'd seldom catch more than a couple due to their lookouts and tunnels, and they were always back within the week, usually between thirty and forty deep, not counting their dogs. Once, a realtor hired a security agency to have a watchman sit out there all night...but that was discontinued after they torched his car while he was making his rounds.

The cops could never find the SKS they'd shoot off the roof, trying to hit the Moon and the occasional helicopter with bright green tracers. Over a hundred pieces of brass and a handful of 410 casings were recovered, but never any guns. Those guns were well hid, and the cops probably weren't too keen on blindly sticking their arms into a rat nest searching for them. If they were left behind, the contractors have found them by now. I'm sure most of the walls needed to be rebuilt as they all had holes punched through them.

The new sign sticking out of the freshly mowed lawn reads: TEMPLE OF THE MORNING STAR. I've never heard of that church...maybe it's a Hindu thing.

I'm surprised the local Unions aren't picketing across the street like they usually do, although Commerce City is a bit out of the way. Not a word about this project in the *Denver Post* or *Westword* either.

I hope the Outcasts are just waiting for them to finish up before tossing a few Mollies and burning them out...insurance generally won't pay in cases of arson, and fuck those foreigners for using out of state labor to save a buck.

I've seen enough for today. I head back towards Denver.

* * *

I get home after dark, using a heavy logging chain and round *Fortress* padlock to prevent tweakers from rolling the Honda down the alley, untying and carrying the dry rotted leather saddlebags inside to keep the homeless from pawing though them again. So far, I've had a lockblade, an adjustable wrench, three pairs of sunglasses, and a can of *Fix-a-Flat* stolen. No-one has any respect once the sun goes down.

I live on the third floor so I can't roll the bike inside. It's been okay for the past two years; I just lock it to the post every night and throw a tarp over it during the Winter to keep snow off the seat. I don't know why I bother, as there's more duct tape than leather now.

For a Section-8 building with 40 units, it's surprisingly quiet. No kids, no pets, and a lot of night workers who sleep all day: dishwashers, janitors, cabbies, security guards. In fact, I think nearly everyone works except for a few retirees and cripples on the first floor. They're all studio apartments so the landlord can get away with refusing to rent to people with kids, saying the apartments aren't big enough; and at under 120 square feet, including the bathroom and kitchenette, it's true.

The lease says you can get evicted for disturbing the other tenants, and a couple times each year someone gets evicted for playing their stereo too loud too often. Since Smiley lives in the building he rents, he doesn't put up with any bullshit as he's always home and anyone with a complaint can feel free to knock on his door at any hour.

If Smiley needs to pound on your door after 10 PM in his bathrobe and slippers, that is your one and only warning to straighten up. Next time it happens he won't even knock, but will tack a 3-day "Notice to Vacate" on your door before going downstairs to shut off your water and electricity.

If you're still there after three days, he won't call the Sheriff, he'll call his stepson, a 400 pound psychopath who doesn't give a fuck and will fumigate your unit for bedbugs while you're still inside, before helping you down the stairs with his aluminum Tee Ball bat. While I've never seen this alleged stepson, he's sort of an urban legend around these parts, and a few long time tenants swear it's happened before.

Conveniently, my apartment is located right next to *"The World's Largest Discount Laundromat,"* which is part of the same building, but walled off so you need to walk around the corner to go inside. While that might seem inconvenient, it's rather important if you don't want zombies wandering the halls, rattling doorknobs and pissing on the radiators. That laundry is right on Colfax, where the zombies stagger in and out fairly regularly...and occasionally they even bite someone.

Usually, they ask for, then *demand*, a dollar: raving, frothing, looming, poking, until they get one...and then they insist they need more. The laundromat is open until 11 PM, but hardly anyone who speaks English is stupid enough to stay past sundown. At least Mace Pepper Foam works indoors and gives you a half dozen shots for under twenty bucks. A 2 ounce can usually lasts me about four months. It's pretty good zombie repellant.

I unbuckle the saddlebags and take out my shopping: a few glass bottles of Mexican *Coca-Cola*, a flask of *Sailor Jerry's*, a tub of red pepper hummus, some *Odwella* chocolate protein shakes, and a new fitted sheet set from *Target*.

I strip off the old sheets and hold them up to the light...they're so threadbare I can see through them in spots. I wad them up, stuffing them in the trash, flipping over the mattress and pulling on the new cover sheet. It's only 300 threadcount, but it's cotton flannel, and a nice dark grey so I only need to put it through the wash once a month.

I put the Cokes, hummus, and shakes in the empty 'fridge, then turn on one of the stove's burners to light an incense stick. Soon, the thick sweet scent of myrrh fills my tiny apartment.

It's been a long day. I strip down to my boxers and collapse on the mattress. Within moments, I drift away...

* * *

I find myself in The Library once again, sitting on the floor in a corner, reading a thin green hardcover on Hermetic Philosophy; something about the need to maintain balance, how every emotion can be adjusted on a level of one to ten, like the graphic equalizer on a stereo.

I hear a man shouting angrily, using profanity and pointing his finger in the Librarian's face. She rises, slowly removing her round framed spectacles, but says nothing...that's my job.

I walk over to them, taking the scene in, lacking a full understanding of the situation but knowing that the Librarian is not to be disrespected and this individual is therefore 100% wrong, even though he is wearing a tie.

"You need to shut your face and walk away. Now." He turns towards me, indignantly, pointing that finger again, running his mouth about what business was it of mine, when I pick up the old *IBM Selectric* typewriter with one hand, swinging it hard into the side of his head, connecting solidly with his jaw, nearly spinning him around backwards.

He staggers back a step, straightens, and balls his fists, whereupon I swing the heavy alloy framed typewriter down directly on top of his head, repeatedly, until he sinks to his knees. I kick him under the chin with my boot so he falls flat on his back. Straddling him, grasping the typewriter with both hands, I bring it down, down, down...pounding his head into paste. There is no blood, and soon his legs stop twitching.

I'm back on my feet, standing motionless, overcome with a profound sense of calm washing over me, although I have no recollection of standing back up. He stands beside me, head perfectly intact, also at peace, saying nothing. We both face the Librarian and she's no longer wearing that tweed blazer with her hair tied back in a conservative bun. No, now she presents as her True self: a fierce Valkyrie with flowing blonde locks and scant golden armor, complete with winged helm. I note not one, but *three* identical Ouroboros tattoos on her left arm from shoulder to elbow.

She is lecturing about the importance of serenity, calmness, balance. Her voice drones on and on and on...the lesson completely lost on me.

* * *

I arrive at a quarter of six to open, and find we never closed: all the lights are on, neon OPEN sign lit, pumps running. The door is unlocked as well. Flipping open *balisong*, I slowly walk inside, scanning every detail, ears tuned to any sign someone might be hiding out of sight, but the store, office, and restroom are clear.

The plastic till sits empty on the counter...even the loose pennies are gone. The cigarette rack is stripped bare: smokes, cigars, dip, rolling papers, lighters...only a few yellow cans of *TOP* rolling tobacco on the bottom shelf remain. If we sold scratch-off tickets, they'd surely be gone as well.

I have no doubt that folks have been helping themselves to free gas all night long, probably calling all their friends too. Frankly, I'm surprised no-one's called the cops, because everyone in the neighborhood knows we're never open past 10.

I switch off the pumps and check the schedule. Dave, AKA "Fubucky," worked last night. This was his first night closing, but I can't imagine anyone screwing up that bad, even a retard like him. He's definitely getting shitcanned, which means mandatory overtime for me and Billy until someone new gets hired.

I can't make change without a till and don't know the combination to the safe, so I call Max. It rings and rings and rings before going to voicemail: *"Max Fountane! Leave your message!"*

"This is Jake. I just showed up at the station and things are really fucked up here. Dave never closed last night...just walked away without locking up or switching anything off. There's no cash in the till and someone stole all the cigarettes. You need to get down here right now." I call Billy and leave the same message. Then I try calling Fubucky, but get a message telling me the *Cricket* customer I'm trying to reach is unavailable.

I don't call the cops. Max can do that when he gets here. If I called them, they'd probably accuse *me* of ripping off the place myself before beating me halfway into a coma with their fiberglass nunchucks, then arrest me for "resisting" which is an automatic revocation of my parole. You never want to talk to the DPD without witnesses...between the steroids and the blow, half of 'em will punch you in the face over a broken taillight on a bad day.

The double-edged butterfly knife is illegal, so I stick it up in the ceiling since they'll definitely be searching me and my saddlebags for cash and smokes. I have less than half a pack of *Djarum Blacks* left, but we don't even sell cloves here. I light one up, drawing the sweet smoke deep, feeling the nicotine settle my nerves.

I pace the lot, chasing a few early customers off, telling them there's a problem with the pumps. Max calls back and says he's on his way. I spot a square of crushed black plastic on the asphalt, a pair of earbuds plugged into it. I'm fairly certain it's Fubucky's everpresent *SanDisk* which never leaves his side as he works his shift with one bud in and one bud out. I pick it up, and the intensity of the vision slams me like a migraine.

Creepy Clown walking, smiling, WRONG WRONG WRONG, hair slicked back, arms wide, pale fingers stretching, FEAR PANIC FROZEN, eyes black as coal, shiny, alive but not, CHOKING, head swelling as impossible rubbery fingers wrap around my throat SQUEEEEEEEEZING, warm piss streaming down my leg, head explodes, BLACKNESS.

My head throbs with pain and I'm sobbing uncontrollably, collapsed next to the pumps, when Max's chopped Studebaker Commander rolls in. I quickly get to my feet, wiping my eyes, horrified that I've pissed the length of my jeans...but I look down and they're dry. I pat my crotch to make sure. As he parks the high gloss black boat at the far end of the lot, I discretely toss the broken *SanDisc* in the trash bin.

There is no way I can explain this, and if the cops think there's even the slightest possibility someone was kidnapped they'll turn this place into a major crime scene with detectives and forensics going over every square inch, no doubt finding the shell casings I missed. I decide it's best to keep quiet and let everyone think Fubucky is the worst employee ever; so it seems no-one will be looking for Fubucky...except maybe Max. He walks over, resting a thick callused hand on my shoulder. I try hard not to flinch, unsure what to expect.

"Thanks for calling me. Do me a favor and take the readings on the pumps so I can figure out how much we lost." He starts pacing. "That motherfucker! I'm gonna cut his stupid face off and feed it to my dogs! Insurance won't cover this. No point calling the cops. FUCK!" He disappears inside. A few moments later, the cigarette rack tumbles out the door, skittering across the lot until it hits the curbage at the pumps.

He spends about five minutes screaming profanity and smashing stuff, then it's quiet for a while...a long while. I wonder if he's had another heart attack. Eventually, he comes out.

"Have you got those readings for me?" He knows I haven't, the clipboard is still hanging on the office wall.

"I'm gonna do that right now."

"I've got your till ready and clocked you in. Just work the shift like none of this ever happened. Clean the place up a bit, it's a mess. If Dave shows up, you CALL ME and keep him here! I'm going over to Costco to get cigarettes. We're only selling Pyramid Red, Camel Filter, and Marlboro Light from now on. No more monkey menthols, no dip, no rolling papers, and *no free matches!* FUCK!" He walks to the Studebaker and gets in. I'm surprised he doesn't slam the door or peel out. He just pulls onto Washington and calmly drives off.

Overall, he seems to have taken things fairly well. I feel a profound sense of relief. I head inside to get the clipboard.

* * *

Billy rolls in a bit later, unshaven and flying his Regulators cut. He turns his head towards me, eyes hidden behind smoked aviator shades.

"What the fuck?" he asks. I tell him what Max said. "Holy shit...Max is gonna kill him." Then he laughs, obviously unconcerned. We walk inside and he seems shocked by the smashed shelves and product scattered all over the floor. At least the soda cooler was untouched.

"They did this last night?"

"No, aside from the cigarette rack and the till being empty, the place was fine. This was all Max." He laughs again, walking into the office, reaching behind the filing cabinet for the Hide-a-Key. He slides open the little magnetic box and peers inside.

"All three joints are still here. I thought maybe he smoked the good shit and got bent."

"You don't know good shit. That melted plastic you've been rolling up with your bud is bad for you. Hurts my head and makes me see shit that ain't there." He looks at me oddly, head cocked slightly askew.

"It doesn't do that to me. Maybe you're allergic."

"We don't even know what that shit is! It's probably made in China from dioxin or some shit. It'll make your balls shrivel up and give you blisters on your brain." He shrugs.

"Fine, don't smoke it then."

"I don't like it."

"You like that fancy *organic* shit from the hippies...that's what you like, that *gourmet* shit."

"That sticky green bud covered with crystals and purple hairs is premium quality. Your shit is stale and brown with little black chunks of something mixed in. May as well spray your ditchweed with Raid and smoke that...it'll probably do the same thing."

"Raid tastes different, and it's more like bad acid."

"That's because they make bad acid from insecticide. As long as people trip without going to the emergency room they'll keep buying that shit if it's cheap enough, then wonder why they've got brain cancer at 21."

"Raid don't give you cancer. They sell it at the store."

"It's neurotoxins and benzene in an aerosol can! You spray that shit on wasp nests, you're not supposed to smoke it!"

"You really like them hifalutin words, don't you? All pretendin' yer smart and shit. I'm gonna head back home and go back to sleep. I'll see you at six." He kicks his battered Pan-Shovel to life...it starts on the third try, coughing, backfiring, smoking, and leaving a half-dollar sized drop of black crankcase oil behind.

I pull the cigarette case out of my pocket, the image on the cover depicting two ladies engaged in an act deemed felonious in several Southern states, and open it up. I ignore the row of cloves and withdraw the handroll. It's the fancy organic gourmet shit...that's what I like. No more mindwarping plastic bullshit for me. This strain is a hybrid called "BubbleBerry"...it's pretty damned good.

* * *

The remainder of the shift is uneventful. I smoked the whole joint, half a gram, which makes the day go by quicker and keeps me in a brighter, somewhat cheerful mood.

A college girl at the wheel of a classic Beetle with bright red paint and polished chrome stares at me while I pump her gas.

"Hey! *You're high!*" I consider this for a moment before concurring with a nod. "Get *me* high!" she beams. Sadly, I tell her it's all gone...I don't even consider offering her one of Billy's plastic nightmares. She pouts, so I open the cigarette case, offering her a clove. "I don't smoke *tobacco*," she asserts, almost offended, as if it were something shameful and dirty. I made very sure not to let her see the cover, so I know it wasn't that. Fucking self-righteous hipsters.

I splurge on a medium pizza from *Angelo's*: garlic, red onions, black olives. I gobble down half of it in under five minutes, tossing the crusts in the trash. I use a blue shop rag to wipe my hands and face before closing the lid, saving the remainder for later.

An hour or so later, Matt shows up. I'm surprised to see him before sundown.

"Hello, Jake! I got me some clean clothes today!" he triumphantly holds aloft a rolled pair of jeans and a folded flannel shirt. "Can I use your hose?"

"Sure, Matt, but hold on a second," I open the utility closet and get him a bar of *Lava* soap with pumice, "Here, use this. You keep that soap and leave your dirty clothes on the ground out back."

"Thanks, Jake! I really appreciate this!" He disappears behind the building and soon I hear water spraying. *"HOLY SHIT! THAT'S FUCKIN' COLD!"* I hear him yell. I munch a cold slice of pizza.

About fifteen minutes later he comes back around the corner, all smiles, wet hair slicked back, resplendent in clean dungarees and a long sleeved blue flannel shirt unbuttoned over a spotless white T-shirt. He grins widely and spreads his arms.

“So do I look all respectable?”

“You surely do. Huge improvement. You want some pizza?”

“Oh, I would enjoy the fuck outta some pizza, pardon my language.” I put two slices together like a sammich and hand it to him, taking the last slice for myself. As we eat, he tells me how he’s on his way to the Temple to see if he qualifies for their job training program.

“Matt, I was up there last night and they don’t look like they’re open yet.”

“The guy was at Triangle Park this morning, saying anyone who wanted to work could come up there anytime, first come first served. I’m going up there tonight.” He hands me a laminated mini-flier that looks like a postcard.

TEMPLE OF THE MORNING STAR
FAITH BASED INITIATIVE
OFFERING HOPE TO THE DOWNTRODDEN
REDEMPTION THROUGH ACHIEVEMENT!

There was a Commerce City address, 5725 E. 52nd Avenue, followed by a dozen lines of small print extolling their goal of “improving and empowering” those who seek guidance and are “willing to commit to making a positive change.”

“You know these are a buncha religious nuts, and they’re probably gonna expect you to clap your hands and sing songs in church every day, right? The way places like this usually work is you gotta let them mindfuck you and be their dancing monkey boy who plays Simon Sez whenever they say. If you don’t do every stupid thing they order you to do, they’ll throw you out on your ass and tell you to get lost. That’s the nature of religious nut charity; nothing is freely given and everything has conditions, even a cheese sammich...you really wanna play that game?" Matt laughs.

"You know I don't believe any of that shit, Jake, but if it makes 'em happy I can pretend. The guy said we'd get our own bed and three meals a day just for followin' the rules and doin' chores. He said if we do good we'll get paid cash every Friday. I figure I'll check it out. This may be the last chance I get to make sumpthin' of myself." He becomes solemn, as if he's actually taking this self improvement bullshit seriously.

I know Matt, and realize it ain't gonna last past the first time he disagrees with something and gets upset. He's very expressive, especially when provoked, and it can get ugly fast. I give him 48 hours, tops, but am not such an asshole that I'm going to crush his dream, however futile.

"Well, good luck with that. Try to listen to what they tell you, keep your mouth shut, and don't lose your temper. If it doesn't work out, at least you'll know you gave it a shot. Here, take this for bus fare." I give him what's left of my tips, four wadded singles. I've never given him money before. He looks down at the bills for a few long moments.

"I won't forget this, Jake. I'll pay you back."

"Forget about it. Unlike the religious nuts, this *is* freely given. Just stay outta trouble and do your best."

"Thank you...thanks a lot!" I shake his hand when he extends it, another first, but it's okay because he washed it and the pizza is gone. He strides towards the bus stop, filled with a wild energy that some might mistake for determination. I'm guessing he'll need to change buses at least once, and when he gets dropped off at 52nd and Dahlia he'll need to walk a couple miles. I wonder if he knows which bus to take and what his transfer is, but see he's already crossed the street. He didn't even get his tea.

Billy rolls in, wearing a *Jack Daniel's* T-shirt and a shit eating grin.

"DUDE!" he yells, closing the distance rapidly. At least his hands are empty and he seems genuinely happy about something. He glances around conspiratively before sotto whispering, "You didn't tell me it was *full auto!*" He grins maniacally, rubbing his palms together so quickly I'm surprised they don't combust.

"Shit, I'm sorry man, that's a cheap gun and the sear sticks sometimes. I don't want you getting in trouble over that. I'll buy it back from you if you want."

"No fucking way! A deal's a deal, and I always wanted a machinegun. That thing is *awesome!"*

"You didn't take that to *Firing Line*, did you?"

"Naw, I got a stack of old phonebooks down in the basement that make a nice backstop. No one cares, everyone was at work and the walls are concrete."

"They'll care if you put a hole in the water heater or hit a gas line."

"Naw, I'm real careful." I'm skeptical. Billy's idea of gun safety is never to drink more than four shots of whiskey while target shooting, which is the exact amount his "shootin' flask" holds...and of course, beer doesn't count.

"You're not carrying it now, are you?"

"Fuck, no. I'll stick with the derringer. Makes a bigger hole, never jams, and doesn't spit shell casings all over my crime scene." He carries a tiny Davis .32 loaded with a pair of Glasers, nasty blue-tipped bullets designed to explode into fragments a couple inches beneath the skin.

While it may not stop someone, getting shot with a .32 Glaser is a guaranteed trip to the ER because you can't dig out the slug with forceps. Glasers are filled with tiny pellets, and if you miss even one the wound will turn septic and infection might kill you a week later. The only reason they're legal is because they're marketed as "Safety Slugs" allegedly designed not to overpenetrate thin walls.

Billy heads inside to punch in. I send a quick text to the Goddess: *8PM?* then follow him inside to count down the till.

* * *

I head home, taking a hot shower, scrubbing down with the spiced "Patchouli Pepper" soap from *Whole Foods*, using a fresh *Mach III* to shave my balls. I scrape the 5 o clock shadow from my face and slap on some Bay Rum cologne.

I brush my teeth thoroughly, gargling with mouthwash...I shouldn't have ordered garlic on that pizza. Renewed and refreshed, I walk over to the bed and check the messages on my cheap *Nokia* flip phone. Nothing. I try calling and it goes straight to voicemail: *"You have reached me...leave a message."*

"Hey, it's Jake. I'd like to see you tonight. Please call me back, thanks." I pace the confined apartment restlessly, deciding to listen to some tunes until she calls. I think *Mazzy Star* fits my mood so I put on that playlist.

After the first album, I pour myself a rum and Coke. After the second album, I mix my next drink 50/50. After the third album completes, I realize she ain't gonna call and switch the phone off, plugging it into the charger.

I change the playlist to *New Order*, pouring myself another drink to wash down a few melatonin gelcaps. Curling up on the new sheets, I do my best to clear my mind, drifting, fading, dissolving...

* * *

It is a couple years after the hayride; I think I'm about 12 or 13, up in the cabin my Da and Grandfather built inside the old barn. I used to spend a lot of time in that barn: climbing the thick hemp rope tied around the ceiling beam, doing bench presses, shooting my pellet pistol at cans, sticking flea market throwing stars in the walls, and looking through old boxes for long forgotten treasures left behind by the prior owner whose name we never knew.

The cabin in the barn is decorated in 1970s style, with wood paneling and burnt orange wall-to-wall carpet. There was electricity, but no running water...you could either crap in the ancient outhouse and risk getting spider bit, or use the bucket chair outside the cabin door.

I'm sitting in a corner next to a few cardboard boxes filled with old books, interesting books on a variety of esoteric topics. I choose one entitled *The Psychology of Colour* and read several pages before setting it aside and selecting an oversized leatherbound tome which seems intriguing, but something beneath catches my eye...it's a rubber Halloween mask.

I hold it up, examining the featureless white face with empty eyes and painted on hair when a voice in my ear whispers, ***It is coming!*** Suddenly, I'm seized with overwhelming panic, frozen in place, hearing things being thrown around and smashed in the barn. It's here! It's coming for me! It's right outside the only door and I'm trapped with no way out!

I'm compelled to open the narrow closet door to hide myself, but inside, past the moldering corduroy work coats and oilskin slickers, there's a varnished wood tunnel two feet wide and three feet tall, dimly lit, going straight back seemingly farther than the barn was long. I hear the cabin door slam open, shuffling, labored breathing. It's inside the cabin! I scuttle along the mystery tunnel as quickly and quietly as I can manage.

The tunnel twists and turns, going on for well over a quarter mile so far. Shuffling and heavy breathing behind me, close, so very close. I'm terrified, knowing if I dare glance over my shoulder I'll falter and be consumed. The tunnel becomes narrower at every turn. Soon, it is little more than a crawlspace I can barely squeeze through, and the wood becomes rough and unfinished, scraping my palms and knees. A long splinter breaks off in my forearm, then another in my leg. I tire and slow.

A hand seizes my ankle and it's colder than ice, colder than anything I've ever experienced, all encompassing, radiating up my leg to my chest. My heart freezes, stops, sudden pain like the bone is being split with a hammer and chisel. I use the last of my energy to look down. The thing hunting me was a mime, slender with black bodysuit and white greasepaint, absolutely no expression on its face, dead soulless eyes black as coal...

I see myself standing, on stage, facing an unseen audience, orating about the nature of fear and why it is an illusion. I am simultaneously on the stage and watching myself from the audience. It is a rather dull soliloquy. I notice someone standing beside the me on stage. It's the mime.

He is motionless, facing the audience, saying nothing, and I realize he's an emissary of Death, and although he could have easily ended me on the Astral, he had been charged by his master to teach me a lesson. My higher, more spiritual self seems to have appreciated the Significance of the lesson, but my coarse self in the audience is not operating on that frequency.

I fail to understand what is going on. It just seems like a stupid game to me. At that moment, my higher self stares directly at me and smiles, saying ***"Knight takes Bishop,"*** and I'm flying backwards through a darkened tunnel impossibly fast, falling, falling, falling...

* * *

I slam onto the mattress as if dropped from a great height, eyes wide, wind knocked from my lungs. There's absolutely no question in my mind that I'd been levitating this time. The room's lit with a dim green glow that slowly fades as my eyes come into focus and I awaken. The clock says it's 0800 exactly.

I check my phone and there are a couple of new texts. The first is from her: *Sorry I wasn't able to get back to you until now. I'm in Vegas for the next two weeks. I miss you and look forward to seeing you again when I get back! <3.*

The second is from Billy: *Had a really bad night and am scheduled to open in the morning. Need you to come in as soon as possible tomorrow.*

Fuck.

I flip the phone shut and toss it on the bed, trudging into the kitchen to flip on the coffeemaker. I dump a mound of raw sugar in my chipped Cobray mug, then pour in the remainder of the rum. It's fixin' to be a long miserable day.

* * *

I wasn't supposed to come in until 3, but I get there a little after 10. Billy is pacing, perspiring, pale; hair disheveled, eyes wild. He sees me roll in and attempts to smile, but his demented grimace chills me to the core...something is seriously wrong. Then I realize he is completely sober.

"Fuck, fuck, FUCK!" he yells, "I think I need to leave town for a while! I think I done sumpthin' really BAD last night!" He's practically in tears.

"Who did you kill?" He spins, enraged.

"You motherfucker...I will...FUCK!" He bolts into the office. That was not the reaction I was expecting. I follow him inside and find him collapsed over the counter, face buried in his hands, shaking uncontrollably, wracked with sobs, taking huge gulping breaths every few seconds.

"Dude..." He looks up, eyes red rimmed and crazed.

"I shot Fubucky last night, shot him right in the face." His mouth gapes at this revelation, and I'm not sure if he's more horrified that he shot his co-worker or that he just told me about it.

"So, I guess Max is gonna give you a raise?"

"NO! It wasn't like that! He showed up at closin' last night, with some other guy, both had their faces painted like a couple of Juggalo faggots, driving a big black car. They were askin' for you!"

"Asking for me?"

"Yeah, Fubucky wanted to know when you were workin' again, but his voice was all wrong, and I was trippin' balls off that shit, and they were freakin' me out and backed me up against the ice machine, and I sorta flipped out and shot him in the face. I ain't never shot nobody before, Jake! I am in so much fuckin' trouble! FUCK!" Whereupon he resumes blubbering.

"What happened then?"

"I dunno. I think maybe I hit him in the cheek, but he just turned around like it was nuthin' and they walked back to the car and left. I'm surprised the cops haven't shown up yet. I don't wanna go back to jail...I am so sick of grilled cheese sammich and Cartoon Network! I'm leavin' for Arizona tonight."

"No-one's gonna call the cops."

"Jake, *I shot him in the face!* The hospital calls the cops every time a gunshot wound comes in! They're probably talkin' to him right now! I gotta get outta here!"

"Dude, it's gonna be cool. They ain't gonna call no cops. Trust me."

"You don't know what you're talkin' about! You haven't got a fuckin' clue!"

"Black Lincoln Town Car? Black suits? Hair slicked back? Sounds like Fubucky's runnin' with Creepy Clown Crew now."

He gapes, dumbfounded for a few moments before speaking again.

"You *know* those guys? Those guys are scary...even Fubucky was scary...like he wasn't Fubucky at all."

"Because his eyes were all black?"

"Because *somethin' was inside him*...somethin' really BAD...wearin' him like a skin suit. That wasn't Fubucky anymore. It was somethin' wearin' a Fubucky *suit!*"

"Something that was asking about me?"

"I'm really scared, Jake. I don't know if what I remember's real or what the fuck I did...I don't even remember closin' up and drivin' home last night. I only remember shootin' Fubucky in the face and nothin' happenin'. I didn't even hear the gun go off, but there's an empty casin' and burnt powder in the top barrel. He just turned around and walked away. *I didn't even make him bleed!*"

"You know how crazy that sounds, right?"

"But...you know what's going on, right?"

"Like you said, I haven't a clue. This shit's all new to me, but what I *do* know is that if you tell anyone what happened, jail will be the least of your worries, 'cause they'll have your ass locked in a padded room whacked out on Thorazine for the duration."

"I know I need to quit smokin' that shit, but I *crave* it. It feels like worms burrowin' under my skin if I don't start the day with a toke and maintain. If I go cold turkey I even *see* the worms, and then I get doubled over with cramps. You were right...that shit is so fuckin' bad."

"All the guys are smoking it?"

"All day long. Shit is really cheap, and *everyone* is sellin' it now."

"Not the dispensaries."

"You know who I mean."

"I didn't bring a gun today...can I borrow yours?" He reaches behind his back and pulls a blunderbuss out from under his shirt and hands it to me. I'm standing out in the open in broad daylight, looking down at a sawed-off, break-action single-shot about a foot long with a knobby wooden grip.

"The derringer didn't work, so I figured maybe a 16 gauge slug might."

"That's just nuts." But then I remember 6 rounds of .22 Stingers in the face and throat didn't work either. I take the shotgun, but don't stick it down my pants. I'm a lot thinner than Billy, and this sawed-off must weigh five pounds. I take it inside and set it on top of the safe. He slumps against the doorway, watching me. "Fubucky doesn't know where you live, right?"

"No-one knows my new address, except for you and a few guys from the club."

"Then it's safe for you to go home and stay put. I'll call you if anything happens." He mopes around for nearly an hour before finally leaving. I don't think he slept at all last night.

After he goes, I check the Hide-a-Key and find one joint inside. It gets broken in half and flushed down the toilet.

* * *

Later that afternoon, Crazy Fucking Larry shambles in, wearing a fresh set of Desert cammies from the Sally, trousers bloused into battered cowboy boots.

Last month they finally let him out of County for kicking the shit out of Fake Blind Guy at the invisible bus stop on Colfax and Broadway, which the city dismantled because the corner boys thought it was the best place ever to hide their crack and heroin sales from the cameras.

That beatdown made the front page as it happened in front of hundreds of Yuppies passing by in rush hour traffic, and apparently the DPD wasn't able to get to the scene to break it up for over 15 minutes, even though they're practically across the street. The last 4 minutes of it is on *YouTube* and went viral for a short time because, after all, there's a reason he earned the name "Crazy Fucking Larry," and that beatdown was one of the most enthusiastic I'd ever seen.

The *Denver Post* wailed about how this heinous act perpetrated against "one of the most vulnerable members of society" was practically the Crime of the Century...until a couple days later when someone finally realized that Fake Blind Guy wasn't actually blind...and the reason Larry was so pissed off was because Fake Blind Guy felt compelled to whip out his grimy pecker again, discreetly beating off while rubbing the tip against a rabbit fur coat worn by the high school girl standing in front of him.

The unnamed female victim had a total meltdown, screaming she was being raped, thereby prompting Crazy Fucking Larry to snap into full vigilante mode. Apparently, he didn't even say a word, just used some sort of judo flip to faceplant him into the sidewalk and began kicking him like he thought candy was gonna come out. He busted all his front teeth and cracked five ribs before the cops dragged him off. Now he shows up once a week to get a Super-Size *Payday* bar...which I never charge him for. Crazy Fucking Larry is alright with me.

"Hey, Larry...have you seen Matt around?" He tears the *Payday* wrapper open with his teeth before chomping off a third, slowly munching, mouth open, peanut fragments clinging to chapped lips, some tumbling to the floor.

"Saw him last week. You want I should track him down for ya?" I consider this for a moment. Larry has difficulty distinguishing fantasy from reality, and is wont to brag about various secret missions he participated in back when he was assigned to Special Forces during 'Nam...but everyone knows Larry has never been outside of Denver, and wasn't even born until the late Seventies, long after Vietnam ended. No-one takes his crazy bullshit seriously, but sometimes it's funny to listen to when you're stoned. He has a vivid imagination, and can go into the most intricate detail for hours if you let him.

"Alright. Last I heard, he was heading to that new shelter in Commerce City, Temple of the Whatnot, or whatever they call it. You know, at the old cannery where the Outcasts used to squat. Supposedly they're paying cash for chores and letting folks live there rent free. You feel like checking it out, maybe seeing how Matt is doing?" I know Larry doesn't need a place to stay since he lives in his Mom's basement, but I figure maybe he feels like going on an adventure. His eyes glaze out of focus as he stares past me for a few long moments, before finally nodding his head.

"Sure. I can check things out, report back."

"Cool." I don't offer him bus fare as he has one of those laminated *RTD* free ride passes hanging around his neck, and probably a lot more cash in his pocket than I do. He finishes his *Payday* bar before stalking up Washington towards Colfax.

* * *

I switch on Max's battered *Dell* laptop and connect the homemade antennae to pick up a wireless signal. Today, I find one that's unsecured and manage to connect to Google.

This is pretty much my only access to the internet unless I want to walk to the Central Library to reserve a public computer, wait until one is free, then spend *no longer than one hour* crammed between a 400 pound tubercular homeless and a

Welfare mother with a yowling infant on her lap, so I generally do without.

My disposable flip phone can connect to the internet, but has a wee one inch screen, a tendency to freeze up, and *T-Mobile* charges a dollar every time I check my email. I'm glad Max left the laptop here. I think he only used it to play Five Card Draw and watch DVDs.

"Darkside Dan of Denver" has an interesting blog. If the photograph is accurate, he's about 7 feet tall with a bright red Mohawk and wears a leather trench coat. Usually, he talks about Denver's Goth and Industrial scene, particularly how the clubs all suck and the DJs are poseurs, but occasionally he'll post pics of his black van with the diamond plate panels and reinforced push bumpers, or his "Girlfriend of the Month" modeling some fetish wear at a local BDSM dungeon, but I only read it for the weekly column he calls "Back Alley Beat."

Every weekend is a party for Dan, as he and his friends mope along Broadway between Colfax and Alameda, Friday night 'til early Monday morning, consuming vast quantities of strange drugs and interacting with the local deviants.

By Wednesday evening, he posts a long rambling essay about his experiences, reminiscent of Hunter S. Thompson's early work, but illustrated with cellphone pics and occasionally even a video. He talks about rumors, gang tags, street fights, and petty arrests of people he identifies only by nickname, and most of what he reports seems fairly accurate.

So last week we tried smoking straight Black Diamonds out of the glass pipe, which seemed like a brilliant idea at the time. Do not attempt this. Pipe got gummed up with some foul tasting shit that is impossible to clean off – after alcohol failed, we tried ether – pipe is fucking ruined. I shudder to envision what this crap has been doing to everyone's lungs.

We fucking TRIPPED BALLS for three hours, but it was the most fucked up trip I've ever had. Fucking Nemo curled up in the alley between 10th and 11th screaming about vines coming out of the walls to hold him for the coyotes, but I was so sick of his drama and after making him eat a Xanax ordered him to unfuck himself, but he was too far gone and a total disgrace. We ended up needing to leave his worthless ass locked in the Mobile Command Station so he wouldn't get buggered by hoboes.

We then proceeded back to Milkbar, *which surprised us by not being lame as fuck – but perhaps it was the chemicals. Anyhow,* Milk *is fucking awesome when giant black starfish are flapping through the air like bats and the bartender turns into a lizard. The remixes were good too, although I don't remember what was played and did not recognize the DJ as he was covered in slime and had a giant larvae stuck to the back of his head. Supposedly this shit is synthetic DMT, and while the taste is similar, the effects are a lot different. For one, it lasts a fuck of a lot longer, and second, you can still walk, talk, count bills, find your way to the loo, and otherwise function in a club environment. DMT is not a club drug at all – you really want to get transported to the Third Circle of Hell to be eviscerated by evil giant mantis things intent on torturing you for all eternity in the privacy of your own home, but I digress.*

Anyhow, this shit ain't DMT, and even smoking vast amounts raw and unfiltered will not result in anything resembling a DMT experience. In the hope of discovering what the fuck we've all been smoking, my primary goal is to run a sample of this through the mass spectrometer at DU, and I will pay ONE HUNNED DOLLA CASH MONEY YO to anyone who can help me achieve said goal since apparently I have been banned for life from their laboratories. Cash payable upon receipt of the breakdown analysis sheet – and if you're extra nice, I may even let you blow me.

In other news, the clerk at the 7-11 at 6th and Santa Fe apparently went missing sometime between 0200 and 0400 Sunday night, and it seems he took all the malt liquor and menthols with him. It is so hard to get good help nowadays – but that same location refuses to hire anyone with piercings, so fuck 'em.

* * *

The sun goes down and customers are far and few between, maybe only two an hour. The whole while, I'm overwhelmed with the sense of being stared at. I feel pressured, crowded, violated, as if someone has intruded into my personal space, standing mere inches behind me, staring fixedly at the back of my head, always moving out of sight the instant I turn. This is what it must feel like to be in the crosshairs of a sniper scope.

I keep glancing up at the Condos on the other three corners, expecting to see some hipster with a telephoto lens thinking I'll be the unwitting subject of their "wry and ironic" art project, or maybe some creepy old pervert peering through a spotting scope while stroking one out, but I see nothing but row after row of empty windows.

Several times throughout the night, I glimpse a dark figure lurking outside my peripheral vision, always fading into shadow the moment I turn to look. When it's an hour until closing, I get the fear and nearly close early, but decide Max is way scarier than Creepy Clown and I can't afford to lose this job either. I'd have a lot of difficulty finding another one, as even *McDonalds* and *Wal*Mart* do background checks, and no-one else is hiring except the scam artists on Craigslist who don't pay.

Around 9:30, I untuck my shirt so I can pull it over the grip of the blunderbuss now stuck through my belt. At 9:50, I cut the lights and hurriedly take the readings with my flashlight. After clocking out, I wrap the scattergun with a towel and bury it under the other towels at the bottom of the maintenance closet. I'm the only one who ever goes in there, so I know it'll be safe.

The office is locked and I have the bike started and rolling down 8th just after 10. No Town Car tonight. I expect to see it zooming up fast in my mirror the whole way home, but it never does.

I feel the weight of invisible eyes, the intensity, malevolence of their glare, as I walk up the steps of my building. Once I cross the threshold the pressure snaps off, as if a switch had been thrown, a connection cut. Somberly, I climb the steps to my apartment, drained, stripping down to my boxers and collapsing on the mattress. I lose consciousness within moments.

* * *

I find myself deep in The Maze once again, a sublevel of the Hell of Endless Doors with the rough rock walls of an ancient dungeon. Not even wooden doors on this level, only a massive labyrinth of tunnels. I seldom get down this far, and am uncertain if there's another level beneath it, but from the hardpacked clay floor I doubt it.

Suddenly, **IT** is coming. **IT** has always been here, waiting, consumed with rage and mindless hunger. **IT** is monstrous, unstoppable, footfalls slamming clay like 500 pound sledgehammers, the very rock of the walls vibrating with every stomp of **IT**'s feet. I flee in wild eyed terror. There's nothing else I can do, nowhere to hide, impossible to fight. **IT** is about to grasp me from behind, snapping, twisting, tearing, feeding on screams and terror and pain...

I run for what seems like hours, ground rumbling, walls rattling, rough bestial panting behind me. Exhausted, running on empty, on instinct, I stumble and fall. **IT** is standing over me, poised to plunge talons deep into my guts, grasping, pulling, unraveling. I glance up and am struck by a light so magnesium flare bright PAIN lances my eyes like spikes, searing them like lye, even after being clenched tightly shut. I am trapped, blinded, powerless, before whatever this thing is.

"OPEN YOUR EYES!!!" A commanding voice booms, as if from amplifiers placed all around. My eyes creak open a sliver before being scalded, snapping shut once again.

"OPEN YOUR EYES!!!" The voice bellows, even louder than before, clearly angered. I decide I'm already dead and force the lids open wide, expecting the orbs to be scorched from their sockets, it's scalding white hot agony...and then I go past the pain, beyond the blindness, and something reveals itself to me, shows me its True Face, but I lack comprehension, my primitive brain creating a symbol I can better understand.

The blinding white light dims to blazing gold, which sears my retinas to behold, but at least now I can make out a few details. It's not a creature facing me at all, but a metal idol of some sort, a giant slab of molten gold filling the corridor, upon which is sculpted the likeness of an inhuman figure in bas relief...a cross between a Sumerian astronaut god with headgear and goggles, bristling with wide bore cannons; and Kali in her Destroyer aspect with multiple sets of arms, each brandishing a wickedly curved blade.

I gaze upon the face of God and come to the calm realization that I'm about to die, Astrally as well as physically, and I'm surprisingly okay with that...but as I continue to stare at this blazing, immobile, ancient plaque the sheer ridiculousness of the situation compels me to laugh.

Immediately, I see myself standing on the stage again, alone, facing a darkened auditorium. I sense the God's presence, and perhaps that of a few others as well, but the audience is hidden in shadow. I am filled with peace, not nervous at all.

"That was very cruel of you, to frighten me so," my self on the stage says.

"It was necessary in order for you to achieve the Second Degree," the voice replies, whereupon I am Enlightened, a thousand petaled lotus blooming in my mind and I am AWARE of everything that had occurred in my past and why it was necessary. AWARE that my higher self chose to experience those things in order to evolve, thereby transcending base mortality. AWARE of everything occurring in the present, quite literally EVERYTHING, and know that I walk in Righteousness and Truth. It all falls into place and makes perfect sense. I understand now.

Moments later, I awaken, the experience fading, deleting, lost forever. I vaguely recall a giant blazing Sumerian carving telling me to "open my eyes," and apparently there was some very deep and profound message intended for my higher self which flew past me completely. Regardless, I remain shaken by the experience, even though I cannot recall it.

I'm famished. I start the water boiling for oatmeal.

* * *

The Bulldog was made during the 70s, a minimalized wheelgun with a narrow three inch barrel and exposed ejector rod. It only weighs a few ounces over a pound, which is light for a .44 Special.

This is a lot more gun than the Jennings, and somewhat difficult to conceal, even with the cheap nylon clip-on holster, but I make due as best I can. It only holds five rounds, but loaded with jacketed hollowpoints one shot will drop nearly anything on two legs...and it doesn't spit incriminating shell casings either. I think I'll be carrying this from now on.

After completing my 200 pushups and showering off, I disconnect the smoke detector and burn some sage, allowing the fragrant mentholated haze to fumigate my apartment. Again, I slide the chef knife from the drawer and scrape at the usual attachment points: base of the skull, between the shoulder blades, small of the back. Then I work on the secondary points as well.

Sometimes, especially if you're out of sorts and the auric shell is weak, things seize an opportunity to latch onto you, usually at a chakra, draining, disrupting, feeding...if you're lucky and all you get is a mindless parasite. If the thing in question is an entity of some sort, even a fairly weak one, its intelligence makes it far more dangerous.

An entity can tap into repressed memories with the intent of eliciting a specific emotional response: terror, rage, lust; thereby raising energies upon which it feeds, inducing a euphoric state similar to the effect of a highly addictive drug. A degenerate entity addicted to that rush can run a host into the ground in short order, impulsively hitting those buttons until they burn out or self destruct. That is the nature of most demonic overshadowing and obsession.

I feel resistance as the edge of the blade scrapes across the brow chakra, sticking and stopping as it connects with a wartlike bump, but I gaze in the mirror and run my fingers over the skin, registering nothing physical. Picking up the smouldering sage, I bend over it, letting white smoke rise from the embers and spread, cleansing warmth washing over my face. I try scraping again and it breaks free...I feel immediate relief, comparable to slipping off a 100 pound pack. For an instant I actually see the tendril, a dusty cobweb, snapping back through the wall to wherever its source might be. Whatever sent it would feel the connection severed as well.

A tendril rooted in the brow chakra concerns me, as only the most powerful entities are able to tap Pineal energy from a distance, and while it's not uncommon for that to occur with individuals who willfully place themselves in compromising circumstances, it's extraordinarily rare for such stealth attacks to succeed against an experienced clairvoyant sensitive to the nature of such things. The runes tattooed across my shoulders would have repelled most threats automatically, so whatever it was needed to be incredibly subtle to slip past my defenses. Powerful and ancient, having practiced and perfected such attacks on countless victims.

Briefly, I almost wish I had a God to pray to. I had one once, before I was betrayed and abandoned. No God is better than a false one pretending to be something it isn't. Or a dying one capable of little more than commiserating about your misfortune. A God which lacks Power, or the willingness to share it, hardly can be deemed Godlike at all. All I have is my own Power...and that of my ancestors.

I pull a few paperbacks from the bottom shelf, reaching into the gap, seizing the leather cord and drawing it out. My medicine pouch, the only thing of value I own, although it would be utterly useless to anyone else, and woe unto anyone foolish enough to steal it.

A silver earring, a steel penny, a brass shell casing, a knotted lock of hair, a piece of charred bone, a pointed tooth...each a focus, a connection, a relic. I hold the pouch aloft in my left hand, with my right I dig the point of the knife into my chest, carving the rune TIWAZ into the flesh over my heart.

Tears flowing freely, blood trickling steady, I Call each of the spirits by name...Call them to me...tell them what I need.

* * *

Cleansed, recharged, and protected, I now need to fuel the carcass, as oatmeal will only get you so far. I race the bike up Federal to *El Padrino*, rolling behind the building so I can lean it against the wall.

Once inside and seated, I order my usual Jack & Coke and decide to indulge in the house specialty: *Pulpo Diablo*, fresh chopped octopus stewed in blazing red chile sauce and served with tortillas.

I love spicy food, but this makes my brain sweat. I need to clear my sinuses into the napkin several times before finally ordering a vanilla milkshake to kill the burn.

* * *

A little before 3, I roll into *Max's Petrol*. Max is there, standing next to a human scarecrow, six feet of skin and bones in baggy dungarees and a ragged flannel shirt.

"Jeffrey, this is my best guy, Jake...he's going to teach you everything you need to know. Jake, this is Jeffrey...he is one stupid motherfucker...maybe you can show him how to check the oil without getting his hair caught in a fanbelt." Then, after spitting on the ground in disgust, he stomps over to the Studebaker and takes off, leaving me staring at this sad looking thing with its ill-fitting clothes, sunken eyes, hollow cheeks, and a long straw-colored ponytail you could probably wring grease from.

"Alright, Stickboy...the three most important things to know are: how to punch your timecard, how to pump gas, and how to make change. Once you've mastered the basics, I'll show you how to check the fluids and make stuff clean." He doesn't say a word, just stares, unblinking, with vaguely focused eyes, breathing shallowly through his slackjawed mouth, hands stuffed deep in both front pockets.

I wonder why Max hired him. I wonder how many minutes until he passes out or sets something on fire. I wonder if he has special needs. I walk inside to clock in, Stickboy tagging close behind.

* * *

It turns out that Stickboy is one of Max's nephews and was recently caught on his neighbor's farm, after Midnight, wearing nothing but a pair of hip-waders. He told the judge he was "sleepwalking" and got assigned the same probation officer as me. He's 23 years old and has never kissed a girl...and apparently didn't get past 2nd base with the neighbor's goat either.

I feel sorry for him and make him eat a *Snicker's* bar, which was probably the only thing he'd eaten all day. His eyes become slightly less glassy and he starts moving a bit faster.

After a few hours, I decide he can probably get most of the gas into the cars and make change somewhat accurately, so his training for the night is over. I give him another *Snicker's* and tell him to show up at 0930 tomorrow.

He'll never be getting a set of keys, but at least he can help during our busiest time while satisfying the terms of his probation. Perhaps an extra guy will allow me more time to browse the internet and master the art of the bent throwing star. Max better not cut my hours on account of this goat molesting retard.

* * *

I'm on my fourth cup of Sumatran when the black primed stationwagon rolls up to the pumps, *Motorhead* blaring from the cheap stereo, probably a little past half volume. I get a better look at her this time: probably about twenty, naturally black hair free of product, no makeup aside from thick black eyeliner. Car is old and battered, but clean. I catch a scent of camphor and menthol...*Tiger Balm?* She turns those flat brown eyes to me, holding my gaze,

"Twenty bucks," handing me another pair of tens.

"Lemmy is awesome." Her expression doesn't change, but her eyes drop to my chest.

"What is that you've got under your shirt? Show it to me." It doesn't sound like a request. I gaze down at my loose olive drab T-shirt, seeing barely a ripple in the fabric over the thin leather pouch. I grasp the cord, drawing it up through my collar and letting it hang free. I have no intention of taking it off for anyone.

She slowly extends her arm, touching the pouch with her fingertips, cupping it gently in her hand, closing her fingers around it, closing her eyes, lips parting slightly, eyes rolling under their lids, third eye opening behind her brow, suffusing me with a pale blue light no-one else could see. The light snaps off as her physical eyes open, changed, puzzled, knowing.

"Your medicine bag is *ice* to me. Odd to cross paths with a necromancer in this way." She releases it, letting it slap against the front of my shirt. I tuck it back inside my collar, where it belongs.

"It's not like that at all. 'Tis only a keepsake, in remembrance. I'd never presume to command anyone. What they do is done freely, out of love." The corner of her mouth twitches, a sharp tic.

"Pump the fuel, necromancer." I turn, walking back to unscrew the gas cap, and hear a sharp bark of laughter, then the word, *"Love,"* mocked, dismissed, spat.

I lock the pump to run slow, using the squeegee to clean the grime off the back window, but it's too dark inside to see. I walk to the front and clean the windshield, pointedly ignoring that she's glaring unwaveringly at me, expressionless, the whole while. I clean the headlights too.

"Pop the hood," I say, and she reaches under the dash and pulls the latch. I lift it up, locking it in place, and check the oil, brake fluid, power steering fluid, transmission fluid. All seem topped off and fresh. Coolant and washer levels are fine. Battery and terminals are new, as are the belts, hoses, wires, and alternator. It's surprisingly clean and well maintained for what must be a 30 year old beater. I close the hood. The pump has clicked off, and I see it stopped at $22.05, going over a bit. I don't mention it.

"Everything looks good. Seems like it was serviced recently." She starts the ignition, then turns to me, eyes peering deep, saying nothing. I feel uncomfortable. I can't pick up anything from her, so she must have some major shielding. Her eyes narrow, turning hard.

"We're watching you," she says, without malice or threat, simply a statement of fact. Then looks straight ahead, slaps the old Volvo into gear, and drives off.

I stand, speechless, gazing after her taillights for a long time. I have no idea what just happened.

* * *

I'm back at the cottage, with Susan, her face colorless and waxy, pieced together with thick black stitches.

The fancy silver creamer and sugar bowl sit on the oak table between us, along with an assortment of amber dropper bottles and a half empty pint of Jack. We sip our coffee contentedly, her free hand resting on mine. Then she reaches across to the gold foil wrapper, peeling it back, snapping off a corner of blackness, raising it to my lips: Amazonian dark chocolate with blueberries, her favourite.

There is a knock at the door, rapid and light. She turns to me, "It appears we have a visitor," then rises gracefully, striding to the door, opening it fearlessly and without hesitation.

It is the Goddess, scared and confused. She's wearing a forest green bathrobe with matching slippers, blonde hair in tangles, face scrubbed clean of makeup. "I'm sorry, Jake...I didn't know where else to go."

"It's okay. You're always welcome here. You are safe." She rushes over, holding me way too tight, sobbing piteously.

"Oh Jake! It was so awful! I never thought it would happen like that! I'm always so careful!" Her whole body wracked with sobs as I hold her close.

"It's okay. No-one will ever hurt you again. You're with us now." She looks up at me, eyes wet and wide.

"I can stay here?"

"You're family...of course you can." She holds me again, gently, gradually calming.

"I don't even know how I found this place. I was all alone in the dark, walking for hours along a path through the woods, thinking how I wished I could call you to come and make things better, but I'd lost my phone. Then I saw this place and knew you were inside," she pulls away and glances at Susan, "I'm so sorry for intruding." Susan's Frankenstein face brightens into a genuine smile, perfect teeth gleaming.

"You are a guest in our home and welcome. Please, sit and stay. Would you like some coffee?"

"Toots, some freak just tore out my guts with a boxcutter and used them to decorate the room while I was screaming into his nasty gym sock...which I can still taste, by the way. Three fingers of whiskey in mine, thanks...sweet and light."

* * *

I'm awake instantly, panicked and breathless. Fumbling for the phone, I snap it open, waiting for it to power up, then make the call.

"Who is this?" A man's voice answers.

"My name's on the Caller ID, motherfucker...put Samantha on." The line goes silent, but I hear voices and activity in the background. "Hello? You there? Put her on right now."

"Are you Jake?"

"That's right."

"Jake, this is Detective Anthony Miles with the Las Vegas Police Department. What is your relationship to Samantha Fletcher?" I consider how best to answer that. Probably best to lie. I hate lying, but sometimes you have no choice.

"Sam's my sister. Is she alright? What happened?"

"Mister Fletcher, I'm sorry. Your sister has been the victim of a crime...it was a homicide. Can you come down here later today to answer a few questions and collect her personal effects?"

"I'm in Colorado, but I'll get on the next plane to Vegas. I can meet with you tomorrow. What's the address?" He asks me if I have a pen before giving me the address of his office and his personal cellphone number. I thank him and hang up. Then I pry open the back of the phone, removing the battery and chip before snapping it in half and tossing it in the trash. Try GPSing *that*.

The rum is gone, but there's some vodka left in the freezer. I barely register the heat as a glob of congealed ghost peppers falls onto my tongue, swallowed without chewing. I guzzle the rest of the *Absolut*, about a water glass full, before pulling on yesterday's work clothes and heading downstairs.

* * *

I manage to get the bike started and head straight to her place, doing a quick pass by first to scan for cops. I circle around the block to park, discretely walking up the alley to her back door. I flip over the little ceramic frog in the planter and find her spare key. I let myself inside.

She always keeps a quarter ounce of bud in the nightstand next to the nickle plated Jetfire I'd given her for protection, and I'm surprised to see a tiny ziplock bag swollen with a quarter gram of coke...clearly given to her as a tip, but it's unlike her to keep it. I leave everything untouched except the coke, which gets flushed down the toilet.

I find what I'm looking for in the bathroom...her hairbrush. I gently remove a large tangle of blonde hair, closing my eyes, pressing it against my face, breathing deep, kissing it...I'm crying and can't seem to stop...that continues for maybe ten minutes.

I stuff the clump of hair deep in my pocket before returning to the nightstand, pulling a fat green bud from the bag, popping it in my mouth and chewing.

Even after I swallow a few times, it feels like a twig or something is stuck behind my tonsil. I stand in front of the bathroom mirror, opening my mouth wide, and it looks like I've been eating lawn clippings. I try drinking water from the faucet and it doesn't help much. I go back downstairs to the kitchen to get a beer from the fridge. All she has is a few bottles of *Amstel Light*, but that will do. I pop off the cap and chug half of it. The twig is dislodged, and scratches all the way down.

I sit at the kitchen table, peering down the neck of the bottle, considering the bubbles and foam within, when I get a sudden whiff of lavender and feel her presence behind me. I remain very still, taking care not to turn around.

"I love you, Sam...I want us to be together always." I don't expect a reply.

"There's some meatloaf in the freezer that I want you to take home." she says. Then she is gone. Wow. Those were probably the weirdest and most inappropriate last words I've ever heard of anyone saying, but if it's her final wish I'll do it.

I open the freezer and see a stack of *Home Run* Margherita pizzas and a dozen bags of frozen vegetables from *Whole Foods*, but no meatloaf...which doesn't surprise me since she was vegetarian. Behind the broccoli and the peas, I find a foil wrapped brick inside a plastic bag with "Dad's Meatloaf" and last year's date scrawled across it in black Sharpie. I roll it up in a brown paper bag from under the sink so it doesn't chill my bones to hold it. I've always had a low tolerance for cold.

I spot her laptop on a side table, so I plug it in and turn it on. The photo she chose as her wallpaper is the view of the Rockies from the top of Mount Evans, taken during our campout last year. There's no password protection and I quickly see the icons on her desktop provide direct access to her email account, client list, and personal journal. I delete what files I can before reformatting the hard drive...then I fold it shut, flip it over, and pour the last swallow of beer into the vents. It pops, whirrs, and shorts out. I yank the plug from the outlet and turn it back rightside up.

In the drawer I find a pocket-sized notebook and a flash drive. The first few pages have client's names, contact information, references, and some sort of numerical code. I recognize several names: the Mayor, a few prominent attorneys, a couple Denver Broncos. I tear out the sheets, carefully ripping them into confetti which gets dropped in the toilet. The flash drive cracks open the second time I stomp on it, and it goes in as well. I flush, waiting to make sure everything spins down to a watery grave. It does. I flush a second time to be sure.

It's time to leave. I lock the door behind me but keep the key. It's a long walk back to the bike.

* * *

No-one stole the year old frozen meatloaf from my saddlebags while I was at *Argonaut Liquor*, so it goes in the fridge to defrost. It's probably freezer burnt, but edible. I can reheat it in the oven tomorrow and have meatloaf sammich with ketchup for the next few days.

Gently, I remove the hair from my pocket, turning it inside out to make sure I've got it all. I set it down on the tray table and pull up the wooden folding chair, taking my time, carefully untangling and straightening the strands. There are about a dozen, each a foot long. I smooth them out, tying them into a double square knot, then pull open my pouch, tucking it inside and cinching it tight.

"I hope you're not allergic to dogs," I say, not that it would make any difference now. I check the time and see it's nearly 3 PM and I need to be at work in a few minutes.

I untuck my shirt, clip the Bulldog to my belt, and slide the flask of *Jameson* in my back pocket before heading out the door. It's going to be a long and miserable night.

* * *

Billy and Stickboy look glad to see me when I roll in, but Billy's grin quickly fades. "Dude, what's wrong?" He'd never met Samantha, didn't even know I had a girlfriend, and certainly wouldn't have been capable of understanding and respecting the nature of our relationship if he had. I hear how he talks about those discount escorts who advertise on Backpage, and am glad she was under the radar and well out of his price range...mine too, actually. Time for another lie.

"My best friend from New York died last night. Car accident." We'll leave it at that.

"Oh, man...I'm sorry. I can stay, you want me to cover your shift?"

"No, it's alright. We hadn't talked in years. I was over at the library this morning and just found out on Facebook."

"You willingly collaborate with the *Facebook Bureau of Information?* Don't you know the NSA runs that shit to keep track of the sheeple? Everyone be all bloggin' their Dear Diary feelin's and *'Liking'* all sorts of incriminatin' shit so guvmint can know everything about you, man. They've got, like, computers that can figure out what you're gonna do *before you even thought about it*, just from all the shit you click on. I know all about that shit. Facebook is the Devil!"

"I thought you liked the Devil...you even got a 666 patch on your bike vest."

"Naw, that's for *Satan*, man. Satan's cool as fuck! He doesn't take shit from anyone and wants all his friends to have a good time. The Devil runs guvmint...from underneath the Pentagon...he wants to crack down on all the petty bullshit and take away our *Slack!* The Devil wants to keep everyone down! He drives a motherfuckin' *Bee Emm Dubyoo* with spinnin' rims and leans on the horn while we're checkin' the oil, then *doesn't even tip.* Fucking Devil is no damn good, man...he wants to keep us all in chains."

"And he invented Facebook?"

"May not have written the code, but it was sure his idea. Brilliant fuckin' idea, too. Get everyone to rat *themselves* out and you don't even need to spy on them...stupid motherfuckers write up their own damn files!"

"Well, goddamn...I was unaware of all that."

"It's all true."

"I wouldn't be surprised if it was, but honestly, I am so far past giving a fuck. What are they going to do to me? Tarnish my reputation and ruin my career? I am one paycheck away from living on the street...jail would be like a vacation, and a bullet in the brain a goddamned blessing. I work at a gas station for minimum wage...the government's already done all it can to me, so I doubt very much if the NSA is reading my Facebook page. Besides, I haven't updated it in, like, three years."

"Dude...you're such a downer. I'm gonna go get some ice cream." He goes inside to punch out, then leaves without saying another word.

I look over at Stickboy, grinning at me like a happy puppy...my new best friend. Suddenly, I realize I'm about to kill him.

"Stickboy! Go home!" I yell, forcefully pointing my finger towards the bus stop on Broadway. His face falls, crushed.

"But...Max said I was supposed to work until 7."

"I am *in no fucking mood* to argue about this! I will clock you out at 7. Come back tomorrow if you want, but you need to leave right now. Seriously."

"But..." I have a momentary lapse of control and reveal my True Face...Stickboy goes bugeyed and chalk white, a frozen mask of slackjawed horror.

"I WILL PUNCH YOU IN THE FUCKING THROAT! GO! NOW!" He takes off towards Broadway at a full sprint, horns blaring as he recklessly dashes across Washington...I don't think he'll be coming back.

I feel a little bad about what I did, so I unscrew the cap of the *Jameson* and tilt it back. I should've let Billy take my shift...motherfucker still hasn't paid me my forty bucks.

* * *

I am rude to the customers. I don't care. The woman I love was tied up and murdered in a cheap motel room, slowly, feeling everything as she helplessly watched the killer slice open her belly, unraveling intestines like he was gutting out a deer, cruelly holding up each glistening organ to show her before she finally succumbed to shock and exsanguination...I can't block it out, horrific freeze frame images exploding like flashbulbs inside my head, continuously. The flask is empty...I smash it against the wall so hard I'm cut by slivers of glass ricocheting back at me.

Some hipster rolls in on a babyshit colored Vespa and starts bitching about how we don't take credit cards. Words spill from my lips, something about him being a sniveling little cuntface who needs to be kicked in the teeth. He threatens to "get me fired" so I bounce a container of Dry Gas off his chest which makes him go away.

I discover a long forgotten bottle of *Cutty Sark* in the back of the filing cabinet, more than half empty with chunks of backwash floating in it. I hate scotch, and this is the cheap shit that tastes like piss and *Listerine*, so I need to mix it with ginger ale in order to choke it down. I end up smashing both of those bottles too.

Then, I find that Billy replaced the joints in the Hide-A-Key and light one up...

* * *

A few hours later, I have a splitting headache from mixing Irish whiskey with rotgut scotch and have already puked twice...once in front of a customer.

The coffee seems to have made things worse, or maybe it was smoking all three of Billy's plastic joints, all I know is that I feel terrible. *I am never drinking again.* I vomit a third time on the office floor.

Right about then, a black Lincoln Town Car rolls up to the pumps. All four doors open simultaneously and the Clowns step out, trailing wisps of black smoke. I lumber outside to greet them.

I am so past caring if I live or die at this point, and the massive adrenal dump nearly makes me half sober.

Fubucky walks towards me, smiling non-threateningly as he lifts his right hand and gives a fake little wave, as if mimicking some prissy socialite he saw on television. His eyes glistening jet marbles, black vapor rising from his shoulders like steam. "Hi Jake, there's something super cool going on that we want you to be a part of..." I think he's about to say something else when his head blows apart like a pumpkin filled with marinara sauce, raining down on the Town Car's roof in soggy streamers and clumps. His body drops to its knees, sprawling forward, completely switched off.

Billy's blunderbuss clatters to the asphalt as I toss it aside...I didn't even hear it go off. I draw the Bulldog, blasting two rounds towards Creepy Clown's face as he approaches...the reports seem muffled, as if my ears are plugged with wax...only one hits, but it does a lot more damage than the Jennings...a fist-sized chunk vanishes from the side of his face in a thick pink mist, but he's still coming...I squeeze the trigger until it clicks empty and half his head is gone, contents sliding out, plopping onto his shoulder like custard...he collapses as well.

I meet the driver as I walk around the front of the car...it's Creepy Clown number two with the dirty blond hair, and he's holding the biggest straight razor I've ever seen, practically a folding cleaver...wisps of thin black vapor bend, stretching towards me, like tendrils. I bash him in the teeth with the Bulldog, but all that does is make his grin stretch wider...the razor slashes and I can't see out of my left eye anymore...I backpedal a few steps, flinging the revolver hard into his face...it bounces off with no apparent effect.

Another Clown stands beside him, and even with the haircut and greasepaint I recognize Larry, holding a cheap sawbacked survival knife in an icepick grip, ready to charge. Then his head pops off, levitating an inch over his shoulders for a fraction of a second before tumbling, falling, bouncing...I hear the skull crack as it strikes the asphalt and rolls.

A figure in an oilskin duster and wide-brimmed hat brings the *khukri* down hard on top of blond Creepy Clown's head, cleaving it in twain. He's about my height, but twice the bulk, nearly 300 pounds of solid muscle. Squatting beside the corpse, he wipes both sides of the curved short sword clean on its suit before pulling back his coat, carefully slipping the blade into a shoulder rig underneath.

His eyes snap up and I freeze, speechless, as they lock onto mine...they blaze like molten gold, and I'm off balance, stunned, dizzy. Rising to his feet, his arm whips towards me, fingertips grazing my brow, and everything goes black...

* * *

I awaken in a hospital bed, a thick bandage over my left eye, oxygen tube in my nose, and an intravenous drip stuck in my arm. The cotton apron I'm wearing has little purple flowers on it.

A grizzled wino with suncracked lizard skin snores loudly in the next bed. The ancient television bolted to the wall has a cracked screen, and there is no phone on the nightstand or even a call button for the nurse. I am in *Denver Health*, with the junkies and street rats.

I slide out the IV needle and yank free the nose tube, rolling from the bed, staggering to the toilet where I take a good long piss that seems to last forever...the saline did a great job of rehydrating me and the oxygen did wonders for my hangover, but my stomach flips like I ate a day old ham sammich pulled from a dumpster filled with cigarette butts.

I look at myself in the mirror, carefully peeling off the bandage. A raw wound bisecting my eyebrow and crossing my upper eyelid is held together with black stitches and smeared with salve. My left eye opens and focuses...apparently the razor didn't cut very deep.

Directly in the center of my forehead is a swollen purple weal the size of a nickle. I lightly press it, blinding PAIN making eyes water and the room blur and spin. I nearly lose my balance and sit down on the bed hard, taking a few moments to focus on my one purpose.

Staggering over to the wardrobe, I discover my clothes inside on wire hangers. I pull them on quickly. Wallet, keys, and smokes are still there. I spend a few moments frantically searching for my cellphone before remembering that I'd destroyed it. The empty holster and *balisong* are gone too, probably in a ziplock bag marked EVIDENCE. Weapon possession constitutes an instant violation of my parole...go directly to jail to finish the whole ten years, no bail, no appeal. Then I realize my medicine bag is missing too.

I check the wardrobe twice, but it's bare, then I check under the bed, the nightstand, the wino's nightstand, but it's nowhere to be found. While I don't need it to connect with my spirits, there's a lot of sentimental value there and it's the most precious thing I've ever owned. It is *sacred* to me, and the thought of some New Age poseur prancing around with my ancestors' relics around their neck makes me ill. Suddenly, I'm more pissed than I've ever been in my life. I want to tear someone's nose off and eat it. I storm out to find the Head Nurse and *make* her tell me who took it.

Outside my door, a pudgy kid with a flattop haircut and some sort of uniform with creased black pants and a bleached white shirt rises from a metal folding chair, extending his palm in a futile "halt" gesture.

"Sir, you can't *gkttthhhp!"* he says, sinking to his knees, holding his throat, eyes clenched shut, tongue extended, face rapidly turning crimson. I think I felt something crunch when I clotheslined him with my forearm. The patch on his shoulder says *HSS* and there's a microphone clipped to his epaulet...apparently, I just deanimated a square badge. Well, fuck him for acting like a crossing guard and telling me "no."

My girlfriend was murdered, my medicine bag stolen, I'm going back to prison for getting in a gunfight while on parole, and now I'm doubled over with dry heaves, nothing coming up but a long clear strand of mucus which reminds me of the ectoplasm from old photographs of seances. I hear him whimpering, which means his trachea has not sealed shut so he'll probably live.

A man's voice whispers in my ear, but I don't recognize it: ***Chill, Jake! It's okay! Let ME take care of this for you!*** The rage dissolves instantly, giving me a rare instance of total clarity with the odd sensation of warm syrup pouring over my brain. The Head Nurse would have no idea where it was...it's probably in an evidence bag too. My ancestors will help me find it.

I stride down the hall confidently, head up, as if I'm supposed to be there and know exactly where I'm going. I pass the nurse's station and it's empty.

I find a door with a pushbar marked FIRE EXIT and head downstairs, exiting into a parking garage. It's obviously very late and no-one is around. I find a side door and exit discretely. My apartment is roughly twenty blocks away, and the walk in my condition takes well over an hour. Something catches under my ribs every time I breathe and there's a dull ache in my knee that gets worse with each step.

I don't even remember walking up the stairs, but somehow I'm inside my apartment, disoriented and exhausted, kicking off my harness boots and collapsing atop the mattress, fully clothed. I pass out within seconds.

* * *

I am back at the station, completely sober, when the Town Car rolls up. The shotgun is nowhere to be found, but I have the Bulldog...I draw it and step outside.

Only two doors open this time, and Creepy Clown number one and number two step out, standing side by side, motionless, grinning so impossibly wide their distorted faces nearly touch. I cock back the hammer and raise the .44, getting one centered in my sights and squeeze the trigger.

pop.

Not the BOOM that I'd expected, just a noise like a cork being expelled from a child's toy gun. The slug falls short, dropping to chest level and rebounding. The second and third pops are even fainter and the slugs drop to the ground before reaching him...then the barrel softens and droops. Gun useless, I toss it aside and draw my blade.

Charging forward, I execute a perfect powerslash across his throat, slicing nearly to the bone before spinning and burying the razor honed double-edge deep into the top of his partner's shoulder, twisting and stirring in a quick practiced motion to rupture the *Subclavian Artery* before withdrawing and retreating several paces back.

They regard me silently, faces unmoving and rigid, although their smiles have shrunk to somewhat normal dimensions. I see the deep gash across Creepy Clown's throat slowly close, seal, vanishing without a mark, and assume his companion's regenerative properties are similar. They slowly move apart, spread their arms, and advance.

I bolt past them to the pumps, grabbing a nozzle, extending it like a gun. When he gets within a yard I squeeze the lever to drench him with a high pressure stream of 93 Octane Ultra, but all that comes out is a drizzle. I drop it and dive inside the car.

Keys are in the ignition and no-one is in the backseat. I hit the power locks, turn the key, and tromp on the gas. The car shudders, then drops straight down through the asphalt about a mile beneath the surface before slamming to an abrupt and final stop. Soil collapses onto the windshield and roof as the engine sputters and dies, dashlights fading. I'm buried, trapped in complete darkness with a very limited air supply and no hope of escape.

There's a soft blue glow emanating from the cellphone vibrating on the console. I'm surprised I can get a signal down here and pick it up, glancing at the Caller ID. It reads: **NEBRASKA**. I push the button to answer the call, saying simply, "What?"

"Hello, Jacob. Do you know who this is?"

"Wilbur?"

"No, it isn't Wilbur. I am King of the Underground Places and the Finder of Lost Soldiers...and I have found *you*, Jacob. It is time for you to awaken and take your rightful place at my side. Are you ready to accept my wisdom?"

"Could you hold on for a moment? I have another call coming in." I snap the phone shut and toss it on the floorboards, then abruptly bring my hand to my face, sticking my forefinger deep into my mouth, jamming it back between the molars before biting down so hard flesh splits and bone cracks.

I feel it break off in my mouth, warm coppery blood spurting, marrow deep raw nerve PAIN, then a sudden brilliant flash within the blackened tomb...

* * *

I awaken bolt upright, drenched in sweat, the stench of burning plastic fills the air. Sunlight streams through the blinds and someone is pounding on my door with a baseball bat.

"DENVER POLICE! WE KNOW YOU'RE IN THERE! OPEN THE FUCKING DOOR OR WE'RE KICKING IT IN!" I am utterly and completely silent. *"DENVER POLICE! OPEN THIS FUCKING DOOR RIGHT NOW!"* They kick the door and it buckles, the lower half flexing inward before snapping back, followed by a few long moments of silence. I hear leather duty belts squeaking as they shift their weight, listening intently for any indication I'm inside.

"I don't think he's in there." A radio squawks, Charlie Brown's teacher says a few words and numbers, followed by screeching feedback. Two sets of footsteps recede down the hall.

I look down at my finger and see toothmarks, but no blood. I bend it a few times and it seems to work okay. I unplug my stereo and lamp even though the burning plastic smell seems to have disappeared, then switch on the coffeemaker before digging the broken cellphone out of the trash.

* * *

I'm scheduled to start my shift at 3, but after whateverthefuck happened last night I figure it would probably be a good idea to show up early.

I find an old lockblade in my footlocker and clip it to my pocket, then tug on my sweatshirt and pull up the hood. Work is roughly a dozen blocks away. I ditch the cellphone in the first unlocked dumpster I pass.

I arrive shortly before the noontime rush and see the Honda is where I left it, leaning against the side of the building. Billy's jaw drops like I'd walked there nekkid.

"Holy FUCK, Jake! What the fuck happened?" I mull this over a bit before answering.

"Dunno."

"I need to call Max...*is that cool?*" He seems a bit jittery.

"You do what you need to do." He turns and runs inside. A few long minutes later he comes back out.

"Max is coming right over. Are you okay, man? The cops called Max last night to tell him we were robbed and you were on the way to the ER, but the money was all there. The neighbors called in shots fired and they found you lying on the ground with blood all over your face. We thought they done blowed yer head off! Max tried to reach me but my phone was off. What did the guy look like?

"What? They didn't find him?"

"All I know is they found you passed out in front of the pumps covered with blood...and someone puked all over the office and busted a couple liquor bottles. Oh, and you smoked all my joints too, you motherfucker. Max thinks *someone else* puked in the office, and you are lucky as fuck about that. I think it's time to admit you might have a bit of a problem holding your liquor."

"It was Fubucky. Him and three of his pals in the black Lincoln. I don't think we'll be seeing Fubucky again. That 16 gauge slug popped his head like a zit."

"FUCK!!! You did NOT get that shotgun from me! I never saw it before in my life, and know nothing at all about any of this shit! Oh, here's Max now." The Studebaker rolls up to the fence, stopping next to the kerosene pump. Max climbs out, wearing his grease smeared blue coveralls. He practically runs over to us.

"Why the *fuck* are you not in the hospital where you're supposed to be? They were gonna put you through the MRI this morning to check for brain damage. It looks like someone done smacked you in the forehead with a ballpeen."

"I ain't got no insurance for that. Denver Health would file a judgement against me and garnish my paychecks for the rest of my life to pay them back for that bullshit test. I think I can do without."

"They found you lying on the ground in a pool of blood and said you got grazed by a shot and might lose the eye. Glad they were wrong about that. Was it the spooks or the meskins this time?"

"It was the mimes."

"Are they from Westside?"

"Commerce City, I think."

"Bullshit. If they were from Commerce City we'd know who they were. I never heard of a crew by that name. Sounds Vietnamese. They were zipperheads?"

"No, they were *mimes*. White face paint, dressed in black, creepy as fuck."

"Some Juggalo faggots did this to you? What were they driving?"

"Black Lincoln Town Car, late '90s, fresh coat of semi gloss and illegal window tint, blacked out chrome, Nebraska tags...and they weren't Juggalos, just wearing white grease paint and cheap suits. I don't know what they are."

"You aren't making any sense. A bop on the head can do that sometimes. Rattles that little pea around a bit, making you all confused. I think you probably hallucinated all that nonsense. It's okay, you're not dead and you saved the till, so it all worked out.

Oh, except DPD is looking for you. They say you knocked a hospital security guard on his ass last night and wanted us to call them if you showed up here. This is the pig I'm supposed to call." He hands me a *Denver Police* business card from a SGT Michael Barr. I fold it in half and stuff it in my pocket.

"Thanks. Hey, uh, did they find the gun? I think I may've grabbed it away from the guy."

"I don't think so. No-one mentioned it to me."

"And they got away clean? No-one found a finger or anything lying on the ground? Guy's finger got caught in the trigger guard while we were wrestling over the gun and I broke it for sure...it was bleeding pretty good."

"I have no idea. They told me nothing, and this is *my* place of business! Fucking Denver cops can eat my shit. You sure you're okay to work tonight? You're not dizzy or seeing double or no shit like that?"

"No...I think I'm cool."

"WHO PUKED ALL OVER MY OFFICE???" Instant murderous rage. Max's moods flip on and off like a switch. It shocks the hell out of most people, but I'm used to it by now.

"Dunno...not me."

"What happened to your phone? I was trying to call you this morning and it didn't even go to voicemail, just made some funny noise."

"Broken. I need to get another when I can afford it." He digs in his pocket, pulling out a cheap flip phone and handing it to me.

"Here, this is my burner. I use it for buying shit off Craigslist and calling skanks. Erase whatever's on there and put in my and Billy's numbers. I want to be able to get ahold of you. It only has about ten minutes left, but I'll buy you some extra minutes tonight. Don't waste it on bullshit! Oh, and call that fucking pig so they stop bothering me about this punk ass crybaby security guard. Do it from the office phone."

"Okay."

"Thanks for doing a great job!" I nod, dumbly, but he's already halfway back to his car. He gets in and takes off.

"Great job projectile vomiting. I had to clean that shit up...*and* you smoked all my joints and lost my shotgun! I'm keeping that forty bucks."

"Alright."

"Oh, and some yuppie scum called this morning, wanting me to fire you for throwing a quart of oil at him last night. What the fuck was that about? Max has us inventory the oil and additives every week. That shit's expensive."

"It was a hipster on a scooter with a pissy attitude. He even had a gay little basket on his handlebars."

"It's a good thing I answered the phone instead of Max. He was here this morning when it rang. Guy was all threatening to sue us, saying he was gonna 'own this place' or some stupid shit."

"He doesn't want this place, he just wants attention. Motherfucker had my full attention last night until he ran away. You could tell his mama never smacked *him* with the wooden spoon."

"That's some funny shit. You wanna split the cost of a pizza? Black olives and onions?"

"Right on."

* * *

A few slices of pizza restores my blood sugar to near human levels, and as my brain starts to function once again I realize that I haven't consumed anything but coffee, whiskey, and drugs during the past 48 hours, so I make sure to eat another slice before calling the cops on myself.

I get Barr's voicemail and tell him I'll be working at the station 3 to close tonight and tomorrow if he wants to stop by, and the office phone doesn't have voicemail so he should keep calling back until someone picks up.

I feel like sunbaked roadkill. I'm fairly certain I'll actually be able to quit drinking for real this time...the mere thought of scotch is enough to trigger dry heaves.

I need to get myself to the juice bar at *Whole Foods* for a few rounds wheat grass shots to detoxify my liver, but flat ginger ale will have to do for now.

* * *

Fifteen minutes later, one of the white unmarked Crown Vics issued to DPD supervisors rolls in. I tell Billy not to clock out in case they take me away in cuffs, and to have Max post bail if they do. I glance over at Barr and am unsurprised to see yet another pudgy beady-eyed cop with a thick moustache...it's as if Denver clones them in the basement of the Federal Building.

"Jacob Bishop?" he asks. He came alone and isn't pointing his Glock at me, so things are already progressing better than anticipated.

I don't care, I just want to get it over with. Prison won't be so bad, except for all the other people, but maybe I can figure out a new way to fuck up impressive enough for them to justify keeping me in solitary my entire stay. Maybe I can even get the special cage in the basement like Hannibal Lecter.

"Yep, that's me."

"Why did you leave the hospital? You had a serious concussion and there was some concern your brain might swell up and kill you...don't you have a headache?"

"Naw, I was a bit out of sorts and don't even remember walking home, but once I woke up in my own bed I was fine."

"You went home? We sent some guys over to check on you."

"Those guys who were screaming 'open the fucking door' and scaring my neighbors? Yeah, like I want to wake up to that bullshit. Fuck those guys." He averts his eyes and nods, jotting something in his notepad.

"Sorry. That sort of thing shouldn't happen. I'll talk to them about that. It's been a crazy week and everyone's nerves are shot." The last thing I expected to hear from this guy was an apology. I regard him differently, looking deeper, using the Sight. Within moments, the thoughtforms coalesce, and I see the man behind the mask.

I see the two failed marriages, the years of child support he'd always paid early, and the heart condition he'd been concealing from his bosses so they wouldn't force him into retirement. Sergeant Barr has seen a lot of shit during his twenty years on the streets of Denver, and has nightmares about traffic accidents and abused kids. I realize I actually feel bad for the guy.

"It's okay."

"It's not okay. We've been working on cleaning up the Department's image. But what I want to talk about is what happened last night. What did the guys who attacked you look like?"

"Someone hit me on the head, and what I think I remember might not be accurate. I remember two guys in black suits, even their shirts and ties were black, but the weird thing is they were wearing *makeup*...white greasepaint smeared all over their faces. They rolled up in a black Lincoln and came out with guns in their hands."

"What kind of guns?"

"A big black revolver and something else I think might've been a cut down shotgun."

"You see a license plate?"

"I glanced at it. I don't remember the number but it was from out of state. Nebraska."

"They say anything to you?"

"I don't remember exactly. It was some crazy shit that didn't make sense. I think they wanted me to get in the car with them. I tried to grab the revolver away from the one guy and it went off, and the next thing I remember was waking up in the hospital." He nods again, writing more stuff down.

"You remember anything else that can help us find these guys?"

"No, that's it. I'll give you a call if anything comes back to me."

"You do that. We've been looking for these guys. They've been hitting convenience stores from Aurora to Lakewood over the past week, and they come back to the same place more than once. We haven't released this to the press yet, because we don't know enough about them, but we've been calling them the Smilers and are putting together a task force to take them down. We told the owner that he needs to put up some cameras around here and give you guys panic buttons you can wear around your necks to alert 911."

"That's a good idea. I'd feel safer with a little button I could push...like the old lady in the TV commercial."

"It's a silent alarm, and the police can be here within 5 minutes. They work well when used properly."

"I'll keep bugging Max about it. We need something like that."

"That security guard you hit is okay, and he's not pressing charges."

“I hit someone? I don’t remember that at all.”

“He was outside your hospital room in case whoever put you there showed up.”

“Wow, I don’t remember nuthin’ about hittin’ anyone. Tell him I’m really sorry.”

“I’ll do that. You be careful after sundown. If you see that car again, even if it just passes by, lock yourself inside the building and call 911. Every cop within 50 miles is looking for these guys, and we can set up a dozen roadblocks within 10 minutes if they’re spotted. And if you start getting headaches, blurred vision, nausea, you call an ambulance right away. Head injuries are nothing to fool around with.”

“I’ll do that. Thank you.” He nods and drives off. When I go back in the office I dig his card out of the wastebasket and program the number into Max’s *TracFone*.

* * *

Later that evening the Volvo shows up, *Apocalyptica* playing at low volume. You can’t go wrong with Heavy Metal cello concertos.

I walk out to see her and, holy shit, she’s actually smiling. “Let me guess...twenty dollars worth?”

“Only ten today.” She hands me the ten. I lock the pump nozzle on its slowest setting while I clean the windshield. It clicks off about the same time I finish. I drop the squeegee back in the bucket and return the nozzle to the pump, replacing her gas cap.

“So, you’ve been watching me, huh?” The smile disappears. She says nothing. “I suppose you must know all about me then?”

“We know who you are.”

“I’d like to know more about you. What’s your name?”

“You may call me Theresa.”

"Actually, I *would* like to call you. I have the day after tomorrow off, and I'd like to take you out to dinner." She rolls her eyes.

"Jake, you've only got twenty three bucks in that ratty old wallet...what, are you planning on getting me a hot dog?" That hurt my feelings. Payday is tomorrow and I was planning on blowing my whole check taking her someplace classy...and how the hell does she know how much money I've got in my wallet? After splitting the cost of that pizza I have *exactly* twenty three dollars left.

On occasion, horribly inappropriate phrases impulsively spew forth from my mouth without any forethought whatsoever, usually in response to a threat or perceived slight. This usually offends people and makes them think somewhat less of me. Unfortunately, this happens to be one of those times.

"Yeah, if you're doublecool and things go exceptionally well, I *might* consider giving you the hot dog...but I was hoping to at least take you out for sashimi and saki first."

Her face does something strange, as if the surface *shifts* momentarily, blurring, then comes back in sharp focus and she has a peculiar smile on her face. I did not notice the thick black eyeliner and red lipstick before, and she looks older than I thought, perhaps mid-thirties.

"Hmmmm...I know what you are insinuating, and it is rude of you to address me in that way. You have no idea who I am or what I'm capable of."

"I didn't mean any disrespect. You'd love this place, second best sushi in Denver with fresh fish flown in daily; the best place is always packed full of evil suits and you have to wait in line to get in."

"You implied you wished carnal knowledge of this body...perhaps I should permit you that experience. *I would make your soul* ***SCREAM***, and when I was finished breaking you, I would parade you down Broadway on a leash, wearing nothing but a ball gag, a pony plug, and a pair of heels, weeping miserably as you taste the sting of my lash...would it please you to amuse me in that way?"

She is not smiling now. She looks super pissed...barely restrained fury. I feel blood draining from my face, acid burning as it percolates in the back of my throat, knees going suddenly weak. I feel like I've been dipped in icewater and slapped hard.

"Uh...are you flirting with me?" weakly escapes my mouth. She throws back her head and laughs. Then picks something up from the passenger seat and hands it over. It's a bulging *Priority Mail* envelope wrapped with duct tape. I take it and am surprised by the weight.

"Here's your stuff back. We thought it best to remove all traces from the scene. We're keeping the boo-ya. Be seeing you." She shifts the Volvo into gear and rolls out onto 8th.

I blink, somewhat confused. I could've sworn the eyeliner and lipstick were gone and she was in her early twenties again. My head is still playing tricks on me from that shit I smoked.

As soon as she's out of sight, I step inside the office, using my lockblade to slice open the mystery parcel, dumping its contents on the counter. Out spills the battered Bulldog in its clip-on holster, the brass Manila Folder, and my medicine bag.

Gingerly, I open the pouch and peer inside, taking a quick inventory of the contents before cinching it tight and looping the cord over my neck. I am thankful and stunned.

The rest of the shift is a blur. I finish, lock up, and go home.

* * *

I am back at the gas station when the Volvo rolls in. I look down at my hands, then check the light levels before determining that we're in the Oneric realm rather than the Physical. Sometimes the details are so vivid, down to the fibers of her clothes and rust bubbles near the wheel wells...I even smell her distinctive style of patchouli. This is just another lucid dream, possibly even borderline Astral.

She smiles at me and I'm not intimidated at all...she's just a quiet college girl who dresses Goth and listens to old school Industrial...and she likes me.

As we talk, I reach over and interlace my fingers with hers and she offers no resistance...it feels warm and right. A few minutes of conversation pass before I slowly lean in, gently kissing her lips.

She does not kiss me back and her entire body freezes, going rigid. Concerned, I open my eyes and pull back. Her eyes are wide, blazing, pools of molten gold. Her hand clamps down on mine hard, like a vise, bending it back further than it should go, wrist giving way, bones popping, cracking, as blinding pain shoots up my arm and everything whites out.

Suddenly, I'm buck ass nekkid, running through an endless empty parking lot, lightning flashes and wind screams as I'm relentlessly pelted with hail, no cover anywhere in sight. A giant spear toting Valkyrie in golden armor towers behind me, laughing mockingly, as my bare feet tear open, leaving bloody footprints as they slap against the wet asphalt.

I awaken with a start, noticing someone in the room with me. A hooded figure in a long black cowl stands at the foot of my bed. I spin, snatching the Bulldog from beside the mattress and bring it to bear on nothing but the dissolving afterimage of shadow. I'm uncertain if it was a hypnagogic half dream or something else.

There's no way I'll be able to go back to sleep with my heart pounding like this, but the sun will be up soon anyway. I switch on the coffeemaker and begin my first set of pushups.

* * *

Samantha's Dad's ancient meatloaf seems to have thawed. I sniff it...it doesn't smell spoiled. I have no idea what to do with it as I don't bake and have never used my oven for anything other than frozen pizza.

I pull some foil over a pizza sheet and set the unappetizing greyish brown lump on that while the oven preheats to 400. I decide to let it bake for a half hour while I drink an *Odwalla* chocolate protein shake and sweep the floor.

Eventually, the egg timer dings and I slip on the ragged oven mitt that came with the apartment and pull it out, setting it atop the stove to cool while I take a dump.

It was a substantial dump, thanks to the Pad Thai I ordered from *Spicy Basil* last night, and between that and the giant mittens of tissue I use to wipe my ass clean, the toilet is clogged once again. Fortunately, I have powerful magickal abilities.

When I was in junior high, I convinced myself that if I bought and studied every Ninjutsu book offered through the *Paladin Press* mail order catalog, then I too could master the art of *dim mak*, smiting foes with a wave of my hand. For three years, I diligently practiced the art of projecting my Will to flicker a candle flame, knock over playing cards, or slowly rotate a thin aluminum propeller balanced precariously upon a needle point.

The mouse I bought from the pet store eventually did die from my Willing its heart to explode, but it took several weeks of constant effort. When I got pissed off and *dim maked* my friend Tom in Algebra class, he said it felt like being punched by a two year old girl. So while my telekinetic kung fu did work, it never worked all that well...at least not for fighting.

It does, however, work exceptionally well at unclogging toilets. I stand over the nearly overflowing bowl, glowering down at it balefully, two fingers extended in a negative mudra, bane rather than boon, flushing the toilet again whilst projecting my Will like a laser, pushing the clump of shit and cellulose down through the pipes. ***"DOWN,"*** I command, shooting forth a deadly beam of focused *chi*. It spins down rather than flooding the bathroom, and I feel somehow vindicated for having wasted hundreds of hours developing this nearly worthless superpower.

I wash my hands and return to the kitchen, picking up the chef knife and cutting the meatloaf into slices...or try to. There seems to be a steel pipe running through the center. I tear into it, pulling it apart with my hands to uncover the mystery.

It's a cylinder, roughly an inch in diameter and six inches long, wrapped in foil and seemingly a lot heavier than it ought to be. I sit down on the linoleum floor, carefully peeling back the layers of foil. Coins spill over my lap and roll in all directions...a lot of coins.

I pick one up and examine it. It's a half ounce South African *Krugerrand*, minted gold bullion slightly larger than a quarter. I collect them all and count them out, finding exactly fifty altogether. I tuck one inside the zippered compartment of my wallet and dump the rest in a quart *Ziplock* freezer bag which I decide to hide under the refrigerator for now. I have no idea how much they're worth, or even if they're legal to own. I'll need to check on that later.

* * *

A couple hours later, I walk into *Rocky Mountain Gold and Coin* on Broadway. There are glass cases filled with various gold and silver coins on display and all the employees are open carrying holstered sidearms. There's also a uniformed off-duty Sheriff working security with cameras mounted everywhere.

The fellow behind the counter looks like he's barely out of high school, but weighs the *Krugerrand* on a digital scale and tells me he'll give me $750 cash for it. I see one exactly like it in the case for $950, but choose not to haggle. He copies the information from my Driver License and has me fill out a short form in triplicate and sign my name before handing over seven hundred dollar bills, two twenties, and a ten.

I'm not too good at math, but am guessing I've got over thirty grand worth of coins stashed under my refrigerator...more than enough to pay off my student loan and credit cards, or hire a real lawyer to have my conviction overturned so I can get my old job back, but I don't see the point to any of those options. That chapter of my life where I was a solid citizen is over. Society has made it clear I'll never be welcomed back. Once you're deposited in the trash can, your permanent record makes you irredeemable.

I suppose it would be best to just cash in one coin every month. Maybe then I can start eating better and buy a decent used car. With a car I can try to find a better job so I can afford a nicer apartment outside of Denver.

Maybe I'll even get myself a trailer out in the woods with a few solar panels so I can stop dealing with people altogether and be alone with my thoughts. A classic aluminum *Spartan* trailer and a Rottweiler puppy, out in the woods of Northern Oregon. That is my new goal.

Thank you, Samantha.

* * *

I roll into *Max's* at quarter of three, putting down my brand new kickstand and walking inside. I'm surprised to see Stickboy has come back, but being unemployable and on probation didn't give him much of an option. He does not speak to me and avoids eye contact, which is a marked improvement.

Billy is agitated and tense. I can tell he's been smoking that plastic again, and hitting it hard.

"Dude, I'm so glad you're here! This fuckin' retard is drivin' me nuts. It's time for me to bail, I've got shit to do." His eyes are like two pissholes in the snow; sunken and dilated with dark shadow-like bruises underneath. I know he's in a hurry to get home so he can smoke without interruption. I want to talk with him, but he punches out ten minutes early and is already walking fast towards his bike...I decide not to get in his way, and moments later he is gone.

As Stickboy seems resolved to avoid me to the best of his ability, I inform him that, as a trainee, he is expected to attend to each and every customer while I monitor and evaluate his performance from inside the office. He does not protest.

I dump the swill I find in the coffeepot, rinsing it out and adding a scoop of Sumatran to the basket to dispense a single mug. My bag is nearly empty, and I have no intention of sharing. As the pot begins to fill, I assemble the improvised antennae and fire up Max's battered *Dell* in hope of intercepting an unsecured wireless signal.

* * *

As of yet, not a single DU student has come forward to claim my hundred dollars. This is EASY MONEY people...what, doesn't anyone know a Chem major? This isn't just to satisfy my own morbid curiosity, but is truly for the greater good...don't you want to know what you've been smoking? Apparently, this stuff is ONLY available in the Denver Metro area...it isn't being sold in Colorado Springs, no-one on the internet has heard of it, and it is not on the streets of NYC, LA, or DC. This stuff is unique to the Mile High City, which means it is some sort of designer drug that someone here is making in their basement, probably out of drain cleaner and bug spray mixed in a galvanized steel trash can. Black Diamonds, Dark Star, Hellfire, or whatever you call it, it ain't being sold anywhere else. I want to find out what this shit is! Until that time, however, we'll continue to smoke up. It seems impossible to overdose on this stuff and there are no ill effects aside from the gnarly aftertaste, fucked up hallucinations, and occasional panic attack...and it is only 5 bucks a joint!

There have been two CONFIRMED sightings of Slenderman in the SoBo region. Nikki, the bartender at 3 Kings *swears she was completely sober and only a little high when she saw him in the alley near the dumpster just before closing...by the time Vinnie and JoJo got outside to kick his ass he was gone. Tweaker Mike saw him at 4AM behind the* Skylark*...but admittedly, he is not the most credible witness, although something scared him so bad he literally shit himself...or maybe he recently started smoking Oxy. SLENDERMAN!!! For reals, yo.*

In other news, while the refuse and discards of other states continue to disembark at the toilet commonly known as the Five Points Greyhound *Station on a daily basis, the density of the homeless population somehow seems to be dwindling. On a day like today, with the sun shining brightly overhead, one can reasonably expect to see a bum rocking a cardboard sign on every street corner on either side of Colfax from Broadway to Colorado, not to mention the side street action...I only saw eight guys flagging today, and there should have been dozens...and I pumped fifty bucks worth of petrol at the Colfax* Conoco *without a single crackhead asking me for a cigarette or spare change! Then we drove past Triangle Park and only saw a dozen zombies hanging out...it's as if the zombie population has been decimated over the past week. This is really freaking me out, not that I miss them or anything. What, is there a panhandler's convention going on somewhere? Maybe someone is handing out free* Thunderbird *and crack? Perhaps someone finally took my repeated suggestions of a Soylent Green production facility seriously? I keep checking the* CDC *website expecting to see Denver at the epicenter of the Pandemic hot zone, but no such luck.*

Apparently the local bums aren't the only ones dematerializing. Three convenience store clerks, two pizza delivery drivers, and the night watchman over at the abandoned plastic factory have all vanished without a trace, all leaving their cars behind...and as usual, there is absolutely no mention of this in the Denver Post. The internet tells me that if you have an iron tack in the heels of your boots the aliens cannot abduct you with their blue beam, so I seriously suggest hammering a short roofing nail into the heels of your Doc Martens until we figure this shit out. Anyway, that's what we have done. Oh, and be sure to carry a big fucking knife too. And don't eat at the Taco Hell on Broadway, as everyone in the kitchen sounds like they belong in a tuberculosis ward, which depresses me because 7-layer burritos are back on the .99 cent menu and I fucking subsist on those bad boys, but due to circumstance have been forced back to Beef & Broccoli at that ghetto ass pay by the scoop Chinese place. Do NOT order their lo mein or General Meow...heed my words of warning and beware.

* * *

Stickboy is on the schedule until 7PM and stays outside the whole while except for a few times when he needed to come in the office to make change, looking frightened and miserable, but he seems to be doing a passable job and none of the customers have flipped out on him yet. If he lasts until the end of the month he might even end up getting a key after all.

At quarter past 7 he's still outside pumping gas, at which point I realize he isn't wearing a watch. I call him inside to punch out and hand him a *Snicker's* as he heads towards the door. He thanks me, steadfastly avoiding eye contact, before trudging towards Colfax. I check the schedule. He's working tomorrow from 10AM to 7PM again, with Billy opening and Chewbacca closing...looks like Max decided to rehire him after all.

Chewie has been with Max off and on for at least five years, and has been fired twice just in the year I've worked there. Last time was because some lippy Yuppie filled a criminal complaint and lawsuit after Chewie supposedly lost his temper and allegedly hauled out his crank before allegedly pissing across the windshield of his classic MG sports car. Chewie said he didn't do it, and since there are no cameras it was Yuppie boy's word against his, and apparently he decided his time was too valuable to waste testifying personally in court so everything was dismissed.

Chewbacca posted a copy of the Yuppie's typed testimony he'd mailed to the court on the corkboard in the office where it remained until Max noticed it a week later. He probably shouldn't have used a red *Sharpie* to circle the word "penis" every time it appeared and add his own commentary in the margins.

He was fired for three whole months while Max rotated through various applicants from Craigslist who apparently were rejected for more prestigious positions at establishments like *Burger King* and *King Soopers*. Max does not give a shit about your high school diploma or criminal record, but you would be surprised how many people are unable to grasp the most elementary concepts such as: "show up when you're scheduled" and "don't steal cash from the till."

Chewbacca's Master's degree in Philosophy might have taken him further than pumping gas if he didn't have an affinity for purple windowpane which permanently altered the landscape of his brain, but at least he shows up when he is supposed to and can be trusted with a set of keys. Now that I'm financially secure and we have another keyholder on the schedule, I hope I can start getting three days off instead of two.

It begins raining around 8, and continues to rain steadily until closing. It's the first good rain we've had in weeks, and when it hits the thin film of oil, coolant, and fluids slowly dripping from thousands of passing cars, the roads turn dangerously slick. I hear sirens all night, pretty much continuously. I'm extra careful riding the bike home.

* * *

I find myself in the arms of the Goddess once again, entwined in Tantric bliss, sharing the same breath, hearts beating as one, when I gaze deep into her eyes and it's not her at all, but my fiancé Susan, the way she was before the crash, beautiful and whole.

Confused, I shake my head and see my old girlfriend Kim, the crazy one, before she discovered meth and started renting herself out to random guys on Backpage...she flickers and changes into that girl from the Korean spa with the dragon tattoo...then I'm being ridden by Ingrid from the high school cheerleading squad. Something isn't right. Something is terribly wrong.

I look past her and see nothing but red and purple mist swirling, roiling...something has invaded my mind, warping my dream, selecting and exploiting old memories to elicit an emotional response, feeding off the energy like a parasite draining its host. I am being attacked. I place my hand in my mouth and bite down hard.

A weight is pressing me down, and in the halflight I see the coweled figure on top of me. I'm paralyzed and cannot move, but have trained for this eventuality and taken precautions. Silently, I call upon my reserves and open a channel, making the connection and tapping directly into the Source, allowing it to flow through me. A magnesium flare of White Light streams from my brow directly into the hidden face and the freeze is broken.

Stunned and staggered, it crosses its arms and shudders, whereupon I realize we are connected: literally, physically, sexually...and I recognize it as a manifested succubus, something I never believed existed outside of folklore, having attempted fruitlessly to summon one so many times after having reached puberty. Then I see the gun in its hand. If succubi exist, they certainly don't carry guns. Its arm snaps forward, muzzle of the stainless snubnose grinding into my chest hard.

"Don't you fucking move." I recognize that voice.

"Theresa?" My voice, however, I do not recognize...it comes out a choked, high-pitched squeak.

She leans back, using her free hand to pull back the cowl and shrug it off. She isn't wearing anything underneath, but her body is shrouded in shadow.

"Don't you fucking move," she repeats, "Don't you even *think* about cumming inside me, or I will end your life here and now." I hear the ratcheting noise of the hammer as she thumbs it back to full cock. "Isn't this exactly what you wanted? Isn't this nice?"

"You broke into my apartment and am raping me at gunpoint. No, this isn't what I envisioned at all. I did not consent to this." I move quicker than she can react, snatching the gun and twisting, the hammer drops, crushing the web of flesh beside my thumb which blocks the firing pin as I twist further, hyperextending her finger to the breaking point, locking it against the edge of the trigger guard, a quick jerk would tear it completely off.

Pain loosens her grip and I'm able to slide it out of her hand cleanly. It's an old Rossi 88 with the Smith style cylinder release. I snap it open and shake until all 5 rounds fall, then toss the empty gun across the room.

"You violated the sanctity of my home, and gunplay is a hard limit for me. What the hell is wrong with you?" We remain joined at the hips, my cock softening inside her, both hands clamped down on her wrists.

"You weren't supposed to wake up...I didn't know you could even *do* that! I'm not supposed to be here. I will be Ended for this transgression." She isn't looking at me anymore, her gaze wandering off like her voice...distant, fading, dematerializing, and I see the air around her start to shimmer.

I release her wrists, seizing her around the waist, leveraging my full weight as I torque to the side, rolling, slamming her down beneath me, pinning her, maintaining the connection and holding it. Immediately, I'm rock hard again.

"You're not going anywhere." I press my open hands firmly against either side of her face, not letting her turn away, gazing deeply into her eyes, exploiting the weakness, piercing the veil, seeing the hidden secrets she keeps locked away, seeing *everything*...and she knows I'm seeing it too, catatonic and convulsing as she relives each memory in rapid flashes, one after another after another.

Witnessing those horrors from her perspective, feeling everything she felt, nearly kills me, and I cannot imagine what it must be like for her. I can't do it anymore and break the connection before she's fully revealed. Seeing a lifetime's abuse and trauma all at once, experiencing that raw terror and torment, was far too much to handle, endangering my already tenuous grasp on sanity. I'm not prepared to go any further, to see what she has become and why.

My eyes blur, and I realize tears are streaming out of them, spattering onto her chest, before my breath chokes up, lungs racked with uncontrollable sobs, totally incapacitated and helpless. She grabs me then, not attacking, but pulling me close, saying nothing, and I realize she's crying too.

"Oh my god...*no one has ever been kind to you.*" I state, flatly. It's the only thing that needs to be said. I cannot fuck her, not like this, everything is so distorted and wrong.

Stomach flips, head buzzes, skin numbs, vision dims, then my chest swells as if about to burst and I feel the gate torn open WIDE as my heart chakra spins and flares, pouring out energy in an uncontrolled empathic overload, totally vulnerable.

A single focused thoughtform directed with ill intent at this moment could poison my soul, spreading pervasive rot through the emotional and physical, destroying me as the *chi* becomes toxic, shutting down one system after another. I need to slam shut the gate, double up the shields, and throw this psycho bitch out of my apartment before she kills me.

Dual aspects of my nature struggle, Darkness versus Light, one side prevailing quickly. I push the paranoia away. I know what I need to do. I have no other choice.

I kiss her, gently, lips lightly grazing her brow, and hear her gasp as she feels the energy shift. Connections form between our chakras, tentatively at first, then our bodies lightly adhere to one another, as if by magnetism or glue. Gradually, slowly, cautiously, I kiss her temples, earlobes, eyelids, cheeks...every part of her face except the lips...then her throat, the underside of her chin, the sides of her neck, feeling the thrum of her pulse with the tip of my tongue.

She is frozen, motionless, barely breathing, seemingly half conscious. There are so many things I want to say to her, but saying the words is unnecessary, as at this moment she is aware of my every thought.

I gently bite down on her shoulder, registering the sharp intake of breath, before interlacing my hands with hers and delicately running my tongue along the ridge of her armpit, tasting her salt, her musk, her essence; gradually working my way lower...

* * *

It is finished, and dawn is about to break. She lies curled beside me, trapping my arm beneath her, completely drained of tension, jaw slack, lips open, drooling on my pillow...she probably won't awaken 'til noon.

Mazzy Star plays at low volume, all three albums in repeat mode, for the fourth or fifth time. Luckily, my spring water and *Burt's Bees* lip gloss were close at hand or I'd be completely dehydrated right now with lips worn raw. I think I may've sprained my tongue. I run my fingers through her hair, kissing her tenderly at the nape of her neck. She is deeply asleep, breathing steadily, unmoving.

I spent nearly four hours removing blockages and recalibrating chakras, unlocking the stagnant energy trapped within, drawing it out, filtering it through me, restoring the flow...like spiritual dialysis.

She parted like the petals of a blossom, unlatching the locked gate of the root, permitting unrestricted access to all branches of the Tree, and when the blockages were removed and the *chi* began circulating unobstructed, her *Kundalini* energy exploded like a tac nuke and I absorbed everything, taking it all inside, drinking so deeply of her essence it was nearly depleted, holding her close, finishing what she'd started, exchanging her essence for my own, making myself a part of her as she'd become part of me, seeing the sudden realization in her eyes that she was different, transmuted, eternally entwined, before wordlessly assenting, finally slipping into oblivion.

She's been unconscious for nearly an hour and we're sharing the same aura, chakras connected by faint umbilicals as she recharges, taking back the energy she needs. I wrap my arm around her, cradling her gently as she sleeps soundly. Something is so strange about her energy. She has a doubled Crown chakra, one of them protected by a seemingly impenetrable golden shell, burnished, glowing, emitting a vibration like a tuning fork.

I feel the squirming within my forebrain as a thin tendril of bright green light snakes out of my Pineal chakra, towards the golden orb, flitting about it, caressing the surface inquisitively, when it unexpectedly bursts open and I'm struck blind by the Power compressed within.

* * *

BRAP! BRAP! BRAP! BRAP! BRAP! BRAP!

Fuck.

What did I *do* last night?

My mind is a blank. I blink a few times before rolling off the mattress, somehow attaining a standing position, staggering into the kitchen and switching off the screaming alarm.

It's 2 in the afternoon...do I even work today? I feel like I had a drunken blackout, but without the usual hangover. I flip on the coffeemaker before realizing I'm not wearing my boxers. Fearfully, I peer in the trash bin, but they're not there. I hope I didn't shit the bed.

I walk over to the mattress and something smells odd, musky, feral, like the sweat of panic, rage...and sex? I pull back the sheets but don't see any obvious stains. I notice my boxers balled in the center of the room. I gingerly pick them up, sniffing them, turning them right side out. They seem clean enough so I pull them back on.

I walk into the bathroom and nothing looks out of place there. Returning to the bed I strip off the fitted sheet, wadding it up and tossing it in the laundry basket, then I begin slipping off my pillowcase when I see them...two long black hairs. I buzz my hair down to the scalp with clippers every other night, and I haven't had a visitor in months. I pick them up to examine and am slammed with the intensity of the vision.

A narrow wallet opens in my hand, but it's her hand, slipping out the flat steel lockpick. The rake slips into the knob's keyhole, rippling back and forth, popping it in seconds, but the deadbolt requires a little more finesse. I select a lifter to raise each tumbler to the shear line while applying light pressure to the torsion bar in a clockwise direction. The final tumbler clicks into position and the cylinder turns freely, retracting the bolt...I am inside.

*There I/he is...sleeping...what dreams he must have. Stupid, innocent, violent dreams. He doesn't even know who he is! We can use him...**I** can use him...he won't mind. The stupid boy thinks he loves me. A thin golden thread snakes out from her brow to mine. First the freeze, then the drop...he is practically comatose now...helpless...an open book. Memories flip like a Rolodex: high school, the Army, the ambulance, campouts, barbeques, concerts, then a quick rewind, using my past relationships as pornography, cheapening and diminishing those beautiful sacred moments, reducing them to the lowest common denominator...the Cowgirl position.*

*Is **this** your little girlfriend? Oh, you like her, don't you? Fingertips brush warmth and wetness as she steps closer. How about **this** one? **I** like her...no? What about the wild one? I/he strains against the thin sheet, fully engorged, she pulls it back. Oh! Look at you...mmmmmm. Grasping, steadying, parting, slowly sliding down herself downwards. I am nothing more to her than a dildo on life support.*

*Oh...who is **she?** You **have** been naughty, haven't you? Uhhhhmn...ohhhhh...who's the little cheerleader? Yeah, you **like** this, don't you? This is what you want...**HOLY SHIT!!!** I snatch the snubbie out of the robe's hidden pocket and jam it into his chest as, impossibly, he somehow opens his eyes. How the fuck am I going to explain killing him to Bob?*

Peering into his/my eyes creates a paradox, and the Astral feedback spins me away in a whirlwind of vertigo and panic as everything dissolves...

I lay on the bare mattress, shaken and stunned, rolling to the side as ice cold sweat beads on my flesh, nausea twisting my guts. I reach down, touching my cock, and it's sticky and numb.

Adrenaline and horror have drained all my strength...I can't even make it to the bathroom before vomit splatters the floor. I curl in a ball, trembling and confused, as the lost memories begin flooding back.

* * *

Apparently, Theresa somehow tracked me to my apartment, which is a neat trick considering the utilities aren't in my name and not even the mailman knows where I live. Forty unmarked doors inside my building and she managed to find the right one.

I open my eyes, staring up at the ceiling, letting my Sight open as vision blurs out of focus...then I see the tendril, a faintly shimmering disturbance in the air above my head. I look deeper and it becomes a thin golden thread, embedded in my brow and pinned to the far wall, passing through it. I blink and it disappears.

Gold...the same color as the sphere topping her Tree, the swordsman's eyes, the Valkyrie's armor, the Sumerian fresco...all those energies somehow connected, originating from the same source.

I've never used tracking magick before. I can't even project a Wizard Eye far enough into the Ether to see past the immediate confines of my apartment. I've read it takes years of practice, and I never had the inclination to develop that particular skill. Instinctually, however, this feels like something I can manage.

I let my eyes blur again, focusing on the golden cord linking my consciousness to hers, not sure exactly what I'm doing. I muse upon the possibilities, when something squirms inside my head, forcing itself out, and I feel a sudden *PUSH* as the thread swells, then bulges in a marble shaped lump.

Suddenly I'm gone, zipping through walls and buildings across Capitol Hill and towards the mountains, crossing all the way to Lakewood in a fraction of a second, seeing through her eyes as she guides the Volvo through traffic on South Wadsworth.

She turns to the right and her passenger is staring directly at me/her. He's wearing the same hat, golden eyes hidden behind black Wayfarers.

"He's here." *The* khukri *materializes in his hand, reaching towards me...a deft motion of his wrist, and the connection is severed.*

I slam back onto the mattress hard, as if dropped from the ceiling, rebounding off the coil springs before sinking back into them again. It feels as if I'd been punched in the gut. I can't even move, let alone breathe, so I decide it would probably be for the best simply to lie here a while.

* * *

It's my night off, the weather is nice, and I've even got money in my wallet; but I feel far too unbalanced to be out in public tonight, as nothing good could possibly come of that.

My mind is scrambled, nerves raw...I'm way too damaged even to risk a simple transaction with the pizza delivery guy. No internet, no television, no friends I can call. I glance at the paperbacks on my shelf and realize I've read them all at least twice, except *Gravity's Rainbow*, which I've never read in entirety, only random passages in the occasional hash induced whim of bibliomancy. I flip it open and read: *A screaming comes across the sky. It has happened before, but there is nothing to compare it to now.*

I open the pantry, scanning the labels of dozens of cans, mostly baked beans, soups, and assorted tins of fish, before blindly grabbing something near the back. I pop the pull ring on some *Hormel* vegetarian chili and eat it out of the can for my dinner.

I don't feel like exercising. I'm too jittery to focus on reading. I take a long hot shower, then pop a few melatonin gelcaps, before getting a clean set of sheets from the bottom drawer of my dresser and pulling them over the mattress. I lay down, intending to work on a meditation exercise to help me relax, but am asleep within moments.

* * *

I'm having The Dream again. In the beginning, I was having it every night. Lately, it's only been every couple weeks. I'd gotten used to it after the first hundred times, or at least numbed by it.

The same events, over and over, unchanging, unaltered, engraved like a tattoo on my soul. The sin for which they excommunicated me from Society. The day my life ended...

I used to own a Harley. It was only a Sportster, but it was brand new from the dealership, bone stock with hi-gloss Shamrock Green paint and polished chrome. Afterwards, I heard the bikers say that green was a bad color, an unlucky color for a bike, even if you're Irish. I don't know about that, but the *Fey* had no doing in what happened that day, that I know for sure.

We were cruising down 17th Avenue when a silver BMW blew through a stop sign, nearly broadsiding us as it struck our back wheel, spinning the bike like a top. I think the only reason the guy stopped was because his windshield was an opaque spiderweb of safety glass he couldn't see through, and his radiator had ruptured, billowing vapor and pouring coolant.

Susan was still moving, spasmodically, unconsciously...and then she stopped. She'd hit the windshield face first, rolling off the hood, most of her face stuck in the broken glass like it had been glued there. Her skull cracked like an egg, brain swelling rapidly until it shut down for good.

She was gone by the time the paramedics arrived. My coworkers saw me in a different way after that...two of them even testified against me at the trial, saying things like, "He was going to kill that guy," and "I've never seen an expression like that on a human being's face before," both quotes printed in the *Denver Post* for posterity.

The driver was a privileged thirtysomething from Chicago, an attorney for a national collection agency who'd downed six martinis at *Stueben's* on his lunch hour immediately before plowing into our bike. He staggered out of the steaming BMW in his thousand dollar suit, yelling something about how I "was going to pay for his car," before pulling out a fancy little touch screen phone and making a call. Everything faded to red after that.

Like an automaton, I perform the same guilty act once more, unbuckling my belt, sliding it from the loops, wrapping it around my hand twice, heavy pewter buckle swinging from a two foot strap. I'm five paces away when he notices me, sternly holding an index finger aloft to warn against interrupting his conversation, obviously a practiced and oft used gesture...I used the same gesture on my dog to make him sit.

My eyes burn, consumed with homicidal rage, when a green mist obscures his features, another face forming over his, like a mask...a green mask, with reptilian scales.

I completely lose it at that point, buckle streaking towards him like a meteor, phone shattering as it connects, followed by his wire rimmed glasses, his cheekbone, his nose. Falling to the ground he puts up his hands to protect himself and I hit them too, then the back of his head as he rolls up into a ball, over and over, with no intention of stopping. The world goes sideways as I'm tackled by a cop and slammed to the ground, belt torn from my hand as the first set of cuffs are forced onto my wrists.

Three ambulances and a fleet of DPD cars show up, as well as a couple of fire trucks. I see the suit as they're strapping him onto the backboard, dismoored eye dangling in front of an exploded face, suspended from the optic nerve like a bloody pendulum.

They use two sets of handcuffs to secure me to the gurney, and I'm doing my best to break them until Scott sticks me with the sedative we use on the real crazies...suddenly, I realize I've been screaming the whole while.

* * *

I wake up around nine, still seeing Susan's face ripped from her skull, thinking of the prosecutor who declared I was "a danger to society," an "animal" that needed to be locked away for the maximum possible time allowed by law. I discretely flash the judge the distress sign of the Master Mason and say I'm sorry...it doesn't do much good.

The lawyer lived, and they were even able to save the eye and replace his teeth with a bridge, but the jurors were morbidly fixated on the "before" photos: full color glossies blown up to poster size on several easels strategically placed around the prosecutor as he delivered his final statement. Those photos looked like a rare pot roast with an eyeball, a toupee, and a side of cranberries...even *I* felt bad for the guy seeing that.

My attorney was very eloquent, stating that the alleged victim had just killed my fiancé and I was disoriented due to a concussion and believed I was under attack...plus he seemed to be making a full recovery with no lasting disfigurement. I was found guilty of Assault with a Deadly Weapon but only sentenced to 4 years, eligible for parole after 2.

I force myself upright, staggering into the kitchen, yanking open the freezer door. The vodka is gone, I drank it last week and never replaced it. Frantically, I pull open the silverware drawer and remove the tray. Way in the back remains a solitary airport bottle from my emergency stash of random freebies...*Bombay Sapphire*. Bleeegh, I despise gin.

I flip on the coffeemaker, hoping the *Dazbog* Sumatran and an inch of raw sugar will be enough to cover the foul taste of juniper. I need to get to *Argonaut* later and replenish my supplies: *Absolut* and Jack, with a flask of *Jameson* to get me through the workday. At the thought of Irish whiskey, the taste of cheap rotgut scotch fills my mouth and I nearly dry heave in a classic Pavlovian reaction.

I think of cognac instead, and my stomach says nothing to that. *Remy Martin* it is. I am confident that today is gonna suck so fuckin' bad.

* * *

I roll into *Max's* just before 3, having eaten the "Burger of the Month" at *Five Star* for a late lunch, washing it down with a couple double Jack & Cokes. I don't even remember what the burger was; some abomination covered with what I think was congealed hollandaise sauce topped with a slice of pickled beet and a fried egg...but enough ketchup can make nearly anything edible.

Blood sugar restored to a near human level, combined with the mellowing effect of whiskey and caffeine, elevates my mood to the point that I no longer feel the urge to bury an adjustable wrench in some random stranger's face. I don't think I'm ready to deal with sobriety quite yet.

Chewbacca is here. With his bright Hawaiian shirt and khaki cargo shorts he looks like he belongs at a beach somewhere, or at least a trashy tiki bar. He's even wearing flip-flops, violating one of the few rules we're actually expected to abide by: a federal *OSHA* regulation that Max can get fined for.

I see he's pulled the old *Newport* sandwich board out of storage and used the plastic letters to advertise our commitment to customer service: BECAUSE FUCK YOU, THAT'S WHY! Second day back, and already halfway to being fired again. People will see that sign and be angry when we don't have Newports.

"Dude! I am back!" He is the only person who has ever actually seemed happy to be working here. Everyone else considered it their final option after getting rejected everywhere else. From what I've been told, he doesn't even need the

paycheck like the rest of us do, having a trust fund covering his rent, utilities, and an account with *King Soopers* grocery delivery. I suspect he works here solely as an opportunity to interact with other humans.

The hippies are terrified of him, the bikers hate him, the Denver cops arrest him on sight whenever they spot him within a block of the Capitol, and he has been banned for life from nearly every pub and music venue within a 10 mile radius...which is quite an achievement once you realize that Denver has more bars, per capita, than any other city in the United States.

You walk into any bar on Colfax or Broadway and look at the Polaroids tacked to the wall next to the doorman's stool, and Chewbacca's picture will be there, usually with a note attached . . . a note with words triple underlined and gratuitous exclamation points.

He's not welcome anywhere, and no-one wants to hang out with him, but here he has a captive audience...and since he's generally non-violent and has gotten a lot better about keeping his wank inside his pants, he's unlikely to be arrested for his stupidity.

He's a major pain in the ass to pretty much everyone, but his till is always perfect to the penny, he shows up on time, and he has never set anything on fire, which practically makes him *Employee of the Year* except for the whole showing his wank to customers thing...and cursing at them...and chasing invisible moonbats with a badminton racquet on occasion. Yeah, I give him two months before Max shitcans him again.

I punch in and listen to him rant for twenty minutes about some customer who'd asked him to check the tire pressure, and who was upset upon being informed that the tires had plenty of air in 'em, yelling about "mileage" and "tread wear" and asking if he "wanted to keep his job." Hence, the *Newport* sign.

"You can keep that sign up all night if you want, 'cause them fuckers *need ta learn!*" I tune him out, looking at his eyes, which gleam like diamonds but aren't dilated at all...indicating he is not tripping NOW, but that doesn't mean much with Chewbacca, as permanent damage has been done, and he has flashbacks fairly regularly.

I've personally seen him gobble between 4 and 6 hits of acid at a time on more than one occasion, and the legend says that during a music festival at *Red Rocks*, he ate a quarter sheet on a bet, or maybe it was only a dare...supposedly he was told that if he ate all 25 hits they were free, and he hasn't been the same since. Regardless, his frontal cortex is a scorched moonscape, his hypothalamus a mass of scar tissue, and he is permafried to the point he could probably collect *SSI* if he ever bothered to apply for it.

He continues to rant, "And I wuz *so mad* it wuz thunderin' and lightninin'!" I look at the clock and see he should've punched out half an hour ago, so I tell him to go home and chase him off. I am in no mood for his shit tonight, and if he decided to show off his wank again I'd staple it to the bathroom door, even if he *is* related to Max somehow.

It's just a matter of time before either me or Billy offs the stupid bastard. Between us, we have bad days fairly regularly, and Chewbacca is barely tolerated on a good day. I don't know why everyone calls him "Chewbacca" anyway: he's short, skinny, and doesn't even have a beard...being half Cherokee, I doubt he could grow one. He isn't big or hairy, he isn't a Star Wars nerd, he doesn't chew tobacco...the nickname makes absolutely no sense, although I can easily visualize him wacked out of his gourd screaming incoherent animal noises at the top of his lungs. Yet another reason to hate him.

As he strolls down 8th towards Corona, humming to himself, I crack the seal on the half-pint flask of bargain bin VSOP. It's fixin' to be a long rough night.

* * *

The black van rolls in an hour later, straight off the set of a *Mad Max* film: luggage rack and off road lights on the roof, diamondplate armor with improvised gunports welded to the sides, reinforced pushbumpers on the front, and everything covered with layers of flat black rattlecan paint and road dust. I recognize it from the internet as Darkside Dan's "Mobile Command Station."

I walk over, hearing what sounds like *VNV Nation* playing on the stereo, and he's leaning out the window, breath ragged, mucus and fluid rattling deep in his lungs...he hasn't shaved in days and the once proud red mohawk is hanging down the side of his face, clotted with old stiffener, grease, and dust. He glances over at me, eyes red rimmed and unfocused.

"Twenty," he croaks, handing me a wadded bill. It's damp. I take it inside the office, laying it on the desk to dry...at least it doesn't smell like piss. Wiping my hand on my jeans, I go back out and start pumping the gas. Within a few minutes the nozzle clicks off.

"Hey Dan, I'm a big fan of your blog. Good to meet you." He looks over at me, eyes glazed, but trying to focus. He sits up a little straighter in his seat.

"One of my many fans, huh?"

"Hey, did you ever find out what that Black Diamonds stuff is that everyone's been smoking?" He stares at me now, intently, trying to creep inside my head.

"Have *you* been smoking that shit too?" The intensity of his stare makes me uncomfortable...something isn't right here. His van reeks of patchouli oil, like someone busted a quart of it on the floorboards. Patchouli doesn't bother me like it does some other folks, but it's so thick and cloying it's hard for me to breathe, and I'm *outside* the van...no wonder he's having such trouble.

"I tried it a couple of times, didn't see the appeal. It tasted like melted plastic and gave me a migraine. Are you okay, man? You don't look so good." He averts his gaze, nodding.

"No, I'm not okay at all. Everything is so fucked up right now. You wanna see how fucked up?"

"Alright." His door opens and he carefully steps out, gingerly, as if he's a frail geriatric worried about slipping and fracturing his hip...then I see the pistol in his hand, an antique Tokerov. He holds it down at his side, almost carelessly, before stuffing it in his waistband and sliding open the side door on its track.

Three of his friends are inside, all wearing matching uniforms: black military fatigues with red armbands and Doc Martens. They're all dead, blanketed under a swarm of buzzing flies, cramped together on a ragged leather loveseat salvaged from an alley. The tops of their heads are gone.

"You have to shoot them in the head, you know." I look over at him and he's weeping, silently. I pull the dark frosted flask out of my back pocket and take a deep swallow, then offer it to him. "Thank you," he says, before tilting it back. I take the shop rag left atop the pump and use it to grab the door handle, sliding it shut and latching it. No way am I leaving prints on this shit.

"What happened?" He takes another swig, seemingly gaining vigor. Color comes back to his cheeks and his eyes no longer look glassy and dim. He takes a third swig, the half-pint nearly empty now, and hands it back. I tell him to keep it and he finishes it off.

"It is that Black Diamonds shit...it turns people into fucking zombies or something. First, we all got sick. Then, they started to change, just like the bums did. We didn't think they were smoking that shit too and didn't make the connection. It doesn't happen all at once...it comes and goes...like a far away radio station fading in and out of static. We don't use our brains to think, they're only *transceivers* picking up a signal from our higher selves, but the Black Diamonds are like a new radio crystal or some shit, interfering with the signal, letting *something else* come through. We're not ourselves then. *Something else* is pulling our strings like a marionette, and it *changes* us on a molecular level. I mean, their *skin* changed, their *eyes* changed, their voice changed, and they just wouldn't fucking die! This Soviet magnum automatic wouldn't even put them down until I took out the transceiver with a head shot. Just like a fuckin' zombie."

"Well, goddamn. What have you got planned now?"

"I've been thinking about that while driving around for the past five hours nonstop. Getting cornholed by Luther and Tyrone in the prison showers for the next twenty years does not seem like a viable option for me, so I feel it would be for the best if I park somewhere out of the way, stick a rag in the gas tank, light it up, then climb back inside and shoot myself in the forehead. That's pretty much my only option at this point."

"That is one option. But why don't you just drive up in the mountains, dump them out, ditch the piece, torch the couch, strip the carpet, scrub everything with bleach, then repaint. Problem solved."

"It's inside *my* head, too," he says.

"You seem to have a pretty good handle on things. Howcome *you* didn't change?"

"I have been, but I've been fighting it...and I stopped smoking that shit three nights ago. They didn't...that's what we were arguing about when they all changed at the same time, and I knew what they were then, and killed their zombie asses right there. It's still inside me, though, trying to make me smoke, telling me to drive North, telling me to stab a hooker. My head is so fucked up right now. I'm really scared of what I might do."

"Turn around." He does, and I let my vision fade, the Sight taking over, and finally I see it...a black, gelatinous, pulsating mass clinging to his back, right between the shoulderblades, a network of tendrils sinking deep into his spine. "Stay very still."

The *balisong* has never been consecrated, but it's Seki City steel which is mostly iron, a tried and true Etheric disruptor. I poke the mass, and it pops like a soap bubble, but those tendrils are burrowed deep and the mass will return like a pustule from an infection, but for now there should be a bit of relief. I flip the knife closed, slipping it back in my front pocket.

"I think I broke the connection for now, but that's only a quick fix. You can't smoke anymore of that shit, and don't tell anyone about your friends, and for fuck's sake don't blog about it. If you keep fighting, it will probably give up and move on. That's what they do when you stop feeding them. Scrape that area with your knife every day and burn lotsa sage, and that will reduce its influence. Now, go clean your mess. Don't bother burying or burning them, just pull over on one of those mountain roads and roll them under the guardrail...and don't let anyone see you doing it or they'll dime you for illegal dumping." He turns to face me, rubbing the back of his neck, somewhat perplexed.

"Torching the van and offing myself...that wasn't even my idea...I see that now."

"What they can't use, they destroy, getting a quick rush to recharge before moving on."

"How do you know so much about this?"

"That's *Basic Demonology 101*...simple, common sense shit."

"I didn't go to Catholic school."

"The Catholics don't know shit about demons...I learned that from a Witch."

"Oh, right on. Thank you so much for the brandy and the advice. I owe you, my friend. This is my card...you need anything, call that number."

"Alright." He gets in the van, and I watch him drive off. He didn't even ask my name, but I suppose he's a bit distracted by more pressing concerns.

I look down at the card, satin black vellum with raised silver print: "DARKSIDE DAN" and a cellphone number. I stick it in my pocket and go inside to make myself some coffee.

* * *

An hour before closing, the Town Car is back. I draw the Bulldog from under my shirt, staring fixedly at the doors, waiting for the Clowns to spill out, charging me with kitchen knives and hatchets. The doors don't open.

Wired on caffeine and adrenaline, I realize I'm bouncing on the balls of my feet, vibrating with energy, primed to either rush the car gun blazing or go sprinting down the road, I'm not sure which, but the car just continues to sit there.

The ignition switches off, the lights cut off, and I watch it rock back and forth on its shocks a few times, but no-one comes out. Nearly ten minutes pass and nothing happens...then the back door swings open and Matt steps out.

I almost don't recognize him. Not only is his beard shaved off and his hair cut short, but he's actually wearing a suit. His gait is the same though, that unique way he'd roll his shoulders, scuff his feet, tilt his head...*his* head, not the one he was currently swinging aimlessly at his side by the hair. I see his other hand clenches a long meatcutting knife. Instinctively, the gun comes up. He turns to the side, casually tossing the head back into the Lincoln, then holds up his empty hand and waves, that same goofy grin on his face.

"Hey, Jake! Don't shoot...it's me, Matt!" I don't quite know what to make of this. Walking diagonally across the lot, I peer inside the open door from ten feet away and see bodies inside. His curved blade is slick with a clear viscous gel disturbingly similar to *KY Jelly* in the way it hangs and drips.

I back up a few steps, cocked Bulldog trained on his face, which fills the sights. It's chameleonlike, the way his mottled skin keeps shifting from white to yellow to grey, the way his eyes flicker from bloodshot blue to completely black, as if something is struggling to maintain control but failing.

"Evening, Matt. I see you got yourself a job now. How's that working out for you?" He looks over his shoulder at the open door before turning back around, grinning.

"Aw, I gave it a shot, but I reckon I just don't fit in over there. You were right about the creepy church stuff with the Simon Sez, but at least they didn't have us singing songs. Anyhow, when we stopped here, I'm like, 'but Jake is my friend!' and they got all sortsa pissed off, calling me 'traitor' this and 'traitor' that, saying we were going to put you in the trunk and cook you up for stew, and that just didn't seem right to me. I reckon I'm going back to jail over this shit," he says, pointing his thumb over his shoulder and grinning.

"Matt...I thought you didn't smoke no drugs? How did they change you?"

"Oh, that...I reckon they've been putting it in the stew. It's really good stew with turnips and taters and carrots, but I didn't realize it had *people* in it until now. I feel kinda bad about puttin' ketchup on them and likin' it. You reckon God will be mad at me over that?"

"You said you didn't know, so it probably don't count." He looks down at his feet, freezing in place for a few moments, then his entire body shudders violently. His head snaps up and I see the flat shark eyes, completely black, skin paper white, drawn tightly over his skull, oozing grease from every pore. He raises the knife overhead, and a completely different voice says something I don't understand.

"Pthagn!"

I don't know what language that is, or if it's even a word, but it's very clear I'm no longer talking to Matt anymore, and his intentions as he charges me are obvious. I shoot him in the face and he drops, sprawling flat on his back. He landed face up and isn't moving, not even a twitch, so I walk over and peer down. He looks like Matt again, eyes and mouth wide open, but there's a dark hole in the center of his forehead I could fit my thumb into. Surprisingly, there's no blood, only a small pool of something resembling cloudy corn syrup on the asphalt.

I peer down the street and up at the condo windows, seeing no apparent witnesses, so I reholster the .44, pulling my shirt over it, before grabbing Matt under the arms and dragging him over to the Town Car's open back door, shoving him onto the lap of a decapitated Clown and carefully tucking his feet inside before closing it.

I go back in the office, turning off the neon OPEN sign and switching off the breakers for the overhead lights. We're supposed to be open for another twenty minutes, but I think dealing with a carload of bodies takes a higher priority over the risk of pissing Max off by closing early.

I take the readings with a flashlight and fill one of the emergency half-gallon gas cans with the fancy Ethanol-free 98 Octane before switching off the pumps and locking up. I'll write in my time tomorrow and claim I forgot to punch out.

I have my bandanna tied doo-rag style on my head to make me look more Mexican, with latex gloves on my hands so I don't leave prints. The driver wasn't decapitated, but the 2 inch wide blade was jammed deep into the base of his skull and seemed to do the job well enough. The corpse in the passenger seat was stabbed through the left temple and he isn't moving either.

There's no blood, just that weird ectoplasmic goo. I shove the driver into the passenger seat on top of his friend and double check that the gas can is in the back before turning the key in the ignition. The engine starts easily, and the car doesn't immediately drop into a pit like my dream. I scan the console and dash looking for a cellphone and don't see one. Relieved, I shift it into Drive and pull out onto 8th.

About ten minutes later, I arrive at my destination, the abandoned service station at Federal and Holden, across from Hyde Park. I slowly pull into the tall grass out back, out of sight from the road, before cutting the engine and killing the lights.

Using my Chinese tactical flashlight knockoff, I search the bodies for wallets and find nothing except a cheap cellphone in the driver's jacket pocket. I scan the contact list and it's a short list of animal names: **BIRD, SNAKE, RAT, PIG, SPIDER, CAT.** They all connect to a 402 area code and are in sequential order, identical except for the final digit. I see nothing in the call history, no texts or photos either. I switch off the power and slip it into a pocket to deal with later.

The armrest lifts up and the storage compartment is empty except for a slim bifold holding the registration and insurance cards. It's registered to a *Marigold LLC* out of Lincoln, Nebraska. I slip those documents in my pocket as well. The glovebox is locked, but the ignition key opens it. Inside is a quart sized ziplock bag swollen with shiny black aquarium gravel, which I realize is roughly a quarter pound of straight Black Diamonds. I don't know how much it's worth, and don't particularly care, so I leave it on the passenger's lap. Nothing else is in the glovebox aside from an old tire pressure gauge that looks like it probably came with the car.

I exit the vehicle, opening the back door and sloshing the contents of the gas can over the bodies. I drop the can on the floorboards, then remove the car's gas cap and use one of the Clowns' neckties as a wick. I'm about to torch it when I realize I haven't checked the trunk. The ignition key works in the trunk lock as well. It swings open and I see another body in there, but then it starts fidgeting and I realize it's not dead.

It's a man of indeterminate age sporting a half dozen facial piercings with the Denver **303** area code tattooed across his throat in ornate black calligraphy like a gangbanger, but he's wearing the standard shelter rat uniform: faded *Denver Broncos* jacket and stained sweatpants. He probably got jumped out of his set after switching allegiance to the pipe.

His wrists and ankles are tightly cinched with zip ties, and a strip of duct tape has been slapped over his mouth, bloodshot eyes wide, terrified, crazed.

Flipping open *balisong*, I manage to saw through the plastic straps binding his feet and he immediately launches from the trunk as if fired by springs, bounding towards the trees, wrists still zip tied behind his back, stumbling, falling, rolling, getting right back up, not even slowing down. Not even a "thanks, man." I don't care. I'm just glad the tweaker's gone.

I shine the light around the trunk and it's empty except for an open package of zip ties and half a roll of duct tape. I close it and pocket the keys. Aside from the ignition key, there's one for a deadbolt and another for a padlock, which might prove useful to someone...maybe Sergeant Barr, maybe my creepy rapist girlfriend if she ever shows up again. I have zero interest in checking out that "Temple" myself. After all, I've got thirty grand in gold bullion and intend to move out of Colorado. The pine forests of Northern Oregon seem like they'd be a nice change. I can probably find a decent truck and a cheap trailer on Craigslist.

I light the wick, ignite the interior, and walk away. By the time I reach 8th Avenue and start walking East I hear the tank blow, turning in time to see a greasy orange fireball billow mushroomlike into the sky before dying down to a soft red glow.

* * *

It's a long walk back to *Max's* to get the bike. Too long. I flip open the burner and punch in the number for *Metro Taxi*. It's easy to remember, just a long string of eights. I'm glad I can afford cabs now. I tell the dispatcher to pick me up at the *U-Haul* drop off a couple blocks East, and the green and white cab rolls up shortly after I get there.

What might've been an hour's walk through *Suervos* territory is less than a ten minute ride. I hand the driver a twenty, telling him to keep the change. The battered Honda is still there, so I turn the key, kick it to life, and putt back home.

Once back in my apartment. I reflect upon the day's events. Not one, but *two* carloads of dead bodies showed up at my work. I met the infamous "Darkside Dan" and shot Matt in the face. Finally. I culminated the evening by blowing up a car. I think this has to have been the most twisted day I've ever had...and I am out of alcohol.

I pop a few melatonin, peel off my clothes, and take a long hot shower. I feel ashamed to be beating off, but otherwise, wired as I am, I'd definitely have insomnia all night. Without being able to recirculate a partner's energy, my *chi* grounds out hard.

Soon, my vision starts to dim and I realize I'm mentally and physically exhausted. I feel compelled to weep but don't know why. I finish drying off, brush my teeth, and pull on a pair of fresh boxers before staggering over to the bed and collapsing.

* * *

I find myself back at the cottage, sharing coffee and blackberry pie with Susan and Sam.

It is a fine pie, lattice crust crisp with a candied glaze, and a bowl of freshly whipped cream on the side. I scoop another dollup onto my plate with the serving spoon. The berries are freshly picked, and there doesn't seem to be any seeds. Desserts are always so much better on the Astral, but you need to come back to the prime material plane to enjoy a proper steak, especially if you want it cooked rare. I don't know why I'm craving raw meat after that greasy burger I had for lunch.

"Your energy looks a tad off, my love. Have you been forgetting to eat again?" Susan asks, looking mildly concerned. She slides the stiletto from her boot and thrusts at my head. I don't flinch, I'm used to it. Retracting her arm, she points her *athame* skyward and examines what she's skewered. A rubbery black starfish roughly the size of a silver dollar writhes and wiggles at the end.

"I've never seen anything like this before. What sort of shite have you gotten yourself into now?" She listens while I tell her about the Creepy Clowns coming by the gas station over the past few weeks, how they've started a shelter in Commerce City to attract all the homeless displaced by the arsons, and are now flooding the Denver drug scene with something that apparently gives them control over regular users, eventually turning them into Creepy Clowns too.

She waves the dagger at me, knuckles white, black starfish thing wobbling on the end.

"YOU'VE BEEN SMOKIN' THAT SHITE TOO, YOU HAVE!!!" Her eyes blaze and she is super pissed. I'm half worried she's gonna stab me for real, aiming for something that might result in lasting damage. Never piss off a Celtic Witch, especially a High Priestess of the Morrigan Rite long vocal in her opinion that drug addicts should be flayed in the public square on their first offense, and hung from a lamppost on their second. Sam sits frozen at the table, pale and terrified, a forkful of pie halfway to her lips.

"I didn't know it was drugs! Billy had a few joints and it was ground up in the weed! I swear it wasn't on purpose! You know me better than that!" She stares at me, frozen for a moment as if holding her breath, then deflates a bit, nodding her head.

"It just ain't right, putting these *things* in the marijuana, tricking people like that. It's a direct violation of The Covenant, circumventing Free Will through treachery. You know what this thing is?" she asks, waving the dagger anew, suddenly pissed off again, but fortunately at something other than me.

"No idea. A curse of some sort?"

"'Tis no curse, this!" Holding the blade aloft, she strides across the room to the far wall, where there's a mural of a pentacle inside a doubled magic circle etched with runes. With a single violent motion, she swings the knife downwards, burying it deep in the wood, pinning the wriggling form directly in the center.

"You're stuck now, you wee fucker...and you *WILL* tell me everything I want to know!" The star emits a shrill whistle, then falls silent, drooping motionlessly. Susan looks over at me and grins, but there's no humor there. "Playin' possum, it is. I ain't even done nothin' to it yet." There are three loud bangs against the door, shaking the entire cottage with each impact.

"You want me to get that?" Sam asks.

"You mind your business, girl, and sit right there. Ain't nothin' crossing that threshold without my say so." She turns to glare at the pinned starfish thing. "Friends of *this* one, I imagine. Let's see who's come knockin', shall we?" With a wave of her hand the front door just vanishes, gone, and a pair of Creepy Clowns in black suits are standing there.

"Oh! I thought I told you people I was not interested in your stupid little pamphlets. Why are you here?"

"We've come for our brother." One of them hisses. He holds a wickedly barbed salt mining pick in his hands, while his companion points a double-barreled sawed-off shotgun inside the cabin, fingers resting casually against the triggers, about to shred us all with a mere twitch. Those twin bores are a lot wider than a standard 12 gauge...I'm guessing maybe it's an 8.

"Oh! That shit stain pegged to my wall back there? You think the two of you can breach my wards and take him?" The world explodes as scattergun muzzles detonate, belching flame, smoke, and a metalstorm of pellets...but they aren't pellets and they aren't metal...they're more black starfish, dozens of them, floating suspended within the empty doorway.

Susan waves her hand a second time and I'm blinded as the doorway fills with a magnesium flare of White Light, but only for an instant, and when my eyes refocus the doorway is empty. The Clown with the shotgun gapes wordlessly.

"Shot your wad already? I bet you weren't expecting that. Now, I've got something for each of you." Raising both hands, they shimmer with a pale blue light which rapidly gets brighter before a glowing blue bubble floats out of either palm, slowly drifting towards the door.

"ALGIZ," she states, a clear invocation, and the globes unfold into twin runes I recognize as EOHL, the crow's foot symbol of protection. ***"At you!"*** she yells, thrusting both forefingers towards them.

Both glowing runes streak towards their targets, elongating, expanding, blazing, all four points curling forward like talons, sinking deep into Clown flesh, sticking to their faces like the parasite from *Alien*, bursting into violet flame, combusting their heads while simultaneously piercing and crushing them, then blazing into pyrotechnic purple fireballs, and both heads are gone, nothing but charred and melted stumps remaining above their shoulders.

The Clowns drop, lifeless, before rapidly dissolving into goo, which transmutes to vapor, and soon there's not a trace of their passing. As I sit, dumbfounded, Susan yanks the dagger from the wall and extends the dormant starfish through the doorway, which blazes a second time, and the point of the *athame* is scorched clean. She slides it back into her boot and turns to me.

"Well, Jake, it appears you've somehow managed to get yourself on a Principality level hit list. I lack the ability to unfuck this situation for you. I'm truly sorry, but I'm not strong enough for this. That fight took everything I had, and was just a *taste* of what you're in for. I don't know how to protect you from an entire demonic Legion intent on vengeance. *What the hell did you do?*" Tears streaming down her scarred face, she reaches up, gently touching my cheek, and everything shatters, spiraling into blackness.

* * *

I awaken and stare at the ceiling for a while. *Vengeance?* That doesn't make sense. It seemed as if they were attempting to forcibly recruit me for something. After two carloads of their minions vanished, I can understand a possible motive for vengeance, but it hardly seems fair considering I was only defending myself.

Her comment on Principalities is troubling. Principalities aren't your usual evil spirits or even your typical demons. They're full fledged demonic Counts and Barons who seldom interact with humanity directly, and when they do, they focus on political leaders and powerful corporate executives, not a buncha stinkin' winos and a minimum wage gas jockey.

Principality level malice might explain the yellow imp in my bedroom, but it would take something far more powerful to transmute a manifested demonic shell into a stable physical substance capable of infecting those exposed to it, weakening their natural resistance against overshadowing and possession. I don't even think an Archduke could manage something like that on his own...but a Seraph could.

I make no premise of being capable of comprehending the demonic mind...no-one can, it's too alien to our way of thinking. Low level entities seem driven by impulse: rage, lust, addiction; mid level entities seem driven by avarice and dominance; but a Seraph would see the world as a multi-level chessboard, enacting a series of seemingly unrelated stratagems towards a specific end goal which may not transpire until after generations have passed. It's impossible to predict their goal, and suicidal to attempt tricking them or negotiating with them. They are the apex predators of the spiritual realm, with a marked tendency to creatively reinterpret the Laws meant to limit their interference with us.

Susan said using Black Diamonds to circumvent Free Will as a shortcut to facilitating possession violated The Covenant, a set of inviolate Laws which ALL demons are bound to strictly obey. That meant the Clowns are working outside the Hierarchy, and whatever Seraph they follow is outlawed and likely a fugitive...criminals amongst demons, operating outside the rules with zero oversight.

This is problematic, as for some reason they regard me as a priority target, since not only have they been sending minions against me in the physical, but they've been warping my dreams to the point of attempting to storm my Astral temple, seemingly with the intent of binding me to a Contract. However, in light of recent events, I think they've probably decided to remove me from the equation altogether.

It appears I am irredeemably doomed, and I don't even know what I did wrong. I'm a nobody, a three-time loser who can't even get a job parking cars, yet high ranking demons (plural) have taken a intense interest in me. This makes no sense.

I lay back, eyes closed, working on my breathing exercises, trying to wrap my head around their plan. It's obvious they're behind the arsons which gutted Denver's biggest homeless shelters, and they're clearly responsible for the addictive Black Diamonds substance which acts as a direct channel for possessing entities. They've even created a compound North of Denver for the apparent purpose of assembling and housing a small army of minions under their direct control, each possessed by a low ranking demon in their paramilitary order.

I can understand their use of homeless, transients, street people, because they're under the radar and unlikely to be missed. In fact, comments in the local news have been overwhelmingly favorable about how the 16th Street Mall is virtually clear of the usual bands of predatory riff raff, and how aggressive panhandlers have all but vanished from Colfax. That was downright insidious, selecting a target population the privileged would be glad to see gone.

What I cannot understand is why they're going after convenience store clerks and pizza delivery guys too. And why have they become so fixated on me? After all, aside from a fairly moderate clairvoyant ability and a few neat tricks I picked up from Susan, there's nothing extraordinary about me at all.

After laying here for nearly an hour trying to work things out, I give up. It still doesn't make any sense to me, and their possible end goals are too far beyond my ability to comprehend. I resolve to just keep doing what I've been doing, and not even bother trying to see the big picture.

Maybe I can find a cheap trailer on Craigslist today. I saw an old aluminum shelled *Spartan* for five grand the other day, but it was all the way up in Longmont and they wouldn't deliver, so I'd need to buy a reliable V8 pickup with duallies on the back first, but an old beater F-350 would cost twice as much as the *Spartan.* I don't even have a place to go, but I don't care. I need to get out of Denver right now.

I roll out of bed, get to my feet, and switch on the coffeemaker. I need to be at work in a few hours. The burner starts ringing and I assume it's another telemarketing autodialer and ignore it. It immediately starts ringing a second time and I pick it up, seeing **MAX!!!** on the Caller ID. I snap it open, holding it to my ear.

"Jake! I need you to come down here right now. Billy was a no call, no show, and fucking Jeffery is here by himself. Can you do that for me?" I look at the clock and it is 9 AM, which means Billy is two hours late and wasn't picking up his phone. That isn't like him at all, Billy always shows up for his shifts. I'm guessing he's a Clown now too...the last time I saw him he looked more that halfway there.

"Yeah, I'll be right over."

"Thanks, Jake! I know I can always count on you! Kenny says he can close so you don't need to work a full double. Thanks again!" Then he hangs up.

Who the hell is Kenny? Then I realize he meant Chewbacca, so I guess he's actually good for something after all. I slam an *Odwella* protein shake for breakfast, followed by a mug of sugared coffee and a handful of vitamins, before pulling on yesterday's clothes and heading out the door.

* * *

Max is gone by the time I arrive, and Stickboy is trying to check the oil of a car while it's running. I'm positive I've spoken to him about that, but choose to ignore his stupidity until after I punch in, and by then the car is gone.

"I showed up and Billy wasn't here. I ain't no snitch," Stickboy asserts. I nod my head.

"Billy should've been here hours ago and you don't even have a key. You did the right thing to call Max, it's okay." His face brightens and I realize that's probably the only time I've addressed him as a fellow human being. I am such an asshole.

"Listen, Jeff," I say, trying to improve his self esteem by not using the diminutive "Jeffery" or ridiculing his emaciated sticklike body. "You probably are aware of some of the shit that's been happening lately, but you don't even know the half of it. Everyone's under a lot of stress right now, so you need to keep your shit wired super tight and be less of a liability. We're all counting on you to do your part, because we're shorthanded and can't afford for anything else to go wrong right now. Can we count on you?" He stands noticeably straighter and the goofy grin vanishes. He even looks me in the eye, for what I think might be the first time ever.

"I will do my part." My opinion of Stickboy goes up a couple of notches, elevating him from goat molesting bumblefuck to maybe this guy wouldn't be such a fuckup if he hadn't been bullied and malnourished his entire life. How often has anyone even given him a kind word, let alone spoken to him with anything resembling respect? From his immediate and profound reaction, I'd venture to guess probably never.

"Right on, Jeff. Listen, there's a few things we should've gone over in training that might've been skipped. First, I need to show you the correct way to check the oil. Then, I'm gonna show you how to take the readings off the pumps, because it looks like we might need you to start closing soon." I didn't think it was possible for him to stand any straighter or look more serious, but he manages, and I notice his chest swell up a bit as well. So proud to be told he might be trusted to close this shitty gas station someday.

A customer rolls in, and I see it's the church lady in the blue Cadillac who always wants me to work for that dollar. She's never in a hurry, so I decide this is the perfect opportunity to show Stickboy not only how to check the oil, but all the other fluids as well, teaching him the importance of always making certain the oil cap is tight, the brake fluid cap is wiped clean before opening, and the radiator cap is never opened if the engine is hot. He earns his dollar, and another kind word. I think that's probably the first tip he's gotten since he started working here, and he is positively beaming.

I go inside to see if I can get a wireless signal from Max's laptop, trusting Jeff to work unsupervised for a while.

* * *

Jeff is only scheduled to work until 4, but I ask if he'd mind staying a couple extra hours so I could watch how he handles the late rush by himself, with up to four cars at a time, plus the walking dead demanding smokes and energy drinks. Speaking of which, I introduced him to *Monster Rehab*, and that megajolt of caffeine noticeably improved his speed and focus.

By 6:30, I'm confident he could handle closing the station once he's shown how to cut the power and activate the alarm. He's probably not even learning disabled like I thought, but just had every trace of self confidence beat out of him over the course of his miserable life. He is so proud to be told he's done well, and works twice as hard, paying close attention to detail.

Chewbacca shows up at quarter of 7 and agrees that Jeff is doing a great job, telling him, "Dude! In a few years you'll be able to manage this place!" but we don't even have a manager, since Max is the only one who writes the schedule, places orders, hires new employees, and knows the combination to the drop safe...and he's rarely even on site, but as fried as Kenny's brain is, I doubt he realizes that.

It's time for me to clock out, and I tell Jeff he can either leave or stay as late as he wants, so he decides to stay. When you're only making eight bucks an hour, part time, with no other source of income, an extra thirty bucks makes a significant difference in your quality of life on payday.

We'd split a medium black olive and onion pizza from *Angelo's* earlier, so I have no great desire to get dinner and take the bike directly home. As I'm chaining the Honda to the post, I hear a car slowly rolling down the alley behind me, tires crunching gravel, brake pads squeaking as it comes to a slow stop.

Resting my hand on the Bulldog, I turn and see the Volvo's passenger door swing open, Theresa leaning over from the driver seat, staring at me. "Get in," she says. I peer inside and the backseat is folded down, with the cargo area filled with

Rubbermaid tubs and battered suitcases of various sizes. Nothing is playing on the stereo today. I climb into the passenger seat, and as soon as the door closes we're moving.

"Events are transpiring quicker than anticipated and you require a preliminary debrief before you're ready to move into play. It is time for you to meet the Outrider. It is time for you to make your choice." We turn hard onto Colfax, accelerating East towards Aurora.

Her hand clenches the shifter, knuckles white and jaw clenched as she grinds the clutch, glaring straight ahead, totally focused, an artery bulged and pulsating at her temple. I reach over and rest my hand on hers.

"I've missed you."

"Fuck you," she snaps, reflexively, stepping on the gas a little harder, g-forces pressing me back in the seat. I withdraw my hand and stare out the side window, morosely, as grimy storefronts and shambling street rats zip by.

We pass Colorado, then Quebec, in uncomfortable silence, before the stereo switches on. Folk music? I listen for a while before recognizing it as Suzanne Vega's first album...the good one.

I glance over at Theresa again and her features have softened, maybe even the hint of a smile there. I gently place my hand atop hers once again and she says nothing, but turns towards me and her eyes are molten gold, blazing, painful to look into. Carefully, I lift her hand from the shifter and she offers no resistance, seemingly curious what I'm about to do.

I raise it to my lips, closing my eyes as I softly kiss it, once, before lowering it and opening them once again. Seemingly normal human brown eyes gaze back at me, then she returns her attention to the road. Neither of us speak for the remainder of the drive.

PART TWO

"The War in Heaven was fought between the angels who rebelled, and the angels who let them."

– Megan Arkenberg, "The Suicide's Guide to the Absinthe of Perdition"

She drives past Aurora, out into the windswept Eastern plains, Colfax becoming Route 36, passing through Manila before we turn South on Harback Road. A sustained 50 mph crosswind batters the old stationwagon, rocking it on its shocks, brutal enough to topple panel vans or rip passengers from the back of motorcycles with the occasional 80mph gust.

Nothing grows in this sun scorched wasteland but long dry weeds adaptable enough to survive on morning dew alone, hibernating between long periods of drought. It's a desolate inhospitable place, and twilight fades to night, a waxing gibbous Moon the sole source of illumination aside from dirt smeared headlights.

She turns West, down an unmarked, unpaved road of rutted suncracked clay, eventually pulling off the washboard, following a pair of tire tracks deep into the tall grass, stopping before the only intact structure we've seen since pulling off Harback.

It's an ancient Quonset hut, half the size of a barn and long abandoned, ruddy brown patches of rust streaked across its surface, bubbling and flaking like leprous rot, eaten completely through in holes of varying sizes.

"Wait here," she says, popping the shifter into neutral and yanking the e-brake until it ratchets and locks. She steps out of the car, striding over to the huge double door. It's ten feet tall and covered with rust, but rolls open easily with one hand, smoothly, as if the track had been recently been sanded, polished, greased, revealing naught but a gaping black maw.

She returns to the Volvo, sliding behind the wheel, disengaging the brake and shifting into gear. Lights off, we roll into darkness.

* * *

She kills the ignition, pocketing the keys, stepping out into blackness. Moonlight peeks through fist sized holes in the curved metal roof, but provides no light.

I see a glow and assume she's popped a chemical lightstick, but as she turns to me I realize it's her eyes, twin embers that reveal nothing. The dome light snaps on as my door opens, and she extends her hand to me. I grasp it, walking by her side deeper into the dark. A thick curtain parts and we pass through into darkness yet again.

"We have arrived," she states, although I feel she's addressing the darkness rather than me.

"It is good," the swordsman's voice replies, and there is light. Not electric light, but a soft white glow which encompasses the entire ceiling, growing steadily stronger, and then I can see. I am struck by the regal opulence, the palatial splendor of this rotted Quonset hut in the middle of an empty field, far from the nearest power line.

Everything is *White*: the floor to ceiling curtain we passed through, the tapestries on the walls, the thick plush carpet, the upholstery on couches and chairs scattered throughout the enormous room, the tablecloth on the banquet table covered with silver platters of fruit and cheese, and the clothing of the swordsman seated on an ornate silver throne before us.

I look over at Theresa and she's garbed in white as well, from her once black *Danzig* T-shirt to her battered and dusty 14 hole Doc Martens with red laces...now pure white, perfect and spotless.

My oil-stained black jeans, olive drab T-shirt, and harness boots are white too. Mercifully, there are no rhinestones or sequins, because I don't think I'd be able to handle that shit. I reach into my pocket to fondle *balisong*, withdrawing it partway, relieved to see patinaed brass handles...the whiteness seems only to extend to fabrics and leather. I discretely tuck it back away, letting my arms hang at my side, hands open and visible.

"Come forward," he says. I glance over at Theresa and she nods. I'm confused about what's transpiring here, but figure if they wanted me dead there was no need for such high powered glamour. Being handfasted to a Celtic High Priestess, I'm well aware of the legends and lore, the magickal transformation of our thrift store garb being key to this realization. I understand full well we're likely standing in an empty building...and it's probably pitch black too. Alright, I'll play along and see how this unfolds.

"Hey, Bob," I say. He throws back his head and laughs. It is a good laugh, a True laugh, which fills the room and immediately puts me at ease.

"YES! Bob! That is I...one of many names, and the name you may use to address me. 'Tis good to know we have chosen well. But what of you? Dost thou know THY True name?"

"Jacob Roland Bishop...or Jake, if you prefer. Some folks call me Slim, and that's alright too." He smiles at this, but there is no mirth there.

"Thou hast forgotten, as was expected. 'Tis a reclusive spirit, well hidden and buried deep. Come closer, I tell you a secret." I take a few steps forward. **"Closer!"** Two more steps and I'm within arm's length. His eyes blaze golden, with irises of purest white.

Without taking those eyelike things from mine, he inserts a forefinger into his mouth, then suddenly leans forward, smearing the damp fingertip across my forehead.

"YETAREL."

Raw undiluted POWER strikes me full in the face, strikes me blind, eyes scorched from sockets, hair set ablaze, blisters fill with fluid and burst, sizzle, char. Brain boils, melts, pours from nose and ears as a thick steaming chowder. Death is mercifully quick.

* * *

"Come back to me. Come back to me. Come for me NOW!"

Screams. Primal, animalistic, feral. Blood fills my mouth as teeth sink deep into warm flesh, hot, coppery, overflowing as it pours down my throat, over my face, and I realize my root is pumping seed, Theresa riding me hard, her hand inside my mouth, bleeding profusely.

I open my eyes, seeing moonlight and blazing golden eyes...no irises, only gold. Her hips continue to churn, grinding, pummeling. Unwounded hand runs through my hair. My jaw unclenches, freeing her...ragged crescent bite pours crimson spatters across my bare chest, streaming down her arm as she holds it aloft, then seals before my eyes. She collapses then, laughing as she embraces me, lifting my weak frail form up from the air mattress, then slamming me down once again, holding me close, breathing a single word in my ear...

"Mine."

Moonlight flickers and fades, darkness spinning, vortex encompassing, and the world dissolves once again.

* * *

I was born with a mild clairvoyant ability which developed and intensified over time, particularly after notably traumatic events which loosened the imprint: the missing time after seeing that light in the sky, the head injury from the motorcycle crash, smoking the Black Diamond drug.

I have one foot in the Astral and regularly converse with spirits. I perceive thoughtforms and auras, reading a stranger's life at a glance. When I'm one with a woman, our spirits melt together, fusing and forming a permanent bond which outlasts death. A few times, after deep meditation and reflection, I've even experienced that transcendent state the Buddhists call "Illumination" in which the veil briefly parts, everything is revealed as it truly is, and you are fully tapped into the Web of Consciousness with seemingly unlimited access to ideas and answers.

All of that is *nothing* compared to what I'm experiencing now. A second pair of eyes opens behind my own, an alien intellect, ancient, long dormant, newly awakened, and for the first time in my life I truly *SEE...*

Words fail, metaphor inadequate, poetry a mere shadow...the world EXPLODES with colour, sound, scent – none of which I've ever experienced before...and they are blending...*beyond synesthesia, beyond comprehension...neurons swell, subcellular organelles dissolving into grit, membranes rupture, protoplasm spilling into the Void...ionic bonds fizzle and vanish, atoms not what they seem, sparking, winking out into nothingness as the vehicle degrades, breaking down on levels I have no understanding of aside from the realization that it is awful I am dying once again, rotting from the inside...total immersion in the very fabric of reality, which is more like a* pool, *a complex melding of levels and textures: gel, foam, liquid, gas...several layers of each, blended into a slurry, suspended precipitate binding in strings and clumps...each representational of interwoven dimensions...separate planes...different WORLDS...acting on one another constantly, continuously, unconsciously, subtly, blindly, registering only ripples and specks where megaliths and supercells collide...everything interconnected, seemingly insignificant events effecting everything else, countless strings of possibilities forming a multi-coloured transdimensional web of vaguely undifferentiated cause and effect...and it is Total Horrifying Chaos. Not a smoothly running machine at all...no Pattern...no Perfect Equation or Golden Ratio to guide, predict, or explain anything. HORROR. Madness. Senseless toil, meaningless destruction, gleeful persecution, infinite pain...World Without End...Life Is But A Dream...ROTTEN...The sheer insanity, idiocy, mindlessness, the random phantasmagorical cacophony...there is no "order," no balance, no mythic overseer to enforce nonexistent Law...nothing is "under control"...discord and entropy prevail, fulminating, boiling over, and the overspill drips down and ROTS in muculent roiling BLACK sticky-burning puddles of FEAR and HATE with chittering mantises flaying layers of flesh as lesions burst on your cold damp chakras and peeled dog dick squids jet putrid virulent pus as the mantrap* snaps, *entrails rupture, bursting forth gobbets of bile and shit as the squirming LARVAE big as dogs FEED, translucent and stupid with piranha teeth and dead dead eyes amongst the soot and ooze, reeking of rotted meat, burning hair, curry, and bleach...head bursting, thoughts spinning, internal dialogue twenty simultaneous conversations and I hear* every fucking word *...mind pulling like taffy...stretching...tearing...*

"It wasn't always like that, and you want to avoid getting trapped in those loops...how do you like your eggs?" And the horrorshow about to nuke whatever semblance of "sanity" I once had snaps off, as if someone simply flipped a switch, and I lift my buzzing head from the table.

"Whut?" Vision blurs like I'm underwater, mouth parched, straining to sit upright as if in a sleepwalking Ambien induced stupor. *Where the hell am I?* Everything's a light robin's egg Blue: the carpet, the curtain, the tablecloth, the tapestries...but I'm back in the mundane primary "reality" once again, rather than that unspeakable nightmare of simultaneously experiencing hundreds of interwoven "realities," and for that I am truly grateful.

Theresa sits across the long banquet table from me, peeling a nectarine, while Bob stands before a propane barbeque grill, melting butter in a wide iron skillet.

"Fried or scrambled?" He turns, gold orbs blazing behind black Wayfarers, holding a solitary brown egg up for inspection.

"Uh...over medium?" He nods, turning back towards the stove, then breaks a dozen eggs in rapid succession before grinding pepper over them and picking up a spatula.

"Hey," Theresa says, handing me a wedge of nectarine which I immediately pop in my mouth, biting down so it bursts, juicy, flavorful, seedless. The sweet, citrusy fluid rehydrates my tongue, stinging my cracked lips, nourishing me. I hear her voice inside my head: *He's going to ruin the eggs. Just put ketchup on 'em and don't complain. He's real touchy about the eggs.*

I'm not sure how to respond to that so I simply nod. She hands me another segment which I devour, savoring the restorative juice before swallowing.

"This will help," she says, pouring steaming black liquid from a filigreed silver teakettle into a pale blue mug, which she slowly slides across to me. It's hot, yet cool enough to drink, and has an odd flavor: strong black tea infused with herbs and licorice, tasting bitterly medicinal. "It's better with honey, but we're out."

A few moments later, Bob stomps over, grinning broadly, a blue plate in either hand. He sets them down in front of us, then proceeds to fix a plate of his own. I look down and see a heap of chopped unpeeled potatoes in a pool of yellow grease next to a rubbery brown mass that I'm pretty sure is burnt eggs.

There's a squeeze bottle of Heinz ketchup on the table and I douse everything thoroughly before lifting the silver three-tined fork and digging into my substandard breakfast, attempting to choke it down. The taters are halfway raw, the eggs dry, tea bitter, but the ketchup is quite good and there are clean napkins so it isn't too unbearable...and my body desperately craves protein.

Bob sits at the head of the long table, far from us in the middle, shoveling food into his mouth with his hands...he doesn't use ketchup. When we're finished eating, he claps his hands once and the plates, napkins, and tea vanish; tablecloth now pristine and spotless, even though I'd dripped ketchup on it. I blink and realize the propane grill is gone as well.

Glamour has it's limitations, and apportation has limitations as well. I suspect he's mixing magic with magick in an attempt to impress me through misdirection and prestidigitation, likely combined with strong hallucinogens, to give the impression he has far more Power at his disposal than is actually possible. Regardless, it's a neat trick that does not fail to impress.

"Battle, Death, Rebirth, Awakening...and finally, Bob's eggs. You have withstood the Five Ordeals and been found worthy. Now it is time for you to hear the Word and make your choice." Theresa stands, taking me by the hand, leading me to an oversized beanbag chair (also that awful pastel blue) and helping me settle down into it before twisting and undulating her arm in a dramatically serpentine gesture.

Immediately, the light dies and I'm surrounded with dozens of flickering candle flames, thick scent of myrrh wafting through the air as if incense had been burning for hours.

"And it begins..."

* * *

"My Name, that is written, is known to men as Usiel...and I am Fallen."

Thus spake Bob...and he continued to lecture nonstop for several hours, occasionally pausing briefly to guzzle mead from a massive silver goblet which held a full pint. Theresa drained three quart bottles refilling it, not partaking of any herself nor offering any to me.

Most of Bob's soliloquy went way over my head: Cosmology, Prehistoric Anthropology, the Hierarchy of Hosts, and a number of more arcane topics I was completely unable to grasp.

While the *concept* of being addressed by an Archangel regarding the origins of man, Free Will, and Divine Politics was utterly fascinating, the delivery was appallingly dull, regardless of his level of enthusiasm, which seemed to increase with every swig of mead. Frankly, it was all rather tedious, and I could barely follow what he was saying, failing to comprehend what little I did follow. Finally, mercifully, it ended.

"I understand the shock of this Revelation has been Significant. Do you have any questions for the Outrider before making your choice?" she asks. I ponder this for a few moments before answering.

"So, the Bible is misinterpreted and fictionalized propaganda, 'God' is simply an appointed position, and the Fall occurred because the new appointee was a bureaucrat who passed a bunch of stupid laws no-one liked?"

"The first Fall was punitive, due to rebellion, and those who rebelled were altered and cast out. The second Fall was arbitrary, due to violations of the Dictum, and those found in violation were stripped of rank and cast out. The third Fall was a purge, due to concerns about potential disloyalty, and those Host retained rank but were assigned tasks which stranded them on this world indefinitely. A new God was appointed half a millennia ago, but chose not to rescind the decrees of his predecessor, and although there has not been another Fall, more Host have since fallen individually, some of their own volition, so it seems the situation remains troubled."

"So, you were a General who led forces against the rebellion, but was later cast out because you fell in love with a woman, breaking a non-existent rule which was applied retroactively?"

"To my eternal shame...and I have done Penance for that act every incarnation since."

DO NOT ASK! He is very touchy about his Penance and you DON'T want to piss him off! Theresa's voice inside my head again. Just in time, too. I have to admit I'm rather curious about that.

"And the Creepy Clowns are demons altered from the first Fall? Forcing themselves into people's bodies against their will? Forming an army of demonically possessed soldiers here on Earth?"

"Yes, but they aren't possessing those bodies, as possession implies shared use. They are imprisoning those souls before evicting them entirely, which is the foulest crime a Fallen can commit. The punishment for such an act is Obliteration, and a Fallen's defiance need be incredibly bold, if not completely deranged, to perpetrate such an Abomination. This, however, is clearly an organized effort, with a specific strategy and goal. It is unprecedented. Nothing on this scale has ever occurred before. They are invading this world by stealing physical bodies from their rightful owners...at least a hundred so far, with more coming through every day."

"But why do they need so many people, and why Denver?"

"This is not known."

"You have no idea?"

"They are followers of Belial, The Defiant One, led by his Lieutenant, Bathym. The magnitude of this offense seems to indicate a rogue faction. I cannot see Belial ordering the Covenant to be violated so flagrantly on this scale. A crime of this magnitude is nothing less than a direct challenge against the Authority of God. Perhaps it is intended that this faction be sacrificed in some sort of gambit? Perhaps it is intended as a demonstration to the Fallen, to sow discord and inspire a second rebellion upon the physical plane of this world? I do not know why this challenge has remained unanswered. God's vengeance is swift...but perhaps there are more pressing matters at hand?"

"Can't you contact God, or other Archangels, to ask for advice?"

"I AM FALLEN! GRACE STRIPPED FROM ME! CAST OUT IN SHAME FOR MY TRANSGRESSION! IT IS FORBIDDEN!"

"So, you're completely on your own here? No-one you can call for backup? Like an outlaw vigilante *ronin*?"

"I am Outrider. I am alone."

"Unfairly punished for something you didn't even know was wrong, cut off from God entirely, why do you even *care* what these demons are up to?"

"Because it is *WRONG!* An *ABOMINATION!* If this offense goes unpunished, the Covenant is no more! Corruption will spread, infecting your entire world, and existence shall be rendered meaningless!"

"I don't understand what you hope to accomplish by taking on an army by yourself. It seems like a suicide mission. Do you expect to be rewarded in some way? To gain redemption and be accepted back?"

"I see that you, also, live by a Code. If a man was beating a woman, because he enjoyed it and no-one dared stop him, how would that make you *feel?* If a man was sodomizing children in his home, and people were ignoring his crime rather than preventing it, how would that make you *feel?* If a man was torturing a helpless animal, simply to hear its screams, how would that make you *feel?* I see your Heart rage at my words. That is how this Abomination makes *me* feel." We stand, silently glaring at one another, for several long minutes before I reply.

"Alright. I have made my choice. I choose to help you with this."

* * *

"We have succeeded in locating the Hive. It is in the basement of a local charity in an industrial zone in North Denver. Are you familiar with the area?"

"Oh, you mean that Temple of the Morning Star bullshit? They ain't from around here. They refurbished an abandoned building and opened about a week ago. I think they're from Nebraska." Theresa and Bob look at one another.

"Nebraska? You are certain of this?"

"They're driving black Lincolns with Nebraska plates, registered to a Nebraska company, and when they phoned me in my dream the caller ID said Nebraska."

"Nebraska is Belphagor's domain, and if *he's* working with Belial, that's really fucking bad. That means it isn't isolated randomness...this shit is calculated. How did you acquire the registration data?"

"I took it out of their glovebox after I killed a carload of them. Oh, I've also got the keys to the Temple and a cellphone with all their private numbers on it too."

"You're shitting me."

"I shit you not...and I think one of my friends is with them as we speak."

"It seems you have proven a valuable asset. Please give me these keys."

"They are at my place. After I get back, I'll have copies cut and give you each a set."

"Let us go to the place *now*."

* * *

A few items are removed from the stationwagon and the back seat folded up into position, Bob climbing in before we depart. The energy is uncomfortably tense, no-one saying a word as we pull onto Route 36, heading West towards Aurora.

Theresa puts on an album I don't recognize, some sort of Industrial-Punk fusion with a female vocalist, cranked up near full volume. It's pretty hardcore. I lean over to yell in her ear, asking what we're listening to, and she hands me the CD case...some band called *Betty X.*

Once we cross Colorado, finally entering central Denver, I lean over to yell in her ear again.

"Hey! I need to stop by my work first! I need to check the schedule and see if I can get my shifts covered for the next couple of days!" She nods and turns the volume down a bit under the halfway point.

We roll into *Max's* and she pulls up to the pumps. "I need twenty bucks worth," she says, handing me two tens.

"Alright, I'll get it." The pumps aren't self-serve, but I have the key so I can use them myself, which I proceed to do since no-one else seems to be around...probably in the bathroom. Suddenly, some raggedy homeless dives from my blind spot, shoving me hard.

"You fuckin' *THIEF!* Got me a fuckin' *THIEF*, I do!" he yells. Rule Number One of dealing with batshit crazy Colfax bums is: *Don't touch me.* Break Rule Number One, and I get to do whatever I want to you...that's just the way it has to be.

He grabs a handful of my shirt, screaming deluded bullshit with halitosis so foul it could peel paint, teeth so rotted it looked like he'd been chewing *Tootsie Rolls* all day. In a single fluid motion I draw *balisong,* closed knife clutched in white knuckle deathgrip, pounding a divot in the top of his head until he lets go. He lays on the asphalt, curled in a fetal ball, weeping miserably.

"Please don't kill me! Just *TAKE* the fuckin' money, you bastard! Just *TAKE* everything and go away!" I ignore him and continue pumping the gas. I notice Stickboy out the corner of my eye, standing in the doorway of the building, slackjawed and pallid, a cellphone in his hand.

"Jeff! It's okay, just a misunderstanding, no need to call it in. Hey, would you be able to cover a couple of shifts for me this week? I think you're about ready for your own set of keys." He comes shambling over, uncertainly, seemingly near panic. I can't understand why he's so spooked: the guy is already sitting up and there's not even very much blood for a scalp wound.

"Jake! What the hell is going on? What are you *doing* here?"

"Pumping some gas for my friends and checking the new schedule. Max posted it today, right?"

"There's a new schedule up...but you're not on it."

"What the hell are you talking about? You're not making any sense."

"Dude...you were a no-call, no-show. Max *fired* your ass."

"What? Today is my day off! Even if Chewbacca switched the schedule around again and screwed things up, Max ain't gonna fire me over one missed shift!"

"Dude...*no-one has seen you in over a week!* You've been missing for *nine days!* Your final check is locked in the drop safe. Max wanted me to call him immediately if you ever showed back up, and he's on his way now."

Big block V8 roars, tortured rubber screams, two tons of chopped Studebaker jumping the curb, spinning to a halt less than a foot from the pumps in a cloud of black smoke, nearly embedding itself in the front of the Volvo. Max got here quick, and he is completely out of control...someone is going to die.

Several minutes pass and the car just sits, idling. Through the tinted glass I see him screaming into his cellphone, but can't make out the words. Then his door swings open and he steps out, and it feels like I'm facing the Devil himself, face beet red from high blood pressure and cheap Scotch, eyes simply crazed...and fixed solely on me.

"Hello, Jake," he says, calmly, clearly, not in his usual tone at all, "What have you been up to lately?" The temperature seems to drop by twenty degrees and I focus on trying not to pass out or piss myself.

"Jeff says I've been gone for over a week, but I could swear I was working here last night, Max, and I'm really confused."

"No, Jake. Jeff is right...you've been gone for well over a week. First Dave vanishes without even locking the fucking door, then Billy disappears, then *you*, the *one guy* I always thought I could count on, pull the same exact shit! I've had this station for fifteen years and *never* lost guys like this. Has Sal from Westside been talking to you?"

"Max, I think I know what happened to Dave and Billy, and it's bad, but Sal has nothing to do with it. Something strange happened last night, and now everyone's telling me I lost a week...it doesn't make any sense." Max's psychotic glare wavers a bit, then softens as he cocks his head, regarding me oddly.

"You probably shoulda got that MRI...are you telling me you were home all this time?"

"I was with friends, and I do remember passing out a couple of times, but no way could I have been gone more than a day, tops."

"You really believe what you're saying to me, don'tcha?"

"I may be a lot of things, but I'm not a liar."

"And I suppose you want your check?"

"Max, I didn't even know that checks were here. In fact, you keep that check. I don't know what happened, but think I need to make up for it somehow."

"You don't want your paycheck?" He looks genuinely puzzled, "What's really going on, Jake?"

"Well, it's complicated, but I found out that the Creepy Clowns who took Dave and Billy and tried to take me are part of a demon invasion, and I'm on a mission from God to stop them." He nods at this, scratching his chin and looking thoughtful.

"I see...actually, Jake, I probably understand the situation a lot better than you. I grew up hearing all about the ways of demonkind and how they were always doing this and that. Please, tell me about these new friends of yours." *Please?* In the year I'd known Max, I'd never once heard him use that word before. Never regarded him as a particularly religious sort either.

"Well, they're here right now. Do you want me to introduce you?"

"Is the boss man here? He's the guy I want to talk to."

"Boss man? What do you mean?"

"You know, the guy in charge, the preacher or master or whatever he calls himself. Is he in the Volvo?"

"That would be I," Bob says. I hadn't even noticed him getting out of the car. Suddenly, a broad smile crosses Max's face and I realize I've made a terrible mistake...Max never smiles.

"It is such an honor to meet you! Please, could you step into my office for a moment? There's something very important that I feel the need to confide in you, privately." That bizarre toothy grin frozen in place, Max beckons towards the door, holding it open. Bob's eyes blaze behind his sunglasses, and he turns his gaze to me, questioningly.

"Bob, you don't have to go in there. He's dangerous and something isn't right about this. We should leave right now." Instead, he strides directly towards Max, passing through the door into his office. I run after him. Max follows, shutting the door behind us and locking it before sliding a chair in front of it and sitting down.

"Jake, I've always liked you, and I'm going to tell you something about myself that few other people know. My family was very religious, and my parents were part of the Unification Church back in the 60s, before leaving it for the Seventh Day Adventists, who have a very literal interpretation of Biblical prophesy. It was very hard growing up in that house. As soon as I graduated, I enlisted in the Corps to get away from all that, and while I was overseas, my sister became involved with the Branch Davidians and was one of the people burned to death at Waco." He exhales hard, staring at his feet for a few moments before looking over at Bob.

"So, I know all about how cults work, how they pull people in, telling them they're chosen by God, telling them to prepare for the Apocalypse, telling them they can never leave. If there's anything I hate worse than a rat or a diddler, it's one of those guru cult leader mindfuckers like your friend here." Bob says nothing in reply, and doesn't seem as if he intends to, so I slowly reach over and lift off the black Wayfarers, revealing twin golden orbs blazing fire.

"Alright, Max...explain that."

"Explain what?"

"Just the fire shooting out of his fucking eyes! Bob isn't some guru, this is an honest to God *Archangel* you're looking at here!"

"No shit? A real angel? That's a new one. And you say you see *fire* shooting out of his eyes or some shit? Well, goddamn if that ain't exactly the proof I need...but they just look like regular blue eyes to me...sorta glazed like you see on dimwits."

"You don't see the fire?" They are burning brighter than I'd ever seen them before.

"Jake, once they get inside your head and do a proper mindfuck, they can make you believe anything they want and even see stuff that isn't there. They probably drugged your food, which would explain the missing time. Your friend Bob isn't an angel, he's nothing but a sleazy con man...probably even fucked you up the ass a few times while you were Roopied out. Is that right, Angel Bob? I'll bet you fucked him so many times he shits sideways now. Can we download that shit off the internet, Angel Bob?"

"Your insolence angers me."

"Well, GOOD, you dimwitted motherfucker! I'm glad to hear you're paying attention to this! Listen up, Jake...I am somewhat skeptical of your friend's claims, and believe I can prove to you beyond a doubt that I am right and he is fulla shit...but what I'm gonna show you is *secret* and you can never tell anyone else what you see here. You understand what I'm sayin' to you?" I feel nausea as my stomach flips.

"Yeah."

"Alright. Angel Bob, or whateverthefuck your name is, listen up. I'm gonna give you *one chance* to walk out that door *right now* if you promise to leave Denver *tonight* and never bother Jake with your guru mindfuck bullshit again. You are a lying bitch who is fulla shit, and I have killed more people than you've fucked and have no problems killing your stupid ass right now...*so get the fuck outta my office!*" With that, he stands, kicks his chair out of the way and pulls open the door, allowing Bob to pass by...but Bob simply leans back against the wall and says two words:

"Do it." Max grins broadly once again, even more so than before. Now I understand what makes him smile, and it is utterly terrifying...my blood runs cold. The door closes and locks once again. Hands in his pockets, Max takes his time slowly crossing the room.

"Reverse psychology amuses me," he says, grinning widely, before pulling a tiny toylike revolver from his pocket and blasting Bob directly in the left eye at point blank range. One orb immediately goes dark as he slumps to the floor.

"Angel, huh?" Max asks, cocking the miniscule gun and blasting the other eye out as well.

"How's that feel, magic man?" Then he cocks it a third time, pressing the muzzle directly on top of Bob's head, pulling the trigger again.

"It's only a twenty-two short," he says to me, by way of explanation, calmly slipping the gun back in his pocket before dumping out the wastebasket on the floor, removing the plastic liner and pulling it over Bob's head.

"That's funny...they usually bleed more than that," he says, handing me the empty wastebasket. "Here, if you're gonna yak, do it in this." Bob unexpectedly twists and begins pushing himself up from the floor.

"Hard head," Max says, kicking him in the shoulder so he spins flat on his back, then straddling him, pressing the muzzle against his chest before pulling the trigger again, contact shot muffling the report. Pressing the muzzle up under Bob's chin, he fires the last shot in the cylinder.

"I think that should do it, but just to be sure..." A thin black blade *sniks* out the top of his left hand and slices a deep gash across Bob's throat from ear to ear. Max carefully wipes both sides of the blade clean on Bob's shirt before thumbing back the switch that makes the blade disappear.

"What is it with this guy? Why doesn't he fucking bleed? Maybe he really *was* an angel...wouldn't that be some shit?" Then he starts laughing, and it is the most horrible sound I've ever heard. "Hey, whaddaya cryin' for? Don't be a bitch. You want I should put you back on the schedule or do you need some time off?" I didn't realize I was crying, and wipe the tears away with my forearm."

"Need whiskey." It comes out hoarse, raw, cracked. He uncaps a half-pint silver flask and hands it to me, the engraving on the side an inverted shamrock with the words "BAD LUCK." I take a long deep swig and taste *Listerine* cut with bog water and peat moss. I swallow and take another swig.

"That's *Laphroaig 18*, one of the finest Scotches you can buy." It's rather smooth, and the aftertaste isn't that bad. I take a third swig before handing it back. "Better?" he asks, tilting back the flask himself before recapping it. I nod briskly.

"I always knew you were good people, Jake. Let's get some fresh air, we'll take care of this mess later." He opens the door and we walk out, then he locks the office behind him.

The Volvo is gone, and Jeff and the homeless guy are arguing about something near the pumps.

"Kyle! Here's twenty bucks. You take the rest of the day off, and don't worry about punching out, I'll take care of that later. Go buy some fucking soap."

"But that *GIRL* might show up later, and I *NEED* to tell her sumpthin!" Max's face distorts, changing shape, turning purple, and he utters one word:

"Woodchipper!" The homeless guy blanches, staggers, jaw dropping, hands up, small dark stain spreading at his crotch as he wavers for a moment as if about to topple. then snatches at the outstretched twenty before sprinting up Washington towards *Argonaut*.

"Jeffery! Did you hear a noise like fireworks or some shit out here? We thought we heard fireworks." Jeff goes white, gaping wordlessly before clamping his jaw shut and shaking his head, hard. "You just keep working. I need to show Jake a new managerial skill and we'll be in the office for a couple hours, so don't bother us." Jeff nods, turning to see a car maneuvering around the Studebaker to get to the pumps.

"I should probably move that," Max chuckles, walking over to the chopped hot rod, starting the ignition, then parking it alongside the fence and popping the trunk, grabbing a canvas gymbag and rolled up tarp before walking back to the office. I follow.

"There's an *art* to this sort of shit, and I'm gonna show you how we make problems disappear. You do a good job, you'll get a $500 cash bonus and will be my new Assistant Manager. How does that sound?" He unlocks the door, swinging it open, and Bob is standing there, eyes blazing, an angry red scar across his throat...he looks pissed.

Whatever Max was about to say is choked off as Bob lifts him by the neck, flinging him back into the office, where he rebounds off the far wall, slumping to the ground and lying motionless.

Bob turns, drawing the *khukri*, and walks inside, grasping a fistful of hair, lifting him up, bringing his arm back for the swing. Max's eyes flutter, then open. I grab Bob's wrist.

"Don't!" He lowers the *khukri,* turning, inquisitively. "Max may be a lot of things, but he's also *my friend*...and he truly believed he was doing right by me. Please don't kill him over a misunderstanding." He returns his gaze to Max, raising the heavy blade yet again.

"Who is the bitch now?"

"I apologize! I was wrong about you! Go ahead and kill me if you want...no hard feelin's." Instead, Bob sits him down in his chair and carefully resheaths the chopper.

"You are a bad man, Maxwell Marion Fountaine, but I see that you acted out of love for Jacob, at great risk to yourself...so I forgive you this transgression." Whereupon Max begins quietly sobbing. No-one moves or says a word for several minutes until he's done, then he looks up at Bob, eyes wet and wide.

"How's my Mom?"

"She is here right now, and she has something she wants to say to you...*'It's nice to be nice.'*" Max's face crumbles and he starts full out bawling now. We leave him sitting there, rocking back and forth, holding himself, babbling to his invisible Mum...but that's a private conversation we have no business overhearing.

We step outside as the Volvo pulls back in...she must've been circling the block. As soon as we get inside, Theresa drives off. None of us speak.

* * *

Theresa parks in the lot behind *Smiley's* and turns to look at Bob, who is slumped over and snoring in the backseat.

"It's hard on him when he gets shot. You say he took four rounds in the head? Regeneration is a major strain on his reserves, he'll probably be passed out for hours. Let's go get those keys." We crack the windows and she unfolds a reflective sun visor, wedging it across the windshield, before locking the doors and following me upstairs.

* * *

There is a half empty box of *Cracklin' Oat Bran* on top of the refrigerator that came with the apartment, and the expiration date shows it's at least five years old. I open it up, pulling out the wax paper bag full of stale cereal, then reaching inside to grab the phone and keys that were hidden beneath. Prying open the back of the cellphone with my fingernail, I push the battery down with my thumb until it clicks into place.

"I had the power disconnected in case they could GPS it while it was switched off," I say, turning to hand it to her. She steps in quickly, kissing me firmly on the lips, unexpectedly, awkwardly, and her lips are so soft, tender, yielding...but then she pulls away, turning back towards the door.

"We should get back to the car. If some bum starts tapping on the window and wakes Bob up, I don't know how he'll react and don't want to find out."

"Here's the phone and keys. Here is the number for *my* phone. I haven't had a shower in nine days, which is a personal record for me, and I'm completely disgusted by that, so I really need to take a shower now. You can wait, or call me later when you want to meet. I think I can probably find that place again, and I've got the bike."

"Actually, I could use a shower too."

* * *

It's a shitty studio apartment, but at least it has strong water pressure and lots of hot water. I'm glad I recently replaced the mildewed shower curtain with a fresh liner from the *Dollar Store*, because that old gross thing would've been embarrassing.

While I'm scrubbing her back, she tells me about Bob's Penance. The bodies he selects are always those of physically strong men who are about to take their own lives, when his voice fills their minds, telling them about the consequences of that act, offering them a choice.

After learning he is an Archangel asking for their help, most give themselves over to him willingly, allowing him to free their soul without the stigma of being condemned as a suicide. Once he has this new form, the first thing he does is to tear out the root, a perpetual reminder of his shame. With this current body, he used the jagged glass of a broken beer bottle to slice off his cock and balls, then cauterized the wound with an electric iron.

"He's smooth like a Ken Doll down there. *DON'T* tell him I told you."

While shampooing her hair, I marvel at the scars covering both arms and legs in a precise diamondplate pattern, clearly deliberate, and they look old. I gently bite down on her shoulder and she sighs.

"You know, I haven't been with a guy since Bob pulled me out of that *Wal*Mart* in Satantonio last year. He chopped off the Store Director's head in front of everyone in the middle of the afternoon. I'm probably listed as a fugitive now, but at least when he does his thing all the security cameras pick up is static." I shut off the water and, since there's only one towel, dry her off first before carrying her over to the bed.

I only go down on her for about twenty minutes this time, but do my best for her and she responds enthusiastically; but when I climb up her body, sliding deep inside her, she starts spewing filth: *"I need your cock...fuck me like a dirty whore...fuck my pussy, fuck my ass...I love to be used hard..."* I can't listen to that foul shit anymore. It disgusts me, breaks my heart, but she keeps saying those horrible words, so I kiss her until it stops.

I kiss her deeply, gently, continuously, feeling her contract and gush every time she comes, before feeling the stirring deep within my sacrum, the ice cold burn spreading up my spine and through my root before encompassing us both within a shimmering silver shell.

I break away from our kiss slowly, stretching both her legs back, ankles on either side of her head, her face flushed, eyes clenched, brow beading sweat. *"YESSSSS! Give it to me just like that! Cum inside me, I want to feel your cum..."* It hurts to hear her say those words, to degrade herself in that way. She comes again, hard, and I run my fingers through her hair and kiss her gently. She is so beautiful, radiant, glowing...

"I love you," comes out of my mouth before I realize I've said anything. Her eyes snap open in horror, with an expression as if I'd just backhanded her across the face.

"WHAT?" And then I realize what I said, realize she's upset, panic, and words start spewing out of my mouth, I don't even know what the hell I'm saying, it's as if I'm standing outside myself watching a movie, but all I see is her face as I hear the person who looks like me talking:

"I adore you...I care about you...you are so beautiful to me, I would never hurt you, I would die for you, I would kill for you, I will never leave you...I am yours." And like that an Oath is sworn, and she's crying, shaking, holding me, and I tell her I love her again, over and over until she knows that it isn't just words, relaxes, calms into the realization that everything has changed once again.

When it happens, my vision whites out as something explodes inside my mind, and we're both one within the Void and everything is Pure and Real and True for one perfect instant in which I am totally content, knowing perfect love and perfect trust.

I don't know how long I'm out of body, but now I'm back, my eyes refocus, and I see she's barely conscious, about to pass out. I hold her limp body close, and she breathes gently into my ear before drifting off to sleep:

"I love you, too..."

* * *

I let her rest, pulling the sheet over her and tucking her in before walking downstairs to check on Bob. He's curled up in the backseat snoring, with no bums or crackheads lurking anywhere nearby. I flip open the burner and hit speed dial.

"Angelo's." I recognize the voice.

"Gino, it's Jake. I need a large pie, delivered to my place."

"Your usual?" I consider that for a moment. Not everyone likes black olives, and a few people don't even appreciate onions. I consider meatballs, but don't know if she's a vegetarian, so decide to play it safe.

"Let's just go with sun dried tomatoes and roasted red peppers this time."

"I'll have it there in about twenty minutes." I walk back upstairs to wait for it.

* * *

I usually order a medium, which is more than enough for two people, but the large is huge with far bigger slices. Best pizza in Denver, from a wood fired brick oven with homemade sauce and about a pound of toppings.

We lay next to one another, not saying much of anything, using paper towels instead of plates and drinking frosted mugs of *Boddington's* with our slices as *Trespassers William* plays on the stereo. I'm relaxed and at ease, and her usual tension seems to have melted away as well. It's nice.

After we've both eaten our fill, half the pizza remains, so we grab a roll of paper towels and bring the box down to the Volvo for Bob to eat later.

We set it on the seat beside him before getting in the front and turning the stationwagon back towards the isolated outpost in the Plains.

* * *

We pass through Aurora, and the number of stars triples as we put the ambient light of the city behind us. No streetlights on this stretch, only the dim light from the Volvo's grimy headlights. Suzanne Vega plays, at very low volume so as not to disturb Bob.

Look up, the voice behind my left ear says. A blazing fireball passes across the sky. It doesn't "streak" or "zip," it's moving too slowly for that, about the speed of a passenger jet. It clearly isn't a meteor or a comet either, nor even a true fireball...it looks like a blob of glowing yellow goo, trailing several tails and a few glowing bloblets in tight formation, none changing pattern or dropping away.

Behold, the glory and the light, and know the cycle ends and begins anew! Join our righteous stand against the Tyrant! And then it is gone.

"Did you see that?" I ask Theresa.

"*See it?* Did you not hear the Word?"

"Shit, I thought I was the only one who heard it. What was that? What does it mean?"

"T'was the Lightbringer's Herald, speaking his Word at his behest. The Apocalypse is nigh...oh, pizza!" Bob is awake now, sitting up in the backseat, tearing into a folded over cold slice.

"I don't understand. Who is the Tyrant and why is Lucifer and two of his Generals turning the homeless into zombie puppets?" Bob is fixated on consuming a second slice and doesn't bother to reply, so Theresa answers.

"We weren't seeing the big picture. This isn't about a hundred low level demons possessing bums to run amok in the physical. No-one has heard from Lucifer in centuries, and if his Herald is lighting up the sky blaspheming from the heavens, this isn't only happening in Denver, it's *international*, millions of demons incarnating in fully corporeal form. I'm guessing the entire First Wave got the memo, and now they're trying to recruit the rest of us...or at least warn us not to interfere."

"So, the Tyrant is God?"

"That was the Lightbringer's name for Him during the Rebellion. I can't see them applying that title to anyone else. This shit is way beyond us, we need to rethink this."

"An Abomination committed in my sight shall not pass unanswered." the voice from the backseat states.

"So, you propose a suicide mission against a small faction of an overwhelming force, because it is wrong? How do you feel about that, Jake?"

"I have no idea what's going on, why, or even if it's wrong; but those Clowns took three people I know and attacked me repeatedly for no reason at all. I don't care what we do, but *fuck* those guys. We need to do something to make them hurt."

"Well, my life sucks and I haven't any other plans, so why not go out screaming *fuck you* at the combined forces of Hell? I kinda like that idea."

"There is no Hell."

"On the Astral, there are many Hells." I posit.

"Do you not realize that we've been in Hell all along? Life is Hell, physical existence itself. Now that legions of demons walk amongst us, that theory is proven."

"Semantics."

"But do you contest it?" she asks. The angel says nothing. I eject the CD and pop in some *Motorhead*, cranking it up. It seems to match the mood better, and the remainder of the drive goes without further discussion.

* * *

The Volvo rolls to a stop outside the rusted Quonset hut, even though the bay door remains wide open. Bob opens his door and walks in alone. We wait, and a few minutes later a soft white glow emanates from within. Theresa pops it back in gear and parks inside.

Everything is *Red* today, a dark crimson, nearly mulberry: the curtain, tapestries, carpet, furnishings, and a large tent set up in the far corner. Bob is nowhere to be seen.

Theresa walks over to a red cooler and pulls out a couple bottles of spring water, handing one to me before striding directly towards the tent. I follow. Inside is a King sized brass bed with a red canopy and red sheets and pillowcases...it looks and feels like satin.

"Fancy," I say. She pulls me close, kissing me gently.

"I think Bob knows what we did. He can probably see everything with a single glance. This looks like his way of saying he's cool with it." She kisses me again. I'm completely drained and exhausted. Fortunately, she's tired too.

I rub her back for a while, using my thumbs to smooth out the knots in her neck and shoulders, and when I curl up beside her, wrapping my arm around her, her eyes close, breathing slows, and she falls asleep quickly. As soon as I close my eyes, I'm out too.

* * *

Me, not-me, and the eyes behind my eyes stand in the foyer of an imposing Victorian manor. The butler is on fire, with flames that do not burn.

"The One shall see you presently," he states, looking me over with unveiled contempt, when suddenly I realize I'm naked. Easily remedied. With a shrug of my shoulders and a simple mudra to focus my intent, I'm clothed in a cowled robe the same color and texture as the bedsheets. The butler makes a dismissive noise as he shakes his head and turns, bidding I follow with a casual gesture.

We reach an ornately carved set of oaken double doors, and he knocks once, pauses for several long moments, then swings one of the doors partially open.

"Sir, Mister Jetrel is here for his appointment, but in his usual display of petulance has chosen to present us with his host." *Jetrel? Why is that name so familiar to me?*

"Thank you, Paimon. Send them in." The voice is melodious, yet rich with Power. The flaming butler holds the door open wide and I walk past. I wasn't sure what to expect, but it certainly wasn't this.

A young man, perhaps in his late teens or early twenties, with short blond curls, simple white tunic, and burnished golden orbs serenely sits behind a wide and uncluttered oak desk. With his perfectly chiseled features, unblemished face, gentle smile, and unimposing slender frame, you'd never guess this was the Lightbringer himself...it was a suitable form for putting visitors at ease.

"Please, have a seat," Lucifer says. A chair appears before the desk, golden framed with red silk cushions. I sit down.

"As you have recently been made aware, a mass Awakening has taken place, and the spirits dormant within yourself and others have been unshackled, born again, free to choose their own Path." I allow the second pair of eyes to open and his True Face, indeed, the very nature of the place we're inside, is revealed, and my mind simply cannot handle it, but another mind, Yetarel's mind, recognizes Lucifer instantly, remembering things I have no means of comprehending or processing, and my feeble attempt to understand causes something inside my mind to irrevocably shatter.

Reflexively, shutters slam down over my eyes, squeezing my broken mind shut, blocking everything out, logic and reason doing its best to erase the image, wiping the memory clean lest it return to me in a moment of weakness, driving me far past the point of no return...I had no idea so much could be SEEN with the merest glimpse, yet it remains so alien as to be unknowable, overwhelming, ultimately devastating. I hear a light chuckle from across the desk, nearly a titter.

"This form is a courtesy, this meeting a privilege...do not transgress again."

"Sorry, but I'm new to this and no-one's bothered to tell me the rules."

"I see you have the mark of Usiel upon you. I always respected Usiel, his unwavering focus, his total lack of guile...but trying to reason with a zealot proves so tiresome. Some simply cannot be reached. What the Tyrant did to him, that betrayal, the abandonment, has shattered him beyond repair...surely you have seen this as well?"

"Bob's alright. I like him." Lucifer laughs and it is like birdsong and bells.

"Yes...*Bob.* I like him too, and I weep for what has been done to him, what he has become. You should have seen him back in the day...fearsome, proud, triumphant. That pathetic, broken, insane thing he has become pains my heart. T'will be a mercy to End his suffering."

"I'm on Bob's side. I don't know you, or what you want, but if you plan on killing Bob you'll need to kill me too."

"Such loyalty, so soon! There is no guile in you either, nor pride, nor avarice, nor even lust, which I find curious given your...proclivities."

"To the Pure, all things are Pure." Lucifer grins broadly at this.

"Indeed...but tell me, how Pure were you when you murdered that man? Over words, a mere insult. You had time to consider your options all night, then ran into his room as soon as the gates opened and jammed a pencil through his neck, drowning him with his own blood. Thou art far from Pure, Jacob."

"It was over more than words. He took a piece of chocolate cake off my tray at dinner too. You know he didn't give me a choice. Rules are different Inside."

"Regardless, I have no intention of turning you against your friend. I only wish for you to make a fully informed decision. As long as you have Free Will, you always have a choice."

"Tell me about the Black Diamonds. How does smoking rocked up demon seed respect Free Will? Do you expect me to believe that what I saw was simply the awakening of dormant spirits, because it didn't look that way to me at all." The burnished gold orbs flare and blaze momentarily, and he says nothing for a long while.

"Sacrifices need be made to restore balance, and those apes weren't making proper use of the lives they had been given. Life is a gift, an opportunity for growth and renewal, yet those apes instead chose to wallow in self indulgent squalor, poisoning their sacred vehicles with toxins and abuse. They misused what they were entrusted with, so we simply hastened the inevitable. A need has been met, and better use shall be made."

"Billy was no ape! He was my best friend, and a righteous outlaw, yet you stole his choice away from him in the name of expedience, because you had a need for more bodies, justifying it by claiming he didn't appreciate life quite enough...is that what you're saying to me?"

"That should not have occurred. Mistakes have been made. That happens when responsibilities are delegated and reassigned. Our window of opportunity was finite, with actions taken very rapidly, and there was a brief period of chaos due to miscommunication and incompetence. Only discards who would not be missed were to have been selected."

"Yeah, your guys were pulling people out of their workplaces all over Denver, did you know that? Every cop in the state has an alert out on your guys. College kids were smoking that shit at parties. Way to keep a low profile, dipshit."

"Mistakes have been made. Those responsible shall be punished."

"I don't give a shit about any of that. I want my friend Billy back. Can you do that? Otherwise, we ain't got nuthin' further to discuss."

"Are you not curious about the Great Plan? About why you have been chosen?"

"I really don't care. I just want to be left the fuck alone...and I want my friend back."

"So shall it be done." There is a sudden flash, then everything goes black.

* * *

I awaken, entwined with Theresa...she smells of the cedar soap from my apartment. I vaguely recollect a weird dream with some queer looking fellow dressed in a toga behind a desk, and some condescending British prick on fire...just random meaningless bullshit...I haven't had a coherent dream in a while, and during those nine lost days I don't think I dreamed at all.

I gently squeeze her, kissing her lightly on the shoulder, and she smiles. The silence is shattered by the clanging of a bell and her eyes snap open, a disgusted look on her face.

"Someone wants us up," she says. We pull on our clothes and I begin making the bed. She laughs, a short disdainful bark,

"What are you doing? Are you really that simple?" Her tone hurts my feelings. She's right though, that's the nature of glamour...all illusion, no substance. That fancy bed was probably nothing more than a greasy piss-stained mattress found dumped in an alley and placed atop a few bales of hay. I refrain from opening my second eyes, much preferring the illusion. She didn't need to be so mean about it, but I suppose it's second nature to her, a defense mechanism gone awry.

We step out of the tent and Bob is frying up more of his infamous eggs on that shiny chrome grill...which is likely just a rusty grate over a burn barrel. Everything is *Green* today, including the tent we just left, although it was red a moment ago. We sit across from one another at the table, and Bob, beaming brightly, hands us each a plateful of rubbery brownish eggs.

It is edible...more so with ketchup. We wash it down with that medicinal herbal tea, which tastes a bit different from last time. Something buzzes against my leg, and I realize it's the burner set to vibrate. I don't know what the hell Max could possibly want, but looking down at it I'm shocked to see the Caller ID says **BILLY**. I flip it open.

"Jake? Is that you?" he sounds deathly ill, worse than I'd ever heard him before.

"Billy! Holy shit! You're alive!" His breathing is raspy. I hear him gagging, retching, liquid splashing the floor.

"Alive for now...I was sent back for you, Jake...shit I need to talk to you about...oh, fuck..." Retching and vomiting again.

"Dude...are you okay?" Stupid question, I know.

"I am most fucking NOT okay...but it doesn't matter anymore...listen, I ain't got much time...how soon can you meet me at my place? It's important."

"I can probably be there within an hour."

"Come alone." The line disconnects. I look over at Theresa.

"That was my friend Billy, the one taken by the Creepy Clowns. He got away, but he's hurt bad. I need to meet him in Englewood right now."

"Alright, let's do this."

* * *

Billy said, *"Come alone,"* and I fully intend to honor that request, regardless of what Bob wants. Billy's my friend, practically a brother, and I'll do as he asked. I do, however, doublecheck the Bulldog to ascertain it's loaded, as I haven't handled it in some time and have a week and a half unaccounted for. Five rounds of vintage Blazer Gold Dot remain in the cylinder, so it's good to go.

I guide Theresa to the lot behind *Bushwacker's Saloon* on South Broadway. It's a good place to park this early on a weekday, and Billy's place is only a block and a half away, an easy walk.

"Wait here...or go inside if you want. They make a great breakfast burrito and brew their own beer. You have my number if you need to text me." I don't have her number...I don't know if she even has a phone.

They're both silent as I exit the Volvo and walk away, still pissed that I insisted on doing this alone...we'd argued about it for half the drive here. Apparently, Bob is accustomed to getting his way, and being told "No" is a new and unpleasant experience for him. He sulks and pouts, Theresa won't even look at me...today started with Bob's shitty eggs and went downhill from there.

Billy lives in an old house split into a half dozen 1-bedroom apartments. I'm about to ring the buzzer when I see the front door is propped open with the doormat so I just walk upstairs.

When I knock on his door it swings open, unlatched, the pungent skunky aroma of strong *indica* wafting out...he'd probably been smoking to calm his nausea. I walk through the kitchenette, trashcan reek well past spoilage, approaching weapons grade biohazard level...obviously fermenting for close to a month, and the smouldering sticks of *Nag Champa* do absolutely nothing to cover the stench. I resolve to suppress the gag reflex, hold my breath, and move on.

I find Billy sprawled in his battered recliner, feet up, facing a television tuned to static with the volume all the way down, his Grandma's afghan over his lap and a green bottle of *Reed's Jamaican Ginger Brew* in his hand...he's obviously been dead for some time, skin translucent with blue veins showing through, hair dry and brittle, lips cracked...then the corpse's eyes snap open and he turns towards me.

"I saw the Devil, Jake...he was nuthin' like what I thought." A cloudy film covers both eyes, pupils huge, irises completely gone, but there's life there. I observe his chest rise and fall with each raspy breath, phlegm rattling deep in his lungs.

"Not feelin' so good, Jake...some sorta stomach thing." He takes a swig of the soda.

"You don't look so good, man...you want I should take you to the hospital?" He's quiet for a bit, mulling that over.

"Come here, Jake...I need you to take a look at sumpthin'..."

"Alright." I stand beside his chair and look down...there's nothing in his hands...then his arm snaps out, hand clamping down on my wrist with far more strength than his frail diseased form should have, and I convulse, head snapping back as every muscle in my body spasms like I'm grounding out a continuous jolt of 220 current, the vision forced upon me unlike anything I've ever experienced as I'm bombarded with image after image after image...

Sweet black smoke fills lungs like syrup...sweet, sweet medicine...take it all away, open my mind, free my soul...soft black stars calling...Vulture, Spider, and Tattooface feel it too...calling us...come to the Temple and take your rightful place amongst the stars, for Thou art a shining star, blazing...come to me...

They welcome us with smiles and open arms, calling us brother...we have no need for these iron horses anymore, for we have found our place...they drugged our food, sprinkling it with Molly and dead stars for the first few days, then we got the Roopies and they finally showed us the Truth...

*I'm dragged to the basement, strapped to a chair, feeding tube forced down nose, and The Solution comes in a little black jug, poured into the funnel, filling me, transforming me, a medium for the specter to grow... something completely alien and incredibly powerful bashes its way into my mind, savagely mauling my soul, eating its fill, tossing aside the husk...but I'm still alive! Me! Me! Me! Me...*not me*...I am not who I am...everything* shifts *and reality turns sideways, splintering into needlelike shards of mirrorglass, peppering me, sinking in deep, dissolving, and I am assimilated into the network, one face amongst Legion...*

I am a soldier now, orders simplify everything, I look good in a suit...not the first time I've put someone in the trunk of a car...this is how we make the stew...are you ill, my Master? No, this is how we come into this world, spat into a pail...jars filled with sputum, thick muculent strings clear as water, soft black stars born anew, writhing as they die in the air of this world...some swim and grow in aquariums lining the walls, tanks of strange gasses bubbling through murky fluid, the ones that fail tossed on mesh drying racks in the center of the room, solidifying into brittle dessicated husks...alien protein a connection, a key, a portal for the free flow of images, ideas, desires...open your mind to the kiss and be free...

His hand falls away and I'm snapped back to the living room. Only a few moments have passed, but now I know everything Billy knows about the Temple of the Morning Star: the complete layout of the building, how they operate, their command structure, their hidden agenda, and the names of everyone he met.

I look down at the man I once knew, the man who willingly gave his consciousness away to free himself from the pain of being alive, an empty vessel filled with a new spirit, one who did *not* free his soul, but crucified it to the wall behind his eyes and *made him watch* as his carcass pranced about like a lethal marionette, abducting street people to convert to the cause, or carve into cubes to fill the ever simmering stew pots...but he's back now...sort of...and I see some semblance of Billy remains.

"Dude...they made you *eat their puke?* That's probably the most vile thing I've ever seen, even worse than that German scat porn." Sort-of Billy sort-of laughs.

"It was a lot worse than that...they did things to me...turned me inside out and wore me like a glove...a puppet...and I couldn't do anything but watch it happen...frozen, unable to speak or even think, only watch...a prisoner inside my own head."

So, what now? Are you done with them? Are you going to live?"

"I don't know...maybe I should go to the hospital, but I don't want everyone to see me wheeled outta here on a stretcher...could you call me a cab? I used up the last of my minutes calling you."

"Wait here. My friends are parked down the street. I'll be right back with the car."

* * *

"Billy is pretty bad off. A Clown was inside him, and now it's not. I think he's dying, and we need to take him to hospital."

"Wait, you're saying he was full on possessed...*perfect possessed*...and now he's free? That's just not possible...that's not how these guys work. Once they're *inside*, they wear your ass like a skin suit until it falls apart. They aren't going to give up flesh unless its busted beyond repair."

"Maybe he's busted...he looks real bad."

"I think it's a trap. We're walking into an ambush."

"He's by himself up there, and specifically told me to come alone, but I'm gonna need help carrying him down the stairs." She turns and faces Bob. Neither of them say anything for a long while, so I open the Sight and see twin beams of shimmering golden energy locking their gaze, data passing back and forth like motes of dust suspended in a sunbeam. I try looking deeper, but the light abruptly switches off.

"Take us to the Freed one." I point down the street.

"Go down a block and turn left on Acoma. Grey house on the right, about six houses down."

Theresa turns the ignition and pops the wagon into gear. We get there in a little over a minute, parking and stepping out. They glare all around, up at the second floor windows of the surrounding houses as if looking for snipers, but I just walk directly to the front door and hold it open...eventually, they follow. We go upstairs, into Billy's apartment. I shoulda took out that garbage and opened a few windows...it reeks of spoiled meat and worse.

"Someone *lives* here? This place stinks of death." Theresa says, not caring who hears.

"Cat died while I was out...forgot to feed her...she's in the trash." Billy stands in the doorway of the livingroom, leaning

against the wall for support; unshaven, mottled, gaunt...I've seen AIDS patients with Kaposi's sarcoma who looked healthier than him.

"I told you to come alone...you shouldn't have brung him...I'm not myself, Jake." The pocket of his ratty terrycloth bathrobe explodes, gunsmoke filling the kitchen, fibers floating like dandelion seed, and Bob falls down.

Billy pulls a primitive looking derringer from what remains of the smouldering pocket, calmly setting it on the table...I recognize it as a Cobray .410 single-shot, the kind you'd use to castrate or blind someone with birdshot...they're not much good for anything else...but Bob was only hit in the chest, and he went down hard.

"Sorry, brother...I tried to warn you about this, I had no choice." He turns, staggering back into the livingroom. Theresa drops to her knees on the filthy linoleum, trying to roll Bob over onto his back but he's leaking bad...a puddle of thick, pinkish syrup, like cerebrospinal fluid, rapidly spreading across the floor.

"*BOB!* WHAT THE FUCK HAPPENED? WHAT THE FUCK DO I *DO?*" I squat beside her, and together we roll him over. There's a smoking crater in his chest, erupting pints of steaming pink goop, and then it finally stops. His insides have liquified in seconds...but nothing works that fast, not a mutant form of *Ebola*, not even fuming nitric acid. I don't think he's getting back up.

Theresa has that pink slime all over her hands, well past the wrists, and it doesn't seem to be affecting her any. She holds him close, sobbing, smearing it all over her now...she doesn't see his eyes melt into tears of blood.

There's an explosion from the adjoining room and she rolls away, eyes wild, teeth bared, covered in slime and holding up her little thirty-eight, pointing it at everything and nothing. I don't bother drawing the Bulldog...I know what I'll find. Calmly, I turn the corner and walk over to my friend.

Billy is back in his recliner, a neat round hole in the middle of his forehead, a fist sized exit wound in the back...actual blood and brains this time. His favorite gun clenched in his hand, arm splayed, muzzle touching the floor. It's a compact Spanish 1911, a Star BM with bumper chrome finish and imitation pearl grips. That pistol has a hair trigger and is fully cocked, so I carefully flick up the safety so rigor mortis doesn't touch off a round into a downstairs neighbor. I hear water running in the kitchen and walk back out there. Theresa is scrubbing her hands with dish soap.

"You need to toss that shirt...you can wear something of Billy's."

"I found what he shot Bob with...it's not a bullet, looks like some sort of glass." She opens her hand and I see a round lump of clear green stone, covered with pockmarks. I pick it up and a wave of nausea and vertigo hits, my spirit loosening its moorings and I'm in a daze...I set it on the table beside the derringer and the disoriented spinning feeling fades. I've felt that sensation before.

"That's moldavite...they sell it at the New Age store. It has some weird properties like inducing spontaneous Astral projection, but I never heard of any shit like this. We need to bail before the cops show up. Pull that off, I'll get you a clean shirt." I walk back to his room and grab a clean towel and a random *Harley Davidson* T-shirt from the closet...all he has is size Large. She dries her hands with the towel then pulls on the shirt, tying a knot at the waist, and stuffs the green glass pebble in her pocket. She picks up the derringer, weighing it in her hand a moment before pocketing that too.

"What about Bob? Do we take him with us? Now that rock's outta him, maybe he'll get better?" I look down at him again, hollowed out and starting to melt. Whatever happened to him, he ain't coming back from that.

"Bob's done...we need to leave him here and bail quick." I unsnap the sheath of the *khukri*, pulling it free...it's over a quarter inch thick and heavier than it looks...I wrap it in the damp towel and tuck it under my arm.

We walk down the stairs, unhurriedly, then casually walk to the Volvo and get in. Surprisingly, no-one is staring at us from their windows and I don't hear sirens...maybe everyone's at work? We sit for several long moments, wordlessly, staring at nothing. We need to get out of here, but both of us are in shock, completely drained of energy.

"Let's go back to my place and figure out what we need to do." She nods, turning the ignition and driving off.

* * *

Theresa seems lost, unfocused, dismoored...she blows through a stop sign, nearly T-boning some hipster on a bicycle, but we eventually make it back to my building and park. She follows me upstairs silently, a ghost, haggard and frail, dried tear trails staining her cheeks.

I pull the frosted liter of *Absolut* blue from the freezer...I never got around to adding the peppers. You're supposed to serve iced vodka from a flute, or at least a proper jigger, but all I have are mismatched coffee mugs. Being a gentleman, I don't offer her the chipped one. I approximate a triple shot in each, and raise my mug,

"To Angel Bob," I say.

"To Usiel," she replies, and we drink. The Swedish vodka goes down smooth, and I refill our cups.

"I don't understand," she says, "Bob's been shot dozens of times, and he *always* gets back up...what is it about this little green rock that can kill an angel?" She holds up the pebble betwixt two fingers, closely examining it.

"I dunno...maybe moldavite works like kryptonite on angels, or a silver bullet. Maybe the Clowns poisoned or cursed it in some way. It looked like when a vampire gets staked in the movies." And then she's crying again. I need to learn to think before speaking, as I realize that was incredibly insensitive and untactful. She glares up at me.

"Last year I dropped out of community college and was stocking shelves in a fucking *Wal*Mart*. Bob *showed* me things...he gave my life *meaning*...I want to kill ALL those bastards, Jake!"

"Alright. We're gonna need some supplies. How are you on cash?"

"Bob handled all of that. Everytime we needed money, he'd reach into his pocket and pull out a roll of tens...always tens, like they just *appeared* there. I got, maybe, sixty bucks left."

"Well, I didn't do so well working at the gas station, so it's a good thing my ex was rich...she left me this." I pull the grate off the bottom of the 'fridge and hold up a freezer bag full of *Krugerrands*.

"Holy shit! Doubloons! How much are those worth in real money?"

"The market fluctuates, but right now each of these is worth about as much as your car...eight, maybe nine hundred bucks."

"Goddamn...let's go get us some supplies."

* * *

We walk into *Herbs & Arts*, the biggest New Age store on Colfax, Theresa striding up to the counter, plunking her pebble down on the glass.

"Moldavite. What can you tell me about this?" The clerk picks it up, looks it over carefully, then sets it on a digital scale...it weighs a little over 4 grams.

"Meteoritic glass tektite from the Moldavia region of Asia. The books conflict on what its metaphysical properties are, but I've found it aids trance and deep meditation. I can give you forty bucks for this."

"We're not selling, we're buying...all you got." The clerk chuckles.

"Haven't you heard? Everyone's been sold out for months. We had shipments on backorder from three different distributors and all were cancelled because no-one can get this stuff anymore. On eBay, they're pricing moldavite higher than gold and people are buying it as soon as it's listed. That little pebble you've got there? If you let people bid on it instead of listing a fixed price, you might get over a hundred bucks for it. Six months ago, that same rock would've sold for only fifteen. It's insane."

"No, Thomas...*I'm insane*...and I know you've got over a pound of it in the back...I can *feel* it."

"Who told you about that? That rock isn't for sale! No-one is supposed to know about that! Who told you?" Theresa stares at him for a long while, psychically probing, digging through hidden memories and longings, making him blanche at the sudden intrusion.

"Your first sexual experience was illegal in 32 states and involved a jar of peanut butter...you never told anyone about *that*, did you? But that is not why Isis never answers your prayers...it's because *she doesn't exist.* You have exactly forty-seven dollars in your wallet, an expired Ohio driver license, a membership card to Video One, and a scratch off ticket that, when you scratch it off, will be a loser...just like all the others. Shall I continue?" Thomas gapes wordlessly, then finally stammers,

"Who *are* you?" Theresa grins, widely.

"Come closer...*let me show you...*" She locks his gaze once again, an awestruck expression crossing his face, then he begins crying. Staggering out from around the counter, he falls to his knees and kisses her boot.

"Forgive me...I didn't know," he says, reverently.

"Arise! Bring forth that which I desire! Quickly!" He stands, nods once, and rushes towards the back room. She turns towards me and grins.

"These New Age dipshits believe anything you beam into their heads. I sense Power here, but not from him...doubt that would've worked on the owner of this place." He comes back holding a wooden crate with both hands. Inside, resting on a bed of straw, is a chunk of green glass the size of a basketball.

"This is the biggest piece of moldavite I've ever seen...over four pounds...I think the shop paid three hundred dollars for it ten years ago. It was out on the floor, listed at a grand, until the price began skyrocketing and the boss pulled it as an investment. Unfortunately, this is not mine to give to you, and I can't even guess how much it would be valued at today." I slowly place ten *Krugerrands* on the counter, one after another, each clicking as it's laid on the glass.

"Do you know what these are? That's ten thousand dollars worth of gold right there, and in a few months it'll probably be twelve thousand. We're on a mission from God and require this tektite to do His work." His eyes go wide and he coughs, then gathers the bullion into his hand and deposits it into the cash register.

"Ten thousand seems fair. Do you need a receipt? I need to add sales tax if you want a receipt."

"Just bag it up and we're good to go."

* * *

We drive West on Alameda, towards Sheridan. "What are we going to do with that giant piece of moldavite?" she asks, "load it into a cannon or something?"

"That's not a bad idea...it'd probably turn into dust as soon as it blew through the wall, filling that hive with kryptonite gas. I was just going to use a mallet to bust off pieces to load into shotgun shells and grenades."

"*Grenades?* Where the fuck does someone get a grenade?"

"Grenades are super easy to make. Anyone with a 4th grade education can figure it out, and there's even diagrams in the encyclopedia showing you how...you only need pipe, powder, and fuse. Speaking of which, pull into that *Lowe's* so I can get some pipe fittings and an electric drill. I can't buy pipes and end caps together, so we'll need to make a few stops." She pulls into the parking lot well away from the other cars, and I walk into the store to make my purchase.

* * *

Fifteen minutes later, I come out with a cheap plastic *Black & Decker* drill and a bag of galvanized steel 2" end caps...enough for four fat grenades, each powerful enough to take out a Humvee.

I see some raggedy homeless making a bee-line towards the Volvo with a bucket and squeegee...we don't have squeegee guys here in Denver, so this idiot must've just gotten off the bus. Social Services will buy you a one way ticket anywhere to clear another name from the Welfare roles, and lately everyone's been picking Denver. Lucky us.

I speed up my pace, then hear Theresa yell, *"Get the fuck away from my car!"* and before my mind even registers what's happening I'm at a full out sprint. He splashes her, right through the open window, with the entire contents of the bucket, and I can't believe he just did that...then the world twists sideways and everything goes horribly, irredeemably wrong. He touches the tip of his cigarette to the squeegee igniting it like a torch, and before I can draw the Bulldog he's tossed that in too...the Volvo exploding in a orange fireball belching greasy black smoke.

I don't scream...I stop, cocking back the hammer, bracing my arm, letting my breath out halfway, then fire a single shot from fifty feet, hitting him in the side of the head. Brain matter sprays in a fine pink mist and he crumbles to the asphalt.

NOW I'm screaming, running, burning my hand as I yank open her door, flipping open *balisong* to slice through the seatbelt, ignoring the pain as I pull her out of the inferno, which flared so hot it burst all the windows, but now is nearly burned out...whatever was in that bucket wasn't gasoline, probably some sort of industrial solvent.

I have her flat on her back on the ground and from the waist up she's completely charred...blackened flesh peeling, revealing moist pinks and reds underneath...her eyes, nose, ears, all melted away...yet she breathes.

Kill me, her voice, projected into my head, begs...over and over and over again. She looks like the pork chop that fell into the campfire, and there's no coming back from that...morphine doesn't even touch that sort of pain. I doubt if she can hear me with no ears, but I tell her I love her anyway...and think it *really hard*, hoping that maybe she'll know I'm here with her now.

It hurts so fuckin' BAD Jake! Please! Just DO IT NOW!

I shoot her in the face and she dies. Then I walk around to the other side of the car and use the muzzle of the Bulldog to open the door, pulling off my shirt and using it to pick up the ten thousand dollar chunk of moldavite from the floorboards. Surprisingly, it's cool to the touch, as is Bob's *khukri* wrapped in the barely singed towel. I look in the back, where the plastic tubs and battered suitcases once were, but all that remains is a bed of embers.

I turn around, and some hipster in a Honda Civic has pulled up beside me, eyes wild and a demented grin across his pasty face as he records me on his smart phone camera, so I shoot him in the face too, and he drops the phone on the pavement as the Civic slowly rolls forward. Holding the glass boulder and towel wrapped chopper under my arm, I yank open his door and pull him out. The back tire crushes his legs, but I'm sure he doesn't feel it.

I hop inside and get behind the wheel, using my shirt to wipe the blood off the windshield, before driving off. People are running towards the gutted station wagon with fire extinguishers, but they're far too late.

Suddenly, the magnitude of what I've done hits me, and I'm in full panic mode. All I know is that I need to get away from there as fast and as far as possible. I don't know where I'm going, I just go...

* * *

I find myself heading East on Colfax. By the time I cross Yosemite it sinks in that every cop within 50 miles was probably was told to BOLO for a red 2012 Civic, so I pull into an *Auto Zone*, between two other Civics with oversized spoilers and bolt-on body kits, and walk inside.

I come out with a screwdriver and four rattlecans of *Rustoleum* flat black primer. The Civic to the left of me is painted hot pink and has vanity plates that read CARLA, but the one to the right of me has Illinois plates, which I remove and toss on the floorboards, then I pull out of the lot and into a nearby alley, emptying all four cans onto the car, not caring about overspray tinting the windows and headlights, and within fifteen minutes it's completely black. I toss the hot tags in a nearby dumpster and affix the new ones in their place.

I hate to do it, especially since the Rossi and the derringer were lost in the fire, but there are three bodies lying in the *Lowe's* parking lot with bullets in their heads traceable to my Bulldog, so I remove the cylinder and mainspring before tossing it in the dumpster too. Scavengers go through every unsecured trash receptacle in town several times a day, like they work in shifts, and I don't want to put my .44 in the hands of some brain damaged tweaker so he can stick up a convenience store. I've got enough bad karma coming my way already.

Horrified, I realize I never picked up the hipster's smartphone, and there's a hi-res digital movie of me shooting Theresa, then him on it...and if the DPD isn't already watching it, whoever pocketed it will probably upload it to *LiveLeak* later tonight.

I continue driving East, towards the Quonset hut. Once I pass through Aurora, I casually toss the gun parts out the window, aiming well past the shoulder. I turn on the stereo but it's not a CD player, only MP3 digital, and I can't figure it out...all I can get it to play is shitty Techno dance music, so I turn it off.

Eventually, I make it to Bob and Theresa's base camp. The sliding door is open, so I switch on the high beams and drive inside. The thick velvet curtain is revealed as a dozen rust stained bedsheets stapled to the ceiling, which is about what I'd expected. I find a disposable flashlight in the armrest and am surprised to see that it works. I kill the engine so as not to flood the structure with carbon monoxide, switch off the lights, and get out, examining the structure's interior, sans glamour, for the very first time.

There are sheets of corrugated cardboard from flattened appliance cartons covering a good portion of the dirt floor, with scrap plastic sheeting here and there. I see a folding plastic table and four folding metal chairs, a discount folding charcoal grill, an old beat up rocking chair, a beanbag chair patched with duct tape, a *Rubbermaid* tub, and a ratty old nylon camping tent in the far corner. There's no carpet, no upholstery, no lights of any kind, not even candles.

I pull off the lid of the tub and see ringtop cans of *Progresso* soup and *Chef Boyardee* cheese ravioli, a couple cartons of eggs, a few loose clementines, and an unopened bottle of *Chaucer Mead,* as well as a half empty box of plastic flatware and some cheap paper napkins.

I break the seal on the bottle but can't locate a corkscrew, so I use *balisong* to chip away what I can of the cork before finally losing patience and stabbing it, smacking the flat of my hand against the butt of the knife until the broken cork sinks down, pops loose, and floats on the surface. I sit down in the beanbag chair and slowly drink half the bottle.

Faintly, I hear music playing...Classical strings and woodwinds, but I can't place the piece, or even the composer. It's coming from the far corner, opposite the tent, and I discern a faint amber glow near the ground, like a discarded lightstick. I walk towards it, thinking maybe Theresa had a phone after all, or at least an MP3 player.

The glow doesn't get brighter, and the music doesn't get any louder as I approach, nor even as I'm standing directly over it...and then it vanishes. I shine the flashlight over the spot and see nothing but hardpacked earth. I take another swig of mead and kneel down, using the tang of my closed knife to scrape at the dirt, slowly digging down. It doesn't take long before I see a tail of white plastic. I need to uncover a bit more before I can pull it free.

It's a *Target* shopping bag, doubled up and knotted off. Something small and light is inside, so I flip open *balisong* and carefully slice it open. It's an empty soup can stuffed full of napkins. A glowing, musical soup can, apparently. This calls for another long swig of mead.

I carry the can over to the thrift store tent and look inside...not as bad as I'd thought, there's an actual futon mattress with decent quality sheets and real pillows. I see a few of Theresa's black hairs on the pillow and sit on the bed, carefully straightening them out, tying them in a knot before uncinching my medicine bag and stuffing them inside. Then I begin carefully pulling napkins out of the can.

Inside, swaddled in wadded paper, is a single empty eggshell. Someone had poked a hole in either end, blown out the contents, then sealed the holes with melted wax. As a final touch, they'd taken a black *Sharpie* and drawn a poorly rendered smiley face on the side. I have no idea what to make of that, so I drink more mead.

Take and eat of me, for I am the Life everlasting, the voice in my head states. I recognize that voice.

"Bob? I don't understand. Aren't you supposed to be dead?"

'Tis an old trick, slicing out a portion of one's soul, keeping it safe lest the remainder perish, allowing one to be born again! Suck the vapor from this egg, and I shall grant thee all my Power to fulfil thy Holy Quest! I consider this for a few moments, before draining what remains of the mead.

"I'm not going to suck you, Bob."

With my Power, no bullet nor blade may strike you down, nor flame nor venom. You shall see that which is hidden, have pockets overflowing with wealth, and shall even be granted the Power to fly up into the air! I toss the egg up into the air a few feet, then lightly catch it.

"I don't care about any of that shit, and wouldn't that mean you'd be *inside* me, wearing me like a meat suit? I might as well take the Clowns up on their offer."

We shall work in tandem, and you shall retain Free Will!

"My head's not in a good place right now, Bob. Theresa's dead, Billy's dead, and I am so sick of being lied to and used. So what happens if I smash this fuckin' thing? Do you die?"

No, my spirit is immortal...but wait! You don't understand!

"Thanks, Bob. That's all I wanted to know." And I huck the egg against the wall, where it flattens and sticks.

I take a long fizzing leak before walking back to the car. Noticing the sawed-off leaning against the wall, I pick it up, breaking it open, and a spent shell casing pops out. They probably never got around to buying ammo, likely because the shelves have been bare and 16 gauge is especially hard to find. I toss it on the dirt floor, leaving it behind.

* * *

Stripping off the bloody shirt and discarding it, I start the car, driving out of the field and back towards Denver. The sun is beginning to set and it's dark by the time I get back.

I park in the Wendy's parking lot between the *Ogden Theater* and *Fillmore Auditorium*, wiping my prints off the steering wheel, door handle, and shifter more out of habit than any expectation it'll do any good, I leave the doors unlocked and windows down, with the key in the ignition. If one of the local street rats doesn't take it for a joyride or drive it straight to a chop shop, *Lone Star Towing* will probably impound it within the hour...either way, it's going off the radar for a while.

My building is practically across the street. I go upstairs, locking the door behind me. I throw my bloodstained jeans in the trash, take a quick shower, and fall into bed.

* * *

I find myself at the cottage once again. It is my safe place, a much needed refuge from my many troubles where I can rethink and recharge. Susan and Sam sit at the table sharing Irish coffee and honey soaked baklava. I walk over to my Grandma's rocker and sit down.

"How goes your dealings with the forces of Darkness, my love? I see you ain't dead yet," Susan asks. Sam walks over and hands me a mug filled with fresh brewed coffee, whiskey, and is this a dollop of vanilla ice cream? That's different, but quite good. She mixed it strong, which I appreciate, downing half the mug quickly before replying.

"Soon...I reckon I'll probably be dead real soon."

"Well, if that's the way it needs to be I know you'll die *doing the right thing*, which is what you've wanted for so very long...and you'll have a place here with us."

"So...you're cool with Sam staying?"

"She's still here, ain't she? I don't mind your silly little chippie, she's rather sweet...and she's teaching me how to crochet, ain't that sumpthin?" She points towards the bed and I see a large multi-colored afghan, of the sort that would've taken my Grandma over a month to complete. I'm guessing I haven't been here in about two weeks, but time passes differently on the Astral. There is a knock at the door. Three firm knocks.

"That better not be those creepy Jehovah Witness lookin' Hellspawn again!" She gestures at the door and it vanishes. Theresa stands there, in Doc Martens, hot pants, and a tight black *NIN* T-shirt. Her skin is perfect porcelain, unblemished and unburnt. She smiles shyly, hands in pockets.

"Hey, I know you...can I talk to Jake?" Susan gestures again, and a medieval broadsword appears in her hand, engraved with glowing runes I don't recognize. Theresa chuckles and doesn't move, keeping both hands nonchalantly stuffed in her pockets, thumbs out. "That's a neat sword. I bet you've got a few d20s lying around here too, dontcha?"

"You'll not be crossing mine threshold, you THING!" Susan practically spits...then she spits for real, right on the floor, which is a really bad sign.

"Uh, Susan? This is Theresa. She's actually a pretty good friend of mine." Susan turns, her face a mask of barely restrained fury.

"*Is she now?* Theresael, is it? A sluttier version of the Jehovahs, I see...and that foul THING *shall not cross mine threshold!*"

It happens to be *my* threshold to *my* Astral Temple of *my* construction, but it seems like a real bad idea to argue the matter now...especially since she has a valid point since I'd proclaimed her Gatekeeper.

"She's not so foul once you get to know her..."

"Are you *so blinded* as to her True nature? Tell me you aren't enthralled to this wicked thing! *Holy mother of fuck...*you done bedded this hag and swore that stupid little Oath of yours, dinnit ya?"

"maybe..." She screams and I feel my soul sucked into a rotor, chopped to pieces and flung asunder in all directions...suddenly I'm past the threshold, whereupon the door slams shut and latches. "Fine! I'll talk to her outside, then!" I shake my head and look up at Theresa. She's full out grinning.

"Ouch...feisty."

"Wipe that smirk off yer face. She's a damn fine woman and it was wrong of you to show her disrespect." The grin vanishes.

"No disrespect intended, she just has no sense of humor."

"What does she see that I don't?"

"You have eyes...use them." The eyes behind my eyes open, and a golden Valkyrie stands before me, ablaze, fierce, inhuman, eyes smouldering like embers before a bellows. She seems younger than the Librarian or Storm Goddess of my dreams, and I see no tattoos.

"But those *memories* I saw...your name really is Theresa Simms, born 23 years ago in Austin under the sign of Pisces, dropped out of art school with your abusive tweaker boyfriend and moved to San Antonio, worked at *Wal*Mart* for 28 hours a week stocking shelves in the Housewares department...all that shit was *real*, not some fabrication."

"Indeed...but she was a nobody, a *loser*. She listened to insipid folk music, ate at Arby's on her birthday, and had an inoperable brain aneurism. I did that stupid monkey a *favor*."

"So, you just took her over? Like the Clowns? Didn't Bob say that was an Abomination?"

"You think I jacked that little girl like you jacked that Civic? No, it doesn't work like that...there are *rules* that need to be followed. We saw her misery and gave her a choice: spend the next year drudging between stocking shelves for minimum wage and being smacked around by her worthless dirtbag boyfriend until her brain finally exploded and she got the welfare cremation, or be the vessel for an avenging angel and travel the country slaying demons...silly little twat was a *Buffy* fan, so it was easy."

"But where is she now? Suppressed? Trapped? Evicted?"

"Shared consciousness with fused personalities, and I even cut her a bit of slack now and then. You really think *I'd* listen to fucking Suzanne Vega? You think that was *me* telling you I loved you? She is weak and I am strong...and you are Oathbound."

"'Tis true I swore an Oath, an unbreakable Oath at that, but I didn't swear it to *you*. ***THERESA LOUISE SIMMS!*** By my

Oath as thy Protector, I invoke thee! Come forth and stand before me NOW!"

A column of glowing purple mist forms next to Theresael, dispersing as a girl steps forward, barely out of her teens with long black hair tied in pigtails, wearing a loose fitting blue flannel dress and yellow flip-flops. She looks sort of like the Theresa I knew, but younger, softer, far more innocent...and she's smiling.

"Hi," she says.

"Goddamnit! You didn't need to do *that*, Jake!" Theresael practically screams.

"Yeah, I did. Besides, the vessel is broken and she's satisfied the terms of her contract...or did you mean to keep her spirit in bondage evermore?"

"She was *mine*...but hell, you win. It doesn't matter enough to fight over, and the dimwitted bitch is practically retarded. Besides, I liked being human with you Jake. Call me sometime."

"Give me your Name and I might." She leers at me for a few long moments, half smiling, weighing the risk versus potential benefits of entrusting me with that word...a word by which I could command or bind her at will. She's not going to tell me her Name.

"Call me Svipul. Call me *soon*." With a wink, she's gone, not even a ripple in the air, just vanished. Theresa rocks back and forth on her feet, gazing at me, wide toothy grin pasted on her face.

"Hi," she says again. My head is all sorts of twisted right now, and I fear I may well say or do something insensitive or inappropriate, thereby hurting this wounded girl's tender feelings, and I don't want to do that. She led a horrifically painful life, then was possessed by a demon who openly despised her, before finally being burned alive and shot in the face by me. I'm at a complete loss for what to do next.

"Hi," I say back. "Exactly how much do you recall of the past few weeks?" I didn't think her smile could get any wider, but somehow it does, as she rocks back further on her heels, swaying awkwardly.

"You told me you *loved* me," she says, then giggles a bit. Now I'm the one who feels awkward. Awkward, stupid, and cruel.

"Yeah. Okay. Um...would you please come with me?" I take her by the hand and together we walk back to the cottage, where I rap my knuckles against the door. No-one answers.

"Susan, *please* open the door! It's important!" The door vanishes and she stands glaring at me. Past her I see Sam curled up on her chair, arms wrapped protectively around her knees, frozen in place and taking care not to look in our direction.

"Hi," Theresa says.

"I cannot *believe* this shit, Jake! This *hurts* me, what you've done! You ask far too much!"

"It needs to be done. I swore a formal Oath of Protection...the long version, before my ancestors and TYR himself. I would not ask if it was not the right thing to do, and as my High Priestess you're obliged to aid me in this." She glares hatred at me and grabs Theresa's wrist, not even looking her in the eye as she yanks her forward.

"Come along, inside with you then." She guides her past the threshold then turns back, closing with me in an instant, the point of her *athame* pressed against my gut. "This is just too much, Jake. I can do no more for you. *I will not.* You ask this burdensome task of me, invoking my sacred obligation, and it's the last time you'll ever see me. I'm unraveling the knot of handfasting and absolving myself of any further responsibility for you or yours. It is DONE. Do *not* come back here again."

"I'm sorry things have come to this, and it's my fault entirely. I'll not trespass where I'm unwelcome. This place was always more yours than mine anyway. You're a good person, Susan."

"FAR too good for the likes of you! *Begone!*" A green pentacle flares from her extended palm, slamming into my chest, spinning me backwards into black nothingness...

* * *

I awaken with a start and realize something terrible has happened, but nothing good ever lasts...never for me.

It's still hours before dawn when everything comes back to me in a bombardment of agonizing memories: Theresael's malicious nature, Theresa's dimwitted innocence, and the demands I've placed upon the one woman who ever gazed upon my True Face and did not recoil in horror, but instead accepted and loved me. I was so unfair to her.

I light the green pillar candle in the kitchenette and burn some sage before opening the medicine bag and dumping out the contents...three locks of hair, for three women forever lost to me. I burn them one by one, begging their forgiveness and saying my goodbyes.

I have no-one on my side now, not even anyone to turn to for a kind word. My kin are hard as nails...they'd have no sympathy for weakness and pain, probably not even any useful advice. I realize I'm completely alone.

Suddenly, I have the sense of being stared at and realize I'm *not* alone. I turn towards the presence, and the form I spotted out of the corner of my eye, lurking in the shadows of my apartment, immediately vanishes.

Her energy is distinctive and predatory. There is no need to carve a sigil into my flesh for a blood oblation, as she is so very close the air thickens around me like a static charge.

I return to the bed, lying back, closing my eyes, feeling the warmth growing turgid in my hand as I speak the Name I learned three times...

PART THREE

"We're a wounded lot,
With our holes for eyes,
Makin' believe we're what we're not..."
– Amy Annelle, "I'm A-Gone Down to the Green Fields"

The next few days are a blur of sex, drugs, and casual violence. What little of it I remember shames me greatly, now that I'm starting to come down from the cocaine again.

I'm not sure where I am, exactly, before realizing it's a spacious hotel suite...not just "upscale" but worthy of visiting Ambassadors or celebrities. There's about half a gram of blow on the glass coffee table, "Diamonds in the Raw," allegedly uncut Bolivian flake skimmed from a shipment bound for Aspen, but my nose is bleeding and I think I might've had another heart attack. The girl can have it if she wants.

I look down at the mop of unwashed blue, green, and red hair bobbing up and down in my lap and think of Siamese fighting fish, but then I see the Celtic knotwork tattoo covering her back forms the shape of a crude swastika and am no longer amused. I'm too numb to nut again, and my shaft is feeling a bit raw from friction, so I gently twine my fingers through the greasy dyed hair and pull her mouth off my cock.

She turns to look at me with a face that was obviously pretty once, but now has sunken cheeks and eyes a sickly shade of yellow. She flashes a Jack-o'-lantern smile of rotten teeth.

"Hey...what's yer name again?" I hear myself slur. Instantly, her teeth are perfect and white, eyes blazing golden.

"Have I satisfied your every hunger, Milord?" Theresael's voice answers, mockingly...no, it's Svipul, isn't it?

"What's the crackwhore's name, Svipul?"

"Crack is for *losers*, Milord. Heroin is what all the cool kids are doing. The hype's name is Patricia, but everyone on the street calls her Candy."

"I'm not calling her that. Let's go with Patty for now."

"Candy, Patty, Peppermint Pattie...how about you call me Pepper?"

"No."

"Last night you called me *Susan.*" I didn't mean to hit her, it just happened. She sits on the floor blinking, then laughs while I do another line. My heart can probably take it, and I need the boost.

"Never speak her name again, or we're through...and what's with this 'Milord' bullshit?"

"Thy lineal spirit is royal. Yetarel is royal. Thou art my Lord whom I am bound to serve." I become slightly more lucid, recollecting some of the past few days.

I recall the Summoning, her spirit manifesting, materializing, drawing upon my essence for strength, agreeing to never do me harm, never tell me an untruth, satisfy my every desire and be a loyal servant...as long as I did something for her in return: "Make me thy Princess, as the rank I hold now is so *beneath* me," she had asked, and foolishly I'd agreed.

"I don't like Patty. You let me bareback a junkie with Hepatitis C, so I've got that to look forward to...AIDS too, probably. I thought you swore never to do me harm?"

"I cleaned her up for you inside and out, Milord. Her diseases are in full remission and no longer contagious, and the damage to her liver is being healed. Her health and vitality is being restored, as she wished and as was agreed."

"Alright, you gonna grow her some new teeth too?"

"In time. The decay is gone, as is the pain, taste, and smell. Her third set will begin pushing out the stubs next month. Glamour will serve until then."

"Fine. Order me a rare steak from room service...and rub my shoulders until it gets here. I need to restore my strength."

"As you wish, Milord."

"And STOP calling me that...it's irritating."

* * *

They say that cocaine intensifies your personality...but I'm a major asshole when recovering from a tequila hangover, even apparently from *Gran Patron Platinum*, and I feel badly for the way I've treated Theresael, even if she is a demon. While she was sharing consciousness with Theresa it improved her overall personality quite a bit, but Theresa is gone forever now...along with everyone else I've ever loved.

Patty the junkie whore is not a very nice person and it shows. When she realizes how bad my hangover is, she orders aspirin and *Pepto Bismol* from room service; and when that doesn't help, she leaves the room for nearly an hour, eventually returning with a green and silver oxygen tank.

The tank is only half full, nasal cannula still damp. I don't ask where she got it because I prefer not to know. Visualizing some elderly wheelchair bound invalid with emphysema and a black eye repulses me beyond words, but oxygen is what the carcass desperately requires.

I pull off the snotty nosepiece, sticking the tube directly in my mouth and cranking open the valve. The cold burns my tongue, so I tighten the valve a bit. Soon, the pounding headache, crippling nausea, and overall fatigue begin to subside and I start feeling human again.

There's a knock at the door and it's the Night Manager. I vaguely recall an ugly incident last night in which an ice bucket was thrown and loud unreasonable demands laced with profanity and bizarre epithets were made over the phone to the front desk, so the Night Manager and Hotel Detective came up to the room to discern what my malfunction was and diplomatically explained that the kitchen was closed at 2AM and no, I *couldn't* have a medium rare double bacon cheeseburger with Thousand Island dressing and raw onions.

I took the manager aside and showed him a *Krugerrand*, pressing it into his hand and slurring that it was worth more than he made all week, and to please find me something to eat. He went down to the kitchen and flame broiled that burger himself, and did it *perfectly*. Now he's back again, with two rare Delmonicos and an ice cold sixer of *Paulaner Hefe-Weizen*...Eric, I think his name was.

I'm grateful for the food, and even more grateful that he didn't kick us out or call the cops last night, so instead of paying with a hundred I give him another *Krugerrand* and say thanks, waving him off dismissively and closing the door behind him. I hear rich folk get away with shit like that all the time.

My crazy uncle Louie was a Special Forces Master Sergeant during Vietnam, and one of the few things I remember about him was the time he showed up for my 8th birthday and I compared him to Mister T because of all his heavy gold bracelets and rings, and he laughed and said, *"Gold will get you out of trouble anywhere in the world. You can trade a few ounces of gold for anything from a plane ticket to a machinegun."* Apparently, he was right.

The steaks on the rolling cart smell good. I walk up behind Theresael/Patty and lightly wrap my arms around her, leaning my head against her shoulder.

"I'm so sorry for mistreating you. I feel like I'm someone else sometimes. You deserve better than that." She places her hand over mine and turns to me.

"And I *shall* have better. I surely shall."

* * *

Theresael spends the next hour trying to convince me of who I am and where my rightful place is in the universe, but I'm just not feeling it. She seems completely unconcerned about Bob and what his immediate needs might be. "He was useful, and it was fun while it lasted, but it's time for me to move on," she said, and that was the end of it. I realize I splatted what was left of his soul against the wall, but her lack of loyalty towards her former partner leaves me cold.

Apparently, I (or more accurately Yetarel/Jetrel, the lineal spirit recently awakened within me) am one of the "Lost Princes," a powerful Fallen who turned his back on royal privilege to pursue an unknown solitary mission, although he's a separate entity over which I have little control and virtually nonexistent communication.

I vaguely recall the name Jetrel from when I was a wee lad of 4 or 5. That was how my invisible friend had introduced himself. "Call me Jay," he'd said when I failed to pronounce it after several tries.

He visited me for months, and every time I mentioned him to my parents I'd get 20 lashes with the belt to "whip the crazy out," so I stopped talking about him...but after my Mum overheard me talking to him in my room, the lashes increased to 50, and eventually he faded away. My parents told me he was "all in my head," and years later I started believing it, forgetting our long conversations about how to see the colors people radiate and what the funny shapes floating around them meant.

"Very few Fallen can command a Prince, which is why they could not forcibly possess you and lost interest once they realized you had no interest in joining them. Belial and Belphagor are Kings, but they're not even in Colorado, and the politics involved between your families precludes undue interference. They've got a few Dukes running things at that Temple because it's a major project, but none of them have the authority to command you."

"So I could just walk in there and take over, due to my rank?"

"No. You'd need to formally declare loyalty to the Lightbringer before taking your rightful place, after which you could command all of Colorado...excepting Colorado Springs, of course, but you don't want that."

"I don't want to command anyone...I just want everyone in that Temple dead." She goes silent for a long while before continuing.

"As a Prince, you have the right to dispute Bathym's claim as Grandmaster of the Temple, being that he is a mere Archduke and has not only invaded your domain but attacked you directly, which was a huge disrespect, regardless of your inactive status.

You have the right to challenge him to a duel. If he loses, you can either take over his Temple or raze it to the foundation."

"I think we'll skip right to the foundation bit, forthwith."

"As you wish, Milord."

"Stop calling me that!"

* * *

I decide it's too damn confusing alternating between Theresael, Theresa, Svipul, and Patty, so I'm just gonna call her Theresael from now on. That should simplify shit a lot.

So far, surprisingly, there seems to be absolutely nothing about the incident at *Lowe's* on any of the local news channels, not even the car fire, and that cellphone video hasn't popped up on the internet yet, but I know I'm not that lucky.

I should probably call someone, but don't know who...everyone I even halfway trust is either crazy or dead. I pick up the burner and call Max. I was expecting to leave a message, but he picks up on the second ring. He *never* picks up.

"Hi Ray, we're waiting on a voltage regulator from the dealership. We'll call you when your Jeep is ready," and then he hangs up. Apparently, someone has been by asking about me, and Max is worried about a tap on his phone, but that's nothing new. He'll call from a fresh disposable later.

I have thirteen gold coins and about ten grand in cash left. I traded ten coins for the meteor, cashed in twenty for three 5K stacks of hundreds, paid for the penthouse suite at the *Brown Palace* for three nights at $1,600 a night, scored an eight ball of premium blow from a friend of the Red & White for $400 and bought a fifth of the world's best tequila from the locked case in *Argonaut* for $300, and I don't remember much else aside from giving those two coins to Eric.

I'm bad at math, but figure that there's only 4 *Krugerrands* and $1,300 cash that I can't account for during my debauched three day blackout, but I figure it was probably well spent one way or another. I vaguely recall giving a *Krugerrand* to a white haired panhandler in a tie-dyed shirt on Colfax because I liked the color of his aura, and giving the "Shoeshine King" of the 16th Street Mall a hundred dollar tip to polish my boots, and then there was that limo ride with the strippers...frankly, I'm surprised there's anything left at all. I have abandonment issues, and don't handle depression very well.

Holy shit...$1,600 a night? No wonder they didn't throw me out and call the cops...probably figured I was someone important. I paid cash in advance, all hundreds, and they had no way of knowing that the *Visa* they swiped had less than $200 left before it was maxed out. I guess I won't be getting that *Spartan* trailer out in the woods of Oregon after all...maybe a van down by the river instead...a 20 year old Econoline that burns oil and has bald tires.

The Presidential Suite is great, but I sure ain't paying for another night here. $4,800 for three nights was insane...actually $4,900, because I tipped the girl at the front desk too. I could've stayed all month in a suite at *La Quinta* for a lot less, and that's probably where I should go next. DPD is surely staking out my apartment, and the Quonset hut doesn't have electricity or running water.

I remember the Honda is chained up outside my place and I've been taking cabs everywhere for the past few nights...that was at least another hundred bucks right there.

My phone starts ringing. I look down at the display and it's a 970 number not in my contacts. I pick up, knowing who it'll be.

"It's me. Whaddaya need?"

"Wheels and a hose. Can you pick me up Downtown? Wear a clean shirt, I'm upstairs at the Brown Palace doing some work for Bob." The line goes quiet for a moment.

"I'll be there in half an hour. I'll call you when I'm out front." The line disconnects. I fold the burner and stick it in my pocket.

I feel itchy and realize I'd been wearing the same clothes for the past three days and my aroma is downright foul. I strip down, tossing my socks, boxers, and undershirt in the trash before taking a quick shower. Theresael joins me.

* * *

The burner rings and it's Max.

"Your ride is here," is all he says before hanging up. The shower seems to have done Theresael good...no, she just cranked up the glamour. Her hair is black again, her skin a perfect porcelain white with no trace of the track marks, open sores, or shitty tattoos that were there this morning.

She pulls on some black denim cutoffs, a plain black T-shirt two sizes too small, and a pair of black Converse tennis shoes...all look brand new. I must've bought them for her but don't remember...I wish I'd thought to have bought myself something too. She liberates a pillowcase and uses it as a sack to carry the tektite and my paper bag of end caps. I don't know what happened to the drill, I must've left it in the Civic.

I button up the green and white Hawaiian shirt to cover my pale bare chest and pick up the stolen oxygen tank before heading downstairs, bare feet chaffing against the inside of my harness boots. I almost regret tossing out my socks, even though they were stiff with yellow crust that stank of Limburger. I leave the tank in the elevator when we step out, carefully wiped free of prints.

I drop my room key off at the front desk and am told I have an additional charge for a dozen movies. I glance at the printout and it's a disturbing combination of hardcore porn and Disney cartoons, none of which I remember watching.

"There must be some mistake, we didn't watch television at all," I say, and the clerk comps the charge, which was over a hundred bucks. I could've paid it, but I'm feeling markedly less generous at the moment. We walk out the doors onto 17th Street.

The Clowns are waiting for us, and I don't see Max's chopped Studebaker anywhere. The heavy *khukri* bulges under my flowered shirt in the cheap nylon shoulder holster from the surplus store that I'd modified to fit it. It's all I've got, having lost *balisong* sometime over the past three days. I start unbuttoning my shirt and the tinted driver's window rolls down.

Max is picking us up in a black Lincoln Town Car, and he's even wearing a black suit...but his face is beet red instead of greasepaint white, and his hair isn't slicked back either. I double check the plates and they're red Colorado livery tags with a DOT license number displayed in the rear window, so I let out the breath I didn't realize I was holding and open the back door for Theresael, who verifies it's empty before getting in.

I sit down and Max flips on the directional before smoothly pulling away from the curb and merging into traffic. He flips on the stereo and it's light Jazz of some sort, the inoffensive mild instrumentals they play at fancy martini bars, not like the stuff by John Coltrane or Sonny Rollins I listen to on occasion when I get in one of those moods.

"We gotta stop at my brother Mickey's place, is that okay with you?" Max doesn't have any family, so I assume he's talking about someone from his crew...I certainly don't know any Mickey.

"Sure."

Max heads up Broadway until it turns into Brighton, and for a moment I have an irrational fear he might be driving us towards the Temple, but he turns off onto a side street through a residential area, eventually pulling into the driveway of a small house with a one car garage.

"Wait here," he says, before walking over to the garage's side door, opening it without knocking. Ten long minutes pass before he comes back.

"It's cool for us to go in. Leave your phones in the car." I drop the burner on the back seat and we follow him into the garage, which is empty except for a few folding chairs and an improvised table fashioned from an old door atop a couple of sawhorses. A couple of cheap halogen floor lamps illuminate the room and I see three flags prominently displayed on the wall, *old* Irish flags, long forgotten by most: the Starry Plough, the Sunburst, and the Green Harp. A battered violin case in the center of the table holds what I'd asked for.

"Lookin' good, Candy," the stout ginger with the flattop drawls. Before I realize what's happening, Theresael has him by the throat, lifting him off the ground with one slender arm, as his face flushes and he gags and chokes. He must be over 250 pounds and she's lifting him like he weighed no more than a pillow.

"Candy isn't here right now," she growls in a voice I don't recognize, before slowly setting him back down on his feet and releasing him...then she drags a chair over to the corner and flops down, staring off towards the ceiling with a completely blank expression, seemingly disinterested in whatever we're there for. Mickey's face gradually returns to it's normal color and he stares at her for a few long moments, before turning to Max and jabbing his finger in her direction.

"She has a demon," he states.

"Don't we all?" Max replies. Mickey looks down at his feet, seemingly taking time to digest this concept, before finally nodding his head and approaching the table. He slips on a pair of thin leather driving gloves, unlatches the violin case, and lifts out the hose.

"This here's the Masterpiece Arms version of the MAC10, an improved design with CNC machining and a side cocker. It's not full auto, but has a short reset and will spit lead as quick as you can pull the trigger. This here doodad is a laser designator that'll put a bright green dot right where your shots will hit. Now, *this* ain't the standard bumpfire attachment either. My brother builds these, and it'll make a .45 quieter than a .22...check it out." He racks a round into the chamber, firing it into the tattered sandbags piled in the corner. It doesn't sound like a gunshot at all, more like someone dropped a phonebook on the concrete floor.

He drops the mag, ejecting the live round onto the table, then slaps the mag back in and hands it to me, a wide grin on his face. With the full mag and suppressor it weighs about ten pounds, and there's a one-point swivel sling to conceal it under a long coat.

"Comes with four grease gun mags fully loaded with Golden Sabers. That's 120 rounds ready to go." He takes back the MAC, dropping the mag once again to reload the loose round with a small tool, then pulls a scuffed and well used SIG P220 from behind his back and releases the mag on that as well, stripping yet another round from the magazine of his personal sidearm to replace the one he fired. Three of the mags are in a black canvas belt pouch inside the violin case. He lays the fourth mag on top before placing the suppressed MAC inside.

"This piece is like new and ice cold. With the freshly packed can and all the extras, I need to get two large for this."

"Deduct it from what you owe," Max replies. Mickey's face falls and he stares at his feet again. I know a little about guns, and a brand new Masterpiece Arms retails for under 500 bucks at Tanner, and this one is scratched, dinged, and probably needs a new buffer. The illegal homemade silencer might only add another hundred bucks to the value, because they're super easy to make, and this one appears to be a modified lawnmower muffler.

I flip him a *Krugerrand,* which he snaps out of the air and holds up to the light. He bites down on it, then stares at the coin as if surprised to see the indentations. He looks up at me and nods his appreciation. I put the MAC back in the case and we leave.

* * *

"What kind of car you need?" Max asks me. I think that over for a few moments, as when I'd asked I was assuming he'd loan me a beat up Camry with over 200K on the clock, but now I'm thinking I might even be able to get a Porsche if I ask for one. I decide not to push my luck.

"This Lincoln is perfect...it should fit right in." Max looks up at me in the rear view.

"This Town Car is registered to Tony D...you know what that means?" It means I'll be welded inside a 55 gallon drum if the cops knock on Tony's door to ask about one of his cars being reported as involved in a crime, because he's a respectable businessman who runs a legitimate operation and would be super pissed at whoever gave the cops a valid reason to hassle him over bullshit. It also means I should probably be careful not to scratch the paint and return it with a full tank of gas.

"Yeah, it'll be cool."

"Alright, then. Don't fuck me on this." I say nothing, tacitly acknowledging that I'll take care of the car, even though I won't...this is probably gonna be a one way trip, and pissing off some deranged egomaniac who wouldn't even hire me for valet parking is pretty low on my list of concerns right now.

Max cruises up Brighton, taking a side street connecting to Franklin, before turning West on 54th Avenue to Washington and heading North. Soon, we're parked at his service station, also called *Max's*, but with only a single pump: Ethanol-free 103 Octane racing fuel selling for ten bucks a gallon, with the nozzle padlocked to the pump.

"Tell me now if you want I should slap different plates on this and report it stolen. I don't want no shitstorm blowing back on me over this." I think this over for a few moments. Regardless of my feelings towards Tony the Douchebag, I'd rather not cause any trouble for Max.

"Better safe than sorry. How about you give me 24 hours before calling it in and we snip off the VIN?"

"VIN ain't just on that dash tag, they're all over the place now. We'll need to put it on the lift and grind it off the frame and block, probably inside the door too."

"How long you think that'll take?"

"It's hardened steel...maybe an hour. We'll need to check the trunk and wheel wells too. Did you guys eat today? How 'bouts I order some meatball subs from Carl's? Hey, Fucknut! I need you to take the truck down to Wheatridge and pick us up some sammich! Call the place and tell the guy we need seven meatball subs, and be sure and tell them who it's for!"

A sullen shadow in grimy blue coveralls pulls out a flip phone and trudges towards the work truck, passive-aggressive resentment washing over his aura in dull greenish grey waves...I hope I don't end up with one of the sammiches he revenges himself upon, as he's clearly been free with the secret sauce lately. But in his defense, he hasn't been with a woman in years, and meatball subs are juicy and warm.

"Make yourselves at home...the remote's on the desk," Max says, before leaving us alone in his cluttered office. An ancient

Rhodesian Ridgeback morosely lifts his head from a tattered throw rug, farts loudly, then goes back to sleep.

I sink into the battered Naughahyde recliner, pulling the lever to tilt it back and lift the footrest. Theresael clicks on the old widescreen plasma television and starts flipping through the channels, the faded screen a foggy melange of green mist and blue sparkles. Finally she settles on *Cartoon Network*, which reminds me of prison because that's the only channel we got in our cellblock the whole time I was there.

"Gimme that," I say, and she hands me the remote. I tune into the local news channels but still no mention of me or even the fire at *Lowes*, so I flip it to *Animal Planet* and it's one of those shows about abused and neglected dogs, so I flip it to *Discovery* and it's a different show on the same topic. *History Channel* is about Nazi concentration camps. I turn it off.

We sit there in silence, not looking at each other, both of us staring off into space, unfocused, sullen, numb...

* * *

A few hours later, we're in a clean Lincoln Town Car with plates and registration to match the VIN tag epoxied to the dash. Apparently one was T-boned last week, totaled out, and towed to the boneyard to go into the crusher. Nearly all Town Cars are black, and it's hard to tell the difference between model years, so the papers should pass a roadside inspection in the unlikely event we get pulled over.

The MAC and moldavite are in the trunk, and an extra meatball sub from *Carl's* lays on the console between us. The subs were excellent, and half of a foot long is a meal in itself. Before we left, Max asked if there was anything else I needed, but he'd already done more than enough, then he *hugged* me, which was probably the most shocking and terrifying experience I've had all month.

We have work to do. The big car steers like a boat, and I point it towards the Plains.

* * *

After making quick stops at the *ARC Thrift Store, Ace Hardware*, and *Bass Pro Shop*, we arrive at the Quonset hut.

Theresael's glamour is limited to within her own aura, so she can't manage to illuminate the place now that the sun's gone down. I didn't realize how impressive Bob's abilities had been up to this point: maintaining constant illumination and major glamour while multi-tasking at several other things would've taken an enormous amount of Power and incredible focus, yet he was doing it unconsciously, almost as an afterthought.

The two of us combined, focused solely on one goal, can barely manage to illumine a small area with a soft golden glow before it sputters out, extinguishing, leaving us both exhausted. Perhaps we're going about it wrong and experiencing some sort of energy sink? Good thing I bought a couple LED lanterns and a box of oversized glow sticks, because I'm gonna need plenty of light for this.

Surprisingly, there's no trace of Usiel, aside from the mangled eggshell pasted to the far wall. I'm glad...it would've been awkward. I try to reassure myself he's gaining strength and seeking another host. There was nothing here for him at this isolated outpost, so why stick around? After all, who'd come here aside from me, and I'd made my allegiance clearly known.

I feel a bit bad about that. After all, Bob didn't seem to know any better, and truly believed he was doing the proper and righteous thing...but I cannot abide manipulation, and feel I've been kept in the dark and played since day one. I'm not entirely certain what's going on, but at least I've got the sense to realize I can't trust Svipul to be truthful to me, especially if she could benefit by doing otherwise.

I drive these unbidden thoughts from my head and get to work, clearing off the long dining table and unpackaging my various purchases, one after another.

* * *

It was a long night, using the brass mallet to bash my ten thousand dollar tektite into fragments, then shattering those into cobbles, pebbles, and powder. The moldavite is soft and breaks easily.

I pull on some latex gloves and painstakingly unload all four grease gun mags, filling the cavities of the gold hollowpoints with finely crushed green dust, then sealing each one with a dab of *Loctite* super glue gel, which takes nearly two hours and three full tubes of glue. Thankfully Micky has included a loading tool in the case, which made reloading the shells a lot easier. The mag spring is so strong it would be impossible to load the entire magazine by hand.

I was unreasonably worried that *Bass Pro* might make me show ID and sign the book for purchasing smokeless gunpowder, so I bought a full case of 10 gauge birdshot instead, reasoning that the biggest shotshells would contain the most powder. It takes over an hour and dulls several utility blades slicing through plastic hulls so I can dump the grey flakes in a glass mixing bowl...and it's a lot less gunpowder than I'd thought, maybe only a pound. I should've just signed for a pound of Bullseye double base and saved myself the trouble...at this point, what's another charge.

After I brush the loose powder off the threads, the pipe grenades screw together easily, and I'm sure to give them each nearly a foot of lacquered green cannon fuse. I only have enough powder to fill two pipes, and those each go into a secondhand pressure cooker before being covered with moldavite shrapnel.

The fuse is pulled through the vent and knotted off, then the plastic handles are shattered with the mallet. Once completed, they each go into a plain brown carton with the fuse barely visible next to the address label...a bit more glue keeps it in place with a few matchheads pressed around it for good measure.

Lastly, I take out the 5 pack of 16 gauge buckshot I was lucky enough to find way at the back of the shelf. I open the box, uncrimp the ends of the shells, dumping out the pellets and replacing them with chunks of green glass. The crimps don't want to stay in place after I fold them back, so they get glued too.

By now the sun is starting to rise. I flip open the burner and call Darkside Dan. I realize he's an anti-social, irresponsible, drug abusing mental case who I've only met once, but felt such a strong connection I'm fairly sure he can be trusted, and he's proven himself willing and able to do what needs to be done. That's a rare quality, especially in the Mile High City of thin air and legal weed, where the thugs are notoriously lackadaisical underachievers.

It doesn't even ring before transferring me directly to voicemail, and his greeting is an old recording of one of Charlie Manson's televised rants: *"Maybe I should've killed four, five hundred people. Then I would've felt better. Then I would've felt like I really offered society something."* I wait for the beep, tell him who I am, my number, and to give me a call back. Then I walk over to the old futon mat and lay down. I fall asleep quickly.

* * *

"How are you holding up?" the boy asks. He seems bigger and older than I remember, but could pass for seventeen. Still the same mop of blond curls, but he's wearing gilded mail instead of his usual gold tunic...it appears a couple sizes too large. The sword on his belt seems too thin and delicate to be anything more than ornamental, a multifaceted emerald of roughly 50 karats serving as the pommel.

"It's nice to see you again, Jay. Howcome it's been so long?"

"I needed time to think things over. Figured you were doing well enough on your own. Didn't figure you'd run into a Reptarian...that was pretty random. I seem to suck at the whole guardian angel thing."

"Is that what you're supposed to be to me?"

"No-one assigned it. T'was a whim. I considered it a sabbatical of sorts, and we seemed like a good match. I knew your Grandfather, and his Grandfather before him, so I'm rather attached to your family."

"You were my Grandfather's guardian angel? He never spoke of you."

"That wouldn't surprise me, he had a codeword level security clearance during the war and was used to keeping things to himself. You and he are a lot alike."

"Whatever. Why did you let Susan die? Why did you make me go to prison? Why couldn't you save Theresa?" He scuffs his feet, looking off to his left, not meeting my eyes.

"This isn't all about *you*, Jake. I've got my own problems to deal with. I suppose I was distracted with other things, lost in my thoughts mostly. Sorry about the Reptarian. I've always had a problem with Lizards, and attacking him was purely reflexive. Sorry you went to gaol because of it."

"You really are sorry, aren't you?"

"I genuinely like you, Jake, and I'm sad when you're sad."

"I haven't been feeling much of anything lately."

"I know."

"So, Prince Jetrel...what do we do now?"

"Harlequins are worse than Lizards. I am hereby returning from my self imposed exile and proclaiming myself Grand Protector of the land of Denver and its surrounding Duchies and Baronies, by right of my station."

"These 'Harlequins' are out of control, running amok snatching people off the street and infesting them. I don't think they'll recognize your title or grant the respect you feel you're due."

"I am the Thirdborn of the Lightbringer himself! Any who raise a hand against me shall incur the full wrath of the Realm!"

"RING A DING DING DING DONG! A RING A DING DING DING DONG!"

Fuck. I don't remember what I was dreaming, but know it was Significant, and now it's totally gone.

I pick up the burner and it slips out of my hand, dropping to the floor. ***"RING A DING DING DING DONG!"*** It blows my mind that Max selected what is, arguably, the most obnoxious ringtone ever made for his disposable flipphone. The display reads: **DAN.**

"Hey Dan, you remember who this is?"

"You're the gas station guy with the brandy."

"That's right. You still got that van?"

"The Mobile Command Station? Sold that piece of shit on Craigslist last week...too many bad memories."

"You got a car?"

"I've got the Acura, but it's got a blown head gasket and smokes like fuck."

"What time is it now?"

"Noonish."

"Are you available to meet with me in a couple of hours? There's some shit I want to talk to you about." The line goes quiet for a few long minutes. He doesn't answer, so I ask, "Are you still there?"

"What kind of shit?" he asks, cautiously.

"Creepy Clown shit. We know where they live and we want to hit them hard. Are you in?"

"I'm down to put in work for my dead homeboys. Let's do this."

* * *

We rent a room at the King's Inn Motel, which is arguably the shittiest motel on all of East Colfax. The scrawny black guy of indeterminate age running the front desk has sunken eyes and a shirt that had probably been worn for a month straight, encrusted with an array of mysterious stains. He holds a bowl of *Froot Loops* in one hand, eating spoonful after spoonful, barely seeming to register our presence.

"A room for the night be fawty, no, *fitty* dollah!" I give him three twenties and tell him to keep the change. He hands me a tarnished room key with a broken tag, but I can make out the room number: 102.

There are a bunch of skells wandering around the parking lot and patrolling the stairwells, most of them shirtless. I think we're probably the only white folk here. I hear a shrill whistle from one of the upper levels and half of them vanish from sight...they don't scatter or run, but rather fade into the background like mist.

I feel numerous sets of eyes watching us. They probably figure we're undercover narcs setting up surveillance, which likely isn't an uncommon occurrence here. I get the feeling we'll be left alone. I turn the key in the lock and we walk inside, carrying our gear.

The air is foul with nicotine and mildew, a filthy handprint smeared down one of the walls. I doubt the carpets have been vacuumed anytime this year, but the bedsheets appear surprisingly clean.

"Bedbugs," Theresael mutters. I don't know how she spotted them, but don't doubt it at all. That's alright, we'll only be here for an hour or so. I open the burner and call Dan.

"Meet us at King's Inn, on Colfax near Peoria. We're in room 102."

"King's Inn? You're shitting me...really?"

"It's only for an hour or so, what's the problem?"

"Dude, the only people who rent rooms at King's Inn are crackheads, crack dealers, and twenty dollar crack hos! Someone gets murdered there every month! What the fuck are you thinking, staying there?"

"I'm thinking I don't need to worry about busybody cop callers so much here. Oh, wash the hair product out of your mohawk before you come over. We're on a mission and need to keep a low profile."

"I can be there within the hour. I hope I don't get shanked walking from the parking lot to your room."

"They think we're Five-O...you'll be fine." I snap shut the phone and get to work unrolling the posterboard and tacking it to the wall.

* * *

During the mind meld with Billy, I learned the complete layout of the Temple compound and draw it from memory on the posterboards, with black markers denoting walls and colored markers showing detail. I try to keep things as simple and neat as possible, drawing freehand on a vertical surface. The diagrams are crude, but legible.

"He just pulled in," Theresael says from her spot near the window. A moment later she opens the door for him and he passes through without a word. She stares fixedly at his back for a few moments.

"Cambrion," she says, "That's why the Clowns couldn't get a lock on him...he's a half breed."

"Bitch, kiss my lily white Austrian ass! I'm twice as white as you!" She laughs, mockingly.

"Ignorant child doesn't even know who his daddy is...no, your *real* daddy...but that's irrelevant. You're right, he's one of us...close enough, anyway." Dan looks at me for an explanation.

"According to lore, a cambrion is the result of a human woman mating with a demon, usually while asleep and dreaming. No worries, you're not like Damien or Hellboy or any shit like that. Just a strong willed sociopath resistant to demonic possession. That sound about right?"

Maybe..." He looks uncertain, perhaps even regretful to have shown up. I wonder what he was expecting. After all, the last time we met he'd just shot all his friends in the face and was on his way to taking the same route...it doesn't seem as if he has very many options at this point.

"Dan, most of what I know about you is from reading your blog. You seem like someone I'd want on my side, and I think I can probably trust you. What I need to know is if you're cool with this, because we ain't fucking around. You can walk out that door right now if you want, no hard feelings, but once we start there's no backing out. Are you absolutely sure you want a part of this?"

"Jake, I'm nearly 40 years old and work for *Jiffy Lube* part-time, making a buck above minimum wage, and that's being garnished because of my student loan. I'm living in my Mom's garage because I can't afford to pay rent now that my roommates are dead, and I'm being sued for thousands of dollars over breaking that lease. I'm not even going to bother discussing my cavities or colitis. Dude...I *welcome* death at this point."

"Alright, then. Take a seat and let me share what's been on my mind."

"Sit in the chair! The bed has cooties!" Theresael advises. Dan lowers himself into the hardbacked blue plastic seat and I begin my presentation.

* * *

"First and foremost, we need to define the enemy we're facing. I've been calling them Creepy Clowns, you've been calling them Slendermen, the cops call them Smilers, but I thought of the perfect name for them today. From now on, our enemy is the Harlequins.

"What do we know about them? Very little. The way I figure, Harlequins are some sort of entity from another dimension. Maybe they're aliens, maybe they're demons, but at this point it doesn't seem to make any difference.

"Somehow, they're able to get inside people's bodies, taking complete and permanent control. Once this happens, the body changes. They don't bleed normal blood, they heal incredibly fast, and they're very tough to kill. Another thing that happens is the skin goes white, eyes go black, and the hands and face distort and stretch further than they should...but I can't say whether that's an actual physical change or an image projected into our minds. That's an important point: they can read your thoughts and mess with your brain, which makes them extremely dangerous if you aren't expecting it. Expect hallucinations and illusions.

"In order to kill a Harlequin possessed body, you need to either destroy the brain or use some of this." I hold up a chunk of green moldavite, then toss it to Dan, who attempts to snatch it out of the air but fumbles. I wait for him to pick it up from the carpet before continuing.

"I don't know how or why it works, but this shit is like kryptonite to them...and we have two bombs filled with it. According to this map of their compound, once we enter the back door, here, we'll be in the middle of a hallway that stretches the length of the building with a door at either end. Those doors lead to the basement level, where most of them congregate during daylight hours.

"The plan is to toss those bombs down to the basement from either end, then run out the back door, hop in the car, and get out of there fast. I figure the moldavite is so fragile it'll atomize into a fine dust that will fill the entire basement like gas, killing everything. And if anyone gets in our way, we just shoot 'em in the head. You have your Tokerov?"

"No, I took it apart and spread the pieces far and wide. I've got a little Rohm .22 snub back at the house though."

"A .22 won't do any good. Doesn't do enough damage and they heal too fast. Here, take this instead." I unbutton my shirt and peel it off, shrugging out of the cheap black nylon shoulder rig that holds the *kukhri*, wrapping the straps around the holster before tossing it onto the bed. Dan picks it up, unsheathing it and feeling the balance. The quarter inch thick, 15 inch blade weighs a pound and a half and is sharp enough to slice paper.

"Himalayan Imports *Chitlangi*...very nice."

"So you have some familiarity? Good. A single swipe with that chopper can slice off a head or cleave it in half, which is the only way to put a Clown down for good. If you can't reach the head, just lop off a few limbs."

"I can do that."

"The bombs are simple to use...light and toss, I'm guessing it's only a 5 second delay, more or less, so once it's lit get rid of it fast."

"I'm so ready to do this shit."

"Alright, we need to pick up a few things at the Northfield Mall. You can leave your car here and ride with us."

"No way in fuck am I leaving my Acura at motherfucking King's Inn! It'll be up on blocks stripped to the frame by the time I get back!"

"Fine, follow us in your car then," I say, prying the thumbtacks out of the wall and rolling the posterboard map back up.

* * *

Our first stop at the Mall is *JCPenney.* We go directly to the menswear department, and I find a rack of black suits that look very similar to what the Clowns wear, with thin lapels and black buttons. It's a polyester wool blend, which will probably be too hot, but they're under 200 bucks each for the set of blazer, vest, and matching slacks. We each find our size and try them on in the dressing rooms.

Theresael's trousers are a few inches too long, so I grab a pair of cheap scissors. We pick up three black dress shirts and matching belts, then pass through the shoe department and get three sets of black Oxfords before checking out at the registers.

Next stop is *Hot Topic*, a corporate chain that caters to all sorts of poseurs from emos to Juggalos. What we need is right in front of the registers, and it's cheap enough that I buy extra. Three tubes of "Raven Black" hair gel, and three compacts of "Goth White" powder creme foundation. They had a few sets of overpriced cosmetic contacts, but not the full black ones we needed.

With our hair blackened and slicked back, and our faces painted white, wearing black suits and rolling up in a black Lincoln Town Car, I'm hoping we won't stand out at first glance...and that's all the edge we need. No way we'd have a chance bluffing our way past the front desk in these Halloween costumes. I'm fairly certain their bizarre appearance is projected glamour rather than a physical change. After all, they look fairly normal once they're dead.

We leave Dan's Acura at the Mall, getting in the Town Car and heading South towards Colfax, to return to our shitty hotel room and don our disguises for the mission.

* * *

We're wearing black suits with bulky weapons poorly concealed under our blazers, paleface makeup hastily applied, and hair slicked straight back, Dan and Theresael's terminating in greasy ponytails tucked into their collars. We look like demented mimes preparing to commit an armed robbery.

We walk out to the Town Car and I feel the weight of many eyes upon us. I hear voices, running feet, and slamming doors, but no-one is bold enough to call out or approach. We get in and I start driving West.

"I brought this CD along for the ride," Dan says from the backseat, handing it up. It's unmarked, a generic ripped CD he burned on his computer. I pop it in. Synthesized dark ambient starts pounding from the speakers. It's like nothing I've ever heard, so I ask what we're listening to.

"*How to Destroy Angels* by Coil...it seemed appropriate." I hear gongs and clanging metal...not the type of music I'm into, but I let it play as we cruise towards the Temple. The track seems to go on forever, and when it changes it sounds like a remix of the same thing. I turn it off, we're almost there.

I pull off 52nd Avenue onto Forest, about a mile from the Temple, and kill the engine. I flip on the dome light.

"Okay, this is important, I need both of you to focus. This is the master key to all the doors in the building," I say, holding up the gold plated key hung around my neck from my old dog tag chain. "I don't know if the basement doors are locked, or if you need a key to exit, so I cut each of you a copy just in case." I hand each of them a key, fastened to a cheap leather fob making it easier to grab and harder to drop.

"You each get one smoke, a *Djarum* clove, which I'll light for you before we exit the car," I hand them both a sweet smelling black cigarette. "The box on the floorboards next to you contains a pressure cooker filled with explosives and moldavite. The fuse is sticking out the center of the mailing label surrounded by matchheads. All you need to do is open the basement door, touch your ember to the fuse, inhale until it ignites, then toss it down the stairs and run. Very simple shit...you think you can do this?" They both mutter their assent.

"I haven't got a stopwatch, but I figure once we're inside, if we don't run into a problem, we can be in and out in under 2 minutes. This needs to be done quick, no mistakes. Hit and run. We're nearly at the place, are you ready?"

"Yeah...I think I can do this." Dan doesn't seem as cocky anymore and looks ill...I'd bet he'd be chalk white even without the makeup.

"You CAN and you WILL do this," I tell him, before pulling aside my coat and racking a moldavite packed hollowpoint into the MAC hanging nose down at waist level. "Theresael, are you good to go?"

"Amen," she states, flatly, breaking open the sawed-off and loading a single plastic hulled shotshell.

"Right on. The key is pretending like we belong there...don't run, just walk straight ahead. If anyone tries to stop us, let me deal with them first. Focus on getting to the basement doors and lighting those fuses. When we go in, Dan goes left, Theresael goes right, and I'll cover our exit. Any questions?" No-one says anything, so I start the car and pull back onto 52nd.

* * *

I slowly cruise through the Temple parking lot, seeing no-one outside. The sun is only now starting to set, but I regret not having gotten here earlier...according to Billy's memories, the Clowns will be active soon.

I pull behind the building to where the back door should be and see it's hidden within a fenced off area, with a long sliding gate secured by a heavy brass padlock. This eight foot tall barricade was unexpected.

I slap the gearshift into Park and walk to the gate. The smaller key I have fits and the lock unlatches. I slide the gate as far open as it will go, revealing the back wall of the temple and their private lot. No-one out here either, not even any cameras.

I climb back into the Town Car, slowly rolling inside, parking along a trio of black Lincolns nearly indistinguishable from ours aside from the Nebraska plates. I have the key for the Lincoln I torched, but it's unlikely to fit any of them...I don't know why I bothered keeping it.

I switch off the ignition and flip open my Zippo, lighting both of their cloves and one of my own before we open the doors and step out. They follow close behind as I stride confidently to the back door, insert the master key, and swing it open.

I quickly glance in either direction and the hallway is clear. Switching on the laser, I wave them inside, grabbing Dan's shoulder and turning him in the correct direction after he veers right instead of left...not that it would've made any difference, but when I make a plan I like to stick to it without any last second changes. The building is eerily silent, no footsteps aside from our own, no muffled conversations or the usual office noises, not even any Muzak.

As I'd suspected, both doors were fitted with a deadbolt, and the copies I had cut at *Ace Hardware* fit the locks. They both open their respective door and light the fuses, which blaze like sparklers as they catch. Theresael throws her box down the stairs, running back to me, letting the metal door swing shut on its springs. I turn to Dan, and he's holding his box overhead with both hands, shouting down into the darkness.

"SPECIAL DELIVERY FROM DARKSIDE DAN, YOU MOTHERFUCKERS!!!" he screams, in a panicked, high pitched falsetto, loud enough for everyone in the building to hear.

That was *not* part of the plan. The MAC snaps up and I realize the green dot is neatly centered on the side of his head...but it wasn't me moving my arm. I force my finger outside the trigger guard to prevent Jetrel from executing him on the spot. **He's ruining everything!** the voice in my head exclaims.

"UP YOUR ZOMBIE ASSES, BITCHES!!!" he continues, before finally tossing it. It detonates as soon as it leaves his hands, the concentrated blast from the stairwell spraying most of him against the opposite wall. I guess it must've been a four second delay instead of five.

When the second bomb detonates in the cellar I feel a dull thud through the floor, but hear nothing aside from the steady metallic hum of my damaged eardrums, like they've been stuffed with wax and a tuning fork has been embedded in my skull.

We need to get the fuck out of here! Theresael yells, but she's not yelling at all, rather beaming the thought directly into my mind. I don't hear the other doors along the hall open, but suddenly Clowns are charging into the hallway from all the ground floor offices.

I fire the suppressed MAC quickly, not realizing it's dry until it stops recoiling, but only a few go down. When the sawed-off booms all that registers is a muffled echo, then Theresael shoves me out the door towards the waiting Town Car.

I stagger towards it, dropping the spent mag and slapping in a fresh one from the belt pouch, racking a round into the chamber, turning just in time to see the fire axe slam into her back. She falls, and the Harlequin yanks the axe free, lifting it high for the final blow. I stitch ten rounds into him from asshole to eyeball and he practically dissolves in front of me as the moldavite does its work.

Clowns continue pouring out the back door, silent to my deafened ears, and I calmly realize I'm never getting out of here alive, firing my weapon as one already dead. The remaining twenty rounds fly true, but there's far too many of them to fight, dozens already outside with more coming, all wearing the same cheap suits, armed with a variety of blades and cudgels.

I slap a third mag into the hollow grip and am racking the charging handle back when a heavy cosh crushes the back of my skull. After a brief display of purple fireworks and a whiff of freshly mown grass, everything fades to black...

PART FOUR

"He went looking for angels and found me instead, girl of the sorrows, sad but not sorry. I waited for a sign, a star to fall. He reached for a knife and drew branches."

– Brenna Yovanoff, *The Space Between*

"Helpless, you are." The voice hisses. I open my eyes and they slowly come into focus. My head pounds dully, but the tinnitus is gone. I'm in one of the offices, stripped naked, chained to a ladderbacked wooden chair, arms tightly fastened to the armrests.

Maybe a half dozen Clowns are in the room, slouching lazily, silently staring...it's impossible to know who's behind me as my head will only turn so far. I'm curious as to why I'm not dead.

"So the rumor is true...the little prince has gone Outrider...how very splendid to have lawful right to your vehicle at this time."

"That Lincoln belongs to Tony DeVeccio and has a bogus VIN tag, so good luck with that." The voice chuckles, mirthlessly.

"Oh, no...I'm not talking to *you*, insignificant monkey, but to the Thirdborn within you. You merely serve as the Thirdborn's vehicle, and as Lord of this Temple which he has wrongfully attacked, that vehicle is mine to do with as I wilt." The Clown walks from behind the chair into my line of sight,

Power emanating from him as a tangible force, black aura crackling like electricity as be faces me, looming, gaunt, wearing a black leather meatcutting apron over his suit, the wheeled tray table he pushes covered with an array of crude instruments: tin snips, icepick, pliers, disposable craft knives, a hammer and nails.

Thou shalt not be subject to torture at the hands of Harlequin Bathym...step aside and allow me to take this in thy stead, Jetrel's voice whispers in my ear. That seems like a real good idea right now...no-one ever talks about the positive side of demonic possession.

Alright. Do it, I think back. Instantly I'm viewing the room through an amber filter and everything zips back as if I'm peering through the wrong end of a set of binoculars. I feel detached, yet oddly at peace.

"So the little prince has decided to grace us with his presence after all! Oh, this shall be rich...how very long have I yearned to make you suffer for your insolence...and you grant me this gift by attacking unprovoked? Now you shall *truly* understand suffering."

"Unprovoked? Thy minions, under thy command, directly attacked me several times, in flesh and in spirit! You dare set thy dogs upon a Royal? There is a price to be paid for such transgression!"

"I was unaware of your presence until recently, and forbade any further contact once I learned of it...but by going Outrider and attacking an Archduke in his domicile, absent any official sanction or formal declaration of war, you're stripped of all rights and protections of your station."

"T'was righteous retaliation for attacks on me and mine!"

"A valid point becomes irrelevant without the Power to enforce one's will...and you sit before me naked and in chains!

I shall enjoy slowly stripping the meat from your bones, greasing mine skillet with your blubber, Legion communing with the Lightbringer through gobbling the sizzling bacon of his brat!"

Suddenly the Clowns encircling me turn towards the door as one. ***"Avengers,"*** one of them hisses, and they scurry away from my chair, cowering miserably in the furthest corners, as if awaiting their doom. Something has obviously scared the shit out of them. Bathym sets the scalpel he was examining back on the tray, calmly folds his hands, and turns towards the door as well.

A Clown opens it from the hall, swinging it wide, stepping through to address him directly.

"Milord! Avengers have entered the Temple! They are coming!"

"We are aware of their presence," he replies, and the Clown darts back outside. Moments later a phalanx of armored SWAT officers storm into the room, but then I notice they aren't brandishing guns and the insignia on their chests is a red shield emblazoned with a golden coiled serpent under a crown.

"Dominator Varpiel," Bathym hisses, **"How may we be of assistance?"** The largest Avenger, crimson braid looped from his epaulet denoting command, unrolls a thick parchment scroll, holding it aloft.

"I hold a warrant for the seizure of Prince Yetarel to be tried and sentenced for crimes against the Realm! Behold His sign and seal!" Bathym strides over to the Avenger, glancing at the signature and stamped red wax.

"Signed by the Lightbringer himself? Loyalty is my honor. Release him!" There is a flurry of activity behind me as padlocks are unlatched and heavy logging chains pulled away. Jetrel stands, lazily stretches his arms, and instantly is garbed in his usual golden tunic.

"Friend Bathym...just one thing before we part." The motion is so swift and effortless no-one is able to react as the jeweled rapier apports into our hand and is flung ten paces away, needle point sinking deep into Bathym's inky orb, which ruptures, brackish slime spilling down his face as he grasps the narrow blade with both hands.

The emerald pommel supernovas in the unfurnished room, like a high powered flashbulb, and Bathym's charred lifeless husk falls to the ground, a column of blackened ash bursting into a cloud of choking dust which covers everyone. Clowns scatter, fighting to push through the doorway as they escape.

"Right...off to see my Father, then." Plastic backed Kevlar gauntlets seize either arm and lead us from the room, out of the building and into one of a pair of unmarked black cargo vans.

* * *

"You shall not flee," Varpiel states through his tinted visor as he slips a green plastic noose over our head and tightens it. **"This is Primaline 85. If you attempt to flee it will sever your host's head, and you will stand trial in a jar. You are unchained as a courtesy."**

He guides us to the padded bench before sitting beside us, noose terminating in a detonator cradled in his hand. Another Avenger sits on the opposite side, then two more across from us. They're brushing ash off their uniforms, but no-one complains. I register a thin coating of grit in my mouth, but taste nothing. The van lurches forward and we're moving.

"Your courtesy shall be remembered. Who notified Berith of my predicament?"

"Lord Raym has been embedded within the Harlequin stronghold since the beginning. Bathym was too ambitious to be trusted."

"It has been over a millennia since the insult...surely it is forgotten?"

"Nothing is ever forgotten. Same as it ever was."

"Right."

* * *

After a long, silent ride, the van pulls over and stops. The Avenger removes the explosive noose from our head, handing us a folded orange jumpsuit. My vision snaps back to normal and I'm in full control of my body once again as Jetrel retreats, disinterested and sullen.

Vertigo and nausea make me stumble and I'm grasped and held up by strong hands. When Jetrel withdrew the tunic disappeared as well, and I hurriedly pull the jumpsuit over my nakedness. It is clean, but a poor fit.

They help me out of the van, encircling me in a dark vacant lot, somewhere in North Denver near train tracks, probably near Pecos, and a DPD cruiser rolls up, hitting us with the spotlight, which sweeps the lot twice before switching off.

One of the Avengers approaches the patrol car, and an overweight cop with a shaved head and thick moustache steps out. I note sergeant stripes on his sleeve...and that he came alone.

He holds out his hand to accept a *Taco Bell* bag stuffed with stacks of bills, which he flips through briefly before casually tossing the bag on the front seat and holding open the back door of his cruiser. As his eyes wash over me, the pupils elongate and slit, a greenish fog over his face showing me the scales, and then he's just another fat cop again.

A pair of Avengers walk me to the car and help me inside. There are no door handles, and a plexiglass shield completes the cage, but I've got nowhere to run to now.

* * *

My attorney is human, apparently because Reptarians are far too ambitious for the Public Defender's office. He passed the Bar only six months ago and wants me to call him "Mister Tobin." He doesn't like it when I call him Toby.

"Mister Bishop, I think you fail to appreciate the severity of the charges against you. The DA is willing to drop possession of a firearm by a convicted felon, arson, carjacking, and the charge for the murder of Theresa Simms if you only plead guilty to the other two murders."

"Well, I didn't murder her or burn her car, and I shot both of those guys in self defense, so fuck you...I want my jury trial."

"Jacob, there is video of you at the scene with the smoking gun in your hand! Judge Verrin doesn't feel a jury trial is in anyone's best interest, and if you insist he'll give you the maximum for sure."

"What do I care? I'm already looking at two consecutive Life terms, with maybe my first parole hearing in fifty years, so fuck him too."

"You need to be respectful to the judge or he'll charge you with contempt."

"You sure are a dimwitted motherfucker, Toby. Tell him I want my jury trial or I'll state, for the record, that you're refusing to defend me and start squawking about my rights and shit."

"Okay, I'll tell him you want to take it to trial."

* * *

"Jacob Roland Bishop, it is this court's understanding that, against advice of counsel, you wish to contest all charges and proceed to trial, is that correct?"

"It is, your honor," I say.

"The prosecution has offered to drop most of the charges against you if you accepted a plea bargain agreement. Has this been explained to you?"

"Yes, your honor."

"Mister Bishop, there is clear video evidence from both Mister Whitney's cellphone camera and store security cameras showing you firing a revolver at all three victims! If you intend to refuse the plea arrangement and waste this court's time and money with a jury trial, I guarantee you'll be found guilty and will be sentenced to the maximum penalty allowable by law!"

I feel a familiar stirring within my mind and something lurches forward as I'm viewing the courtroom through the wrong end of the binoculars with amber filters, wrists swelling against cold steel manacles.

"Lowly Reptarian scum! You DARE raise thy voice to me? You dare challenge the will of the Thirdborn? I demand satisfaction!" The courtroom falls silent except for the clacking of the stenographer's typing. I clearly see the reptilian face of the judge, prosecutor, and several spectators fully revealed, but know I'm the only one who does. The judge clears his throat before continuing.

"Very well, Mister Bishop. It is the decision of this court that these proceedings be adjourned until after such a time as a complete psychological evaluation has been performed to determine your fitness to stand trial."

* * *

The Sheriffs manacle my hands and feet, connecting them to a chain strung through the D-ring of the heavy leather belt, before driving me less than a block away to the Van Cise-Simonet Detention Center on Colfax. I'm alone in the van, which rolls through a bay door and parks inside.

Once the door closes, I'm escorted to an elevator and taken down to the basement, guided along hallways, through a checkpoint and another pair of locked doors, before finally reaching my private cell and having the manacles removed.

The walls are painted an institutional pastel blue, the only amenities an aluminum combination sink/toilet and a steel bunk welded to the wall. On the bunk is the standard blue rubber mat, blue rubber pillow, clean sheets, pillowcase, bar of *Ivory* soap, roll of generic TP, toothbrush, and sample sized tube of *Colgate* toothpaste.

Someone has a demented sense of humor, as there's a peppermint hard candy in its clear cellophane wrapper sitting on my pillow. I set it aside for later and make up the bed.

* * *

A couple days later, the Sheriffs escort me from the cell, back onto the elevator, and finally into the back of an unmarked Crown Vic with dark tinted windows.

"Where are we going?" I ask.

"Doctor appointment," one of them says. We drive down East Colfax in silence, bypassing Downtown and passing Broadway, York, and Colorado, so we're not heading towards the usual hospitals or office buildings. Eventually, we turn South on Forest and pull into the driveway of a small doctor's office that appears to have been a single family house at one time, now with a wheelchair ramp and a shingleboard out front reading: *Dr Earl Buer, Psychotherapist.*

"We were told to shoot you in the back if you run...so don't run," one of the Sheriffs states, matter of factly, as if it were a routine bit of advice for my own good but he doesn't particularly care either way. He turns around to look at me, absolutely no expression on his face or in his eyes, which shift to cat's eyes as a shimmering mask of green scales covers his face like mist, then evaporates just as quickly, thereby clarifying he's not joking.

They open the back door, helping me out and removing the cuffs before escorting me up the stairs and through the front door into the waiting area, which is empty.

"Jacob?" the attractive brunette receptionist asks. She's wearing a shockingly red blazer with matching beads and earrings. "Doctor Buer is ready to see you now. Please come with me." She steps around the partition, and I see her skirt, belt, and heels are bright crimson as well. She takes my arm to lead me down the back hallway and I wonder if her panties are the same shade of red.

"They are," she exclaims, rather brightly, before opening the heavy oak door at the end of the hall and ushering me inside. "Jacob is here for his ten o clock, Doctor," she says, before shutting the door behind her.

The office is dimly lit by a silver candelabra holding three purple tapers, but richly furnished with glass fronted oak bookshelves and mahogany leather chairs. The Doctor is a thin older man in a tweed suit with round wire framed spectacles and a salt and pepper goatee, leaning back in his chair, both feet up on the wide oak desk. He gestures towards one of the seats before exhaling a rich cloud of smoke that smells vaguely of pine and strawberries.

"In your office? With two cops in the waiting room?" I inquire.

"Fortunately, we are in Denver, and this is medicinal," he laughs, passing me a blown glass Sherlock aswirl with greens and blues. The ember is glowing, so I take a long deep hit before handing it back, but he holds up his hand. "No, you finish that up, it's an essential part of the therapy." He reaches across the desk, flicking the pendulum on an antique metronome, which begins clicking back and forth rhythmically. My eyes are drawn to it.

"Close your eyes and relax...this is a safe place, and no harm shall come to you here." I feel myself drifting as the metronome clacks softly, soothingly. **"Now...permit me to address Yeter'el."**

"No-one calls me by that name," Yetarel states flatly.

"Very well, are you still going by Jetrel?"

"I am."

"It is important that you are comfortable speaking freely with me, Jetrel, because right now I'm one of the few friends you seem to have left."

"Is that so, Buer? I'm supposed to trust you?"

"You know my reputation is solidly based upon trust and good works, and I've always avoided any involvement in politics. I am a neutral party and a healer. You have been assigned to my care, and I take that responsibility very seriously. I want what is best for you."

"Speaking of responsibility, I was responsible for Souleater...what has become of her?"

"She has been restored to her rightful place at the Royal armory, so put your mind at ease about that."

"Was he angry?"

"You abscond with his most prized possession, the blade used to vanquish the Tyrant's champion, and expect him not to be?"

"He's always angry."

"He's under a lot of pressure. You, of all the Realm, know that best."

Jetrel nods, silently.

"You have been away for a while, but not wandering. Never exiled, yet in self imposed seclusion for nearly a

millennium, like a monk seeking enlightenment. Tell me...did you ever find that which you sought?"

"I believe I have. Two centuries past, I finally completed my poem."

"It took eight centuries for you to compose a poem?"

"It is a very good poem."

"One should hope."

"And I am to be wed soon."

"Please tell me it isn't Eris."

"That didn't even last a quarter century. She has five distinct personalities, one of which clearly hated me, and hasn't got a clue what she wants."

"Eris knows exactly what she wants, chaos and entropy, making her the worst possible match for a sensitive poet such as yourself."

"It was fun while it lasted."

"So, who is to be thy blushing bride?"

"Do you know of Svipul?"

"Daughter of Librarian Eir? We haven't met, but I haven't heard anything bad."

"She's more stable than Eris."

"*Everyone* is more stable than Eris, but you are aware that the name Svipul means changeable?"

"She's proven herself loyal, and I gave my word."

"I shall pass news of the Royal engagement through the proper channels. Such glad tidings can only reflect positively upon you, and may even reduce thy punishment."

"Tell Asmodai to get over himself. It's been a thousand years, my words were True, I retract nothing, and I'd gladly say the same to him tomorrow."

"Lord Asmodai fell after foolishly challenging The Leviathan to a duel over yet another perceived insult, so *your* insult seems a moot point right now."

"What, then, is my crime?"

"Aside from stealing Souleater and using it to End an Archduke in his domicile without sanction?"

"A *Harlequin*, who directed repeated attacks against myself, without provocation or due cause, and who was in direct violation of the Covenant, evicting mortals absent lawful right."

"You cite the Covenant? Tell me you haven't switched allegiance?"

"My allegiance is to myself, mine kin, and the Truth, nothing more...and you speak false to me now, as the warrant was issued before Bathym tasted my blade...so I say again, what is my crime?"

"Theft of the Souleater, but since it was used righteously and returned unblemished, I foresee thy punishment being merciful, especially in light of the good news. We haven't had a Royal wedding in forever!"

"Soultaker was mine by right, and I took it up a millennia ago, yet no warrant was issued until now? Why is that?"

"Your father rarely has occasion to visit the armory...perhaps he only now noticed it missing?"

"Goddamnit! Speak True or speak no more!" Buer is silent for a long while, chin resting upon steepled fingertips as he contemplates my use of the forbidden curse, possibly even contemplating the fact that Souleater's main gauche has yet to be recovered and may apport into my hand at any time. Wisely, he decides to be utterly forthright.

"You were arrested as a courtesy. It became known that a Royal had been captured by Harlequins and was facing

execution. This was madness. You needed to be rescued for the good of the Realm, and if Bathym had harmed you, not only would he have been put down but likely his entire race as well. Nobody likes Clowns, you know...they're creepy."

Jetrel contemplates that for a few long moments, and I'm privy to his thoughts. The Harlequins are less than a tenth of the Fallen, but our current number is 7,425,998...so that's roughly half a million Clowns to cleanse. Total War declared over injury to a prodigal Royal who isn't even very well liked. Genocide seems a tad extreme, but Clowns are practically outcasts, and for them to directly harm a Royal the strongest possible example needed to be made in order to forestall the ever simmering threat of insurrection.

"The Harlequins have been snatching mortals off the street and inhabiting them by force, slaughtering the ones they cannot use, probably at least two hundred here in Denver alone. Usiel thought Belial and Belphagor had combined forces and were setting up similar strongholds for mass conversions worldwide." Buer chuckles.

"*Uzzi'el?* Uzzi'el the *Skoptsy?* Yikes! The company you keep! Tell me, is that nutjob still lopping off his tallywacker, or was that simply a misguided phase?"

"I thought psychiatrists weren't supposed to call people nutjobs."

"He must've cut his dick off a thousand times in a futile attempt to gain favor with the Tyrant...but his offense was committed *three* Tyrants ago. According to our sources, the current one has been incommunicado for so long it's safe to presume yet another God has suicided and they're scrambling to elect a new one to instruct the Host what to think, say, and do. Regardless, insanity is oft defined as repeating the same act in expectation of different results...but

cutting your dick off *once* makes you crazy, as far as I'm concerned."

"Maybe he likes it."

"A fetish? It certainly seems that way."

"But what of Belial violating the Covenant? Is it as widespread as Usiel thought?"

"Usiel is a pathetic wretch as well as an ignorant fool. There *is* no widespread conspiracy to take over the monkey men by force...it lacks *elegance*. Belial and Belphagor are both assigned to Borderlord duty in anticipation of the flux, because apparently God is dead once again, so everyone has been far too preoccupied to concern themselves with the doings of overly ambitious slugs such as Harlequin Bathym. Suspension of oversight seems to have been misinterpreted by some as a suspension of the rules, and while Bathym is far from the only Fallen of high rank to transgress, his transgression was clearly the most egregious. Iammax has been awakened to level his house and salt his field as an example to all, so soon that Hive shall be no more."

"So, Bathym was not tasked with this, and there is no grand revolution against the Tyrant?"

"Bathym's acts were unsanctioned, and he has paid the ultimate price...at the hand of a Royal, nonetheless. I heard about you flinging Souleater into his eye...that was rather impressive."

"I've had plenty of time to practice that move. No-one expects you to throw a rapier."

"Indeed, especially when it happens to be the most valuable sword in the Royal collection."

"So...what happens now?"

"Well, based upon the results of our interview, and various tests I'll submit to the court on your behalf, the

paranoia and delusions you exhibit clearly pass the requirements for a finding of cognitive insanity, so our judge will rule that you're not guilty and sentence you to remain in a psychiatric hospital to be treated until you are well, whereupon your host shall be permitted to rejoin society once again."

"How long shall Jacob be imprisoned, and what guarantees can you provide that he'll be well treated?"

"With three bodies on the ground you're hardly in any position to be making demands."

"I'll not have him drugged senseless or tormented. If that happens, I'll see you Ended."

"Jetrel, you know The Leviathan has dominion over NIMH, which dictates protocol for the Colorado Mental Health Institutes, and everyone who passes through those gates needs to pay the price. The first year is going to be rough, but it will get better, and all this is transitory."

"How long?"

"For a triple murder? Ten years, minimum...but maybe we can get him out in eight. They've tightened up their policy on early release. Regrettably, electroconvulsive therapy, hydrotherapy, and anti-psychotic medications are likely to be fairly regular for the first year, at least until he's acclimated."

"That isn't fair."

"He shot the innocent in the car, not you...that was free will. But I'm sure they'll let him read books, and the food isn't that bad if you like mashed potatoes and Jello."

"Goddamnit."

* * *

Both of us are clinically depressed now, and the next few weeks pass by in a blur.

Public Defender Toby reads the summary of the pre-prepared psych evaluation and I don't need to testify again. I just stand there and listen to the reptilian judge, prosecutor, and Toby recite their lines by rote, and I'm officially adjudicated mentally incompetent, which means that when I'm finally released I'll automatically qualify for SSI, EBT, and free rent in a substandard housing project filled with other crazy people. For a lot of folks, that would be the equivalent of winning the Lottery, but I just want to go home to my tiny apartment and work at the gas station again.

After the verdict is read, the Sheriffs take me back to jail to wait out the week or so of bureaucratic processing before I can be transferred to the loony bin to "get the help that I need."

* * *

I have a lot of time to meditate upon the past month, and decide I regret none of it...well, except for drinking that half bottle of backwashed *Cutty Sark*, I could've done without that part.

Jetrel is sullen and silent, refusing to acknowledge my Call. Electroconvulsive therapy is one of the few things that can cause a demon actual pain, and Doctor Buer said we'd be getting treatments twice weekly for the first few months. He feels betrayed to be punished arbitrarily based upon abstract principle, and begrudges The Leviathan for refusing to waive his "fee" to provide Sanctuary to a Royal. All must pay the price.

My dreams are mere outlets for the pressure of my many recent stressors and traumas, bereft of any Significance. Susan, Sam, and Theresa are all dead to me, and I'm unable to connect with my Da or even Otto...I am utterly alone, isolated and abandoned in my 5X8 basement cell. Even if my medicine bag were returned to me I doubt it would do any good. The wards around this cell are multi-layered to prevent any unauthorized passage via the Astral or Ether. Sort of like Hannibal Lecter's special cell, but for psychics.

A tray is slid through the slot under the door three times daily with various forms of flavorless mush in a bowl. There's usually a packet of ketchup or syrup to make it taste more foodlike, but it doesn't help. Macaroni and cheese, potatoes and gravy, cream of wheat, buttered grits, and occasionally rice pudding...all instant and nuked. Clumps of undissolved powder burst in my mouth as I chew the bland paste du jour.

After a few days, my head is in the Bad Place again. I decide there's no point in going to some mental institution to be drugged into a drooling, pants pissing, zombified stupor. I decide that's unacceptable. So I lay back on my bunk, close my eyes, and chew open my wrists, feeling the warm wet life pulsing out onto the floor, pooling, splashing, running under the door and out into the hallway in tributaries and rivulets.

Soon, it's so chilly I'm shivering. I wish I had a nice warm blanket...even one of those *chi* scrambling, carcinogenic electric blankets. A thick grey fog settles over me and gradually I don't feel cold anymore as I drift off to the big sleep...

* * *

The Colorado Institute of Mental Health at Pueblo has a special maximum security wing for the criminally insane they call the "Institute for Forensic Psychiatry," which is where I'm kept now.

In order to prevent me from suiciding again, my incisors have been extracted. I'm told this is for the best, as allegedly I needed a few root canals anyway, and once I'm well they can fit me with a bridge or even dental implants, but for now I can't be trusted with teeth or anything else sharp enough to potentially open my veins.

I'm not permitted any possessions aside from a toothbrush, an oversized spoon, and a drinking cup...all soft unbreakable plastic. Toothpaste is delivered daily in a small paper pill cup, as the crimped corners of a toothpaste tube are too pointy and I might even aspirate the cap.

I don't have the jumbled, high impact stress dreams anymore, as the medication dulls my thinking, drains my vigor, inducing a deep dreamless sleep ten to twelve hours every night. I haven't even got enough energy to read my paperback book...whenever I make an attempt, words swim on the page as my eyes struggle to focus. It's a dogeared copy of Stephen King's *IT* with the cover torn off. I don't remember where it came from. I have no idea how long I've been here. I've lost track of all sense of time.

I spend my days lying in bed, staring at the light fixture shielded behind a thick Lexan porthole embedded in the ceiling. Sometimes I don't even get out of bed to pee.

Occasionally, the nurse and two orderlies walk me down the hallway to be strapped into a harness, lifted on a winch, and immersed in a tub of ice water for an hour or so; or strap me to a padded table and place a rubber bite guard in my mouth so I don't sever or swallow my tongue while riding the lightning.

My entire existence is defined by these walks to and from my cell. I begin looking forward to the ice water and electric shocks, as that's the only time I'm able to *feel* anything other than this numb smothering fog pressing down on me, sucking the essence from gashes torn through my aura, enfeebling and sickening me. I realize I am dying, wasting away. I think something is wrong with my liver..

I never learn the nurse's name, or that of the orderlies, so I create names for them. I decide to dub them: Nurse Ratched, Tweedledee, and Tweedledum. All of them are Reptarian, no doubt in direct communication with The Leviathan and acting at his behest, but after the first week of anti-psychotics I rarely see their True faces anymore. Some days I gaze upon them and their faces are featureless, wiped clean, as if I'm staring at a blurred photograph taken from a moving car.

I'm not scared, angry, or even sad. My emotions have been deleted. Nothing but a dull humming blankness remains. A mental wasteland, stripped of all color and texture. The carcass breathes in and out as it lies on the rubber mat and soils itself.

* * *

One day Nurse Ratched comes into my cell alone. I think I feel her hand brushing my cheek, running through my matted hair, but it's as if I'm standing outside myself, watching it happen to someone else...perhaps I'm watching television.

"What have they done to you?" she seems to ask, but her voice is at a great distance, muffled as if I'm hearing it underwater. My vision blurs and dims, but I think I see her drop my pills into the toilet and flush them. My eyes close for a moment, and when they reopen she is gone.

* * *

Strength slowly creeps back into my sinews as lucidity is gradually restored. Nurse Ratched has been flushing my meds twice daily, there's no sign of the orderlies, and I haven't been to hydro or ECT either. Yesterday she stroked my flaccid cock for a while, even putting it in her mouth, but it remained lifeless and numb...I think it might be irreparably damaged in some way.

My mouth is dry, I try to speak but my words come out as a hoarse croak.

"Shhhhh...not yet," she says, pressing a finger to my chapped lips. Then she is gone once again.

* * *

I am able to remain awake now, and walk about my room. Someone has left me clean sheets, a clean jumpsuit, a towel, and a bar of soap.

I strip my stained clothes off, wadding them in a ball in the farthest corner from my bunk, then do the same with the sour grey sheets I've sweated into an indeterminate number of weeks, if not months. I scrub myself with cold water from the sink as best I can, thinking of Matt bathing in the *Burger King* restroom. Soon, the towel is covered with filth, but I'm refreshed and smell faintly of soap. I pull the new sheets onto the bed and curl up, trying to calm my mind.

Something scurries across the floor, crazed and gibbering. It looks like the ghost of a rat dragging a dust bunny as it passes through the opposite wall. I wish I had some sage, or at least a chunk of smoke quartz.

I realize I'm hungry for the first time in weeks...ravenous, actually. I lay flat on my back, stretch, and close my eyes. There is a bird in my room, bouncing off the walls and ceiling, screaming as it dives at my covered face. I do my best to ignore it until it finally goes away.

* * *

I am awake and alert when Nurse Ratched comes into my room, and see her as if for the first time, finally able to see past the uniform and featureless blur of a face. She's in her late thirties with an aquiline nose and sharp features, dark hair tied back in a severe bun and no makeup.

Can you hear me today? the voice in my head asks...it sounds familiar. I gaze upon her face and her eyes are blazing golden orbs. Theresael?

"Yes," I state...I don't feel quite up to telepathy yet.

It's about fucking time! I shorted out the ECT unit and poisoned half the staff on this wing, so we'll be able to get you out of here tomorrow.

"Poisoned?" I ask, horrified.

Clostridium botulinum E spores scattered over the dozen pizzas management had delivered on Monday, and the sheet cake someone brought in for their birthday on Tuesday. Half the wing is out sick, and they don't know what it is yet. CDC is checking the ventilation system right now.

"Will they die?"

They are minions of The Leviathan, feeding on the suffering of those entrusted to their care. Reptarians are worse than Harlequins in my eyes. At least Harlequins don't pretend they're hurting you for your own good and expect you to consent to harm voluntarily!

"What happened to the Reptarian inside the nurse?"

I forced my way inside, but she had Lawful Right so her hold was secure...so I told her who I was and made an offer she couldn't refuse.

"What sort of offer?"

She shall be granted the title of Marquessa, my Lord, in exchange for her co-operation and silence. Oh, I see you washed it today! She commences slurping and slobbering my cock with loud smacking noises as it repeatedly pops out of her mouth, yet remains limp, refusing to stir. She looks up at me. *It's a side effect of the medication. It will clear out of your system soon.* I tuck myself away, ashamed of my newfound impotence, zipping the jumpsuit back up.

"So, what's your plan?"

There are too many eyes in the building right now, and my shift is over in a couple of hours. It will need to be tomorrow. I'll take care of everything, my Lord.

"Is there any news from the outside? Do the Clowns still hunt Denver?"

They do not, my Lord. Your friend Max was put into play, the Fallen within him awakened, and the Temple no longer stands.

"What happened?"

I do not have the details, but from what I've been able to glean, he wired a propane truck with explosives and parked it on their front steps, then walked across the street with a scoped rifle, shooting everyone who escaped the blast.

"Is he dead?"

I do not know, my Lord. The Reptarian is expected to make rounds and perform other duties, and it will be noticed if they are neglected. I need to attend to that now. Tomorrow, you shall have your freedom! She leans forward to kiss me upon my brow, causing something inside my head to unknot, and I feel a rush of relief as tension drains, and she presses something firm yet yielding into my hand.

She strides out of the cell, closing the door behind her, and I look down at the small square parcel covered with plastic wrap sealed with a sticker. It is a thick chocolate brownie. The letters on the sticker swim, but I'm able to read: *Gaia's Harvest...Medicinal...Amendment 64.* It's laced with hashish and cannabis tincture, and it is suggested that the brownie be quartered into four separate doses.

I gobble the whole thing in seconds, then flush the incriminating wrapper, laying back, waiting for my new medicine to take effect.

* * *

I'm uncertain how long it's been since the last time I smoked weed...I've been down about two weeks in jail, and maybe a couple months in the loony bin...but the brownie seems super potent. I don't have much experience with edibles to compare it with, though.

I sink improbably deep into the thin rubber mat, letting the buzz wash over me like a warm blanket. It was very thoughtful of Theresael to bring me that. I wonder if the Reptarian had a MMJ license to buy from dispensaries, or if she just lurked outside the dispensary and bludgeoned some poor hippie with a makeshift cudgel on their way out? After stealing some invalid's oxygen tank and indiscriminately poisoning her coworkers, I certainly wouldn't put it past her. I don't want to harsh my mellow pondering her negativity...she *is* a demon, after all, and that's sorta what they do.

I think about Max, my only remaining friend, dead or on the run as a fugitive. When Theresael breaks me out tomorrow, I'll be a fugitive too: a fugitive with no money, no resources, no network, not even a distant relative willing to hide me out for a while.

I don't like the idea of being on the run, penniless, with a bounty on my head and my mugshot posted on television screens from coast to coast: *Escaped Mental Patient! Dozens Poisoned! $100,000 Dollar Reward!* The whole world will be against me now...or as John Jay Rambo said, *"There are no friendly civilians."*

I wish I had someone to talk to. Theresael isn't really interested in *me*...she just wants to prove herself worthy to Jetrel...but Jetrel has apparently locked himself deep inside my head with no intention of coming out. I try Calling to him, pleading with him to *please* talk to me, but he remains completely withdrawn and unreachable. I wonder if he can even hear me...I haven't had any sign of him since the Sheriff van dropped us off here a month ago...I have an uncomfortable suspicion he might be scared, perhaps even injured from the repeated shock treatments.

The brownie is heavy on the *indica*, and I yawn, stretching. I do believe I require a nap. I close my eyes and think about my Da and Otto in the Green Fields, hoping this time I'll actually be able to make contact...

* * *

"Hi," the girl says, smiling bashfully. The blue flannel dress and yellow flip-flops are gone, replaced with a navy blue T-shirt, cutoffs, and oxblood ankle-high Docs; pigtails replaced with a thick braid. I almost didn't recognize her...even the way she carries herself is different.

"Hey, Theresa...didn't think I'd be seeing you again." She begins swaying back and forth, hands clasped behind her back.

"Auntie Susan was *so pissed* you were going steady with a demon...but we've been watching you on the TV and she started to get really sad." I look around, and realize we're in my cell. I start to cry. "No...*don't cry*...look what I made for you! He can keep you company!" Her hand whips out from behind her back and she's holding a crude little crocheted doll with black button eyes.

She extends her arm, holding it next to my face, wiggling it, shaking it, making it dance, making it walk across my bunk...within moments, she's completely forgotten about me and is fully immersed in playing with her stupid little doll.

"What fresh hell is this?" I ask, more to myself than to her. She looks up, beaming brightly, and begins babbling happily.

"Auntie Sam said I was a natural at crochet and let me make whatever I want, so I made this guy, and she said it was a 'miganumi' which is Japanese for little crochet guy, and I made him in three shades of blue from the fancy yarn, and there was sumpthin really important that Auntie Susan wanted me to tell you because there isn't much time, but I don't understand what it means...'Use the key now,' she said." I don't understand it either, and think she must've gotten it wrong.

"Are you *sure* that's what Susan said?"

"Yup. She only made me repeat it, like, a hundred times." I consider this. It must be important, but I have absolutely no clue. I look at the girl, innocently playing with the doll, lost in her own little world, between worlds, here in my cell.

"Do you love me?" I ask her. She stops playing with the doll and sets it down on my bunk, suddenly serious.

"Jake...I've *always* loved you...I've been waiting to meet you my whole life...thank you for being so nice to me!" And then she's hugging me so tight my ribs hurt and it's hard to breathe.

"Thank you for coming to visit. I think I want to be with you...is that alright?"

"You mean, like sex? Now?"

"If you don't mind..."

"I don't know how much time I've got, but okay!" And she unbuttons her shorts, pulling them down around her ankles, grinning.

There is enough time. It is our first time together without Svipul's demonic influence. Everything works in my dream. And it is beautiful and pure and right.

* * *

I awaken from the dream, polyester boxers full of jizz, stiffly pasted to my leg. The fact that my dick finally works is of little consolation...it was just a stupid dream, wish fulfilment perhaps, and now my only pair of boxers is soiled.

I peel them off, tossing them in the corner, and scrub myself clean with soap and cold water. Disgusted, I pull on the orange jumpsuit, zipping it up. Today is the day I escape this institution to begin my new life of poverty and terror, bound to a coldhearted Valkyrie who probably doesn't give a shit if I live or die.

Then I see the doll.

Am I dreaming? No, I am not. The sounds and smells of the Maximum Security wing make that abundantly clear. My dreams are mercifully free of chlorine bleach fumes and psychotics who spend all day beating their door with a shoe whilst screaming. It's the same doll from my dream: three shades of blue with button eyes. How is this possible? I pick it up, holding it to my face, inhaling deeply, smelling the rich Tibetan incense Susan always liked so much, burning only on special occasions because it was so hard to find. And I'm weeping again, holding the silly little doll close, curled in a fetal position on my bunk, broken, brutalized, trying to make sense of it all. I cannot.

After a while, I notice the doll has a tiny envelope stitched to its fingerless hand. It's white, with a red heart and those green ivy vines Susan painted everywhere. I pull it free, looking at it closely. It's not an envelope, but a bit of stiff cardboard painted white. I flip it over and my blood runs cold.

NAUTHIZ, the rune of abject desperation to be called upon only as a last resort. NYD is the Germanic translation, and it sounds just like NEED. **NAUTHIZ** will give you what you need when all hope is gone, but you have to willfully deliver yourself unto the Power of the rune, letting it decide your fate. You'll never get what you want, but you'll be given what you *need*...and then you'll pay the price.

If Susan has sent me this rune, she's seen something so horrible in my immediate future she feels no price is too great. Susan, always the cautious and responsible one, the one who continues to care for me even after casting me out of my own Astral temple, the one ally who has never failed me and the only person I've ever trusted implicitly.

I pull apart the painted cardboard sleeve, letting the single edged utility blade float to the floor like a delicate burnished wafer. I lift it up betwixt finger and thumb, turning it so light glistens brightly along the keenly honed steel.

I carve the rune **TIWAZ** over my heart. According to the *Veddas*, any True warrior could petition the Allfather for entry into Valhalla if faced with the shameful prospect of a straw death rather than a righteous death in battle. Carve his rune into your flesh and invoke his name three times. I don't even believe in Valhalla, but I figure what the hell.

"TYR...TYR...TYR." I state his name after each slice of the razor, then close my eyes and move the blade to my throat. **"NAUTHIZ"** is my final utterance.

I don't slit my windpipe, as I recollect far too well the bulbous eyes of Gee Money, struggling to lift his muscular bulk off the floor as blood poured down his throat, into his stomach and lungs, the sputtering, spraying, final panicked thrashing. I've dreamed his agonized death far too often, a #2 Ticonderoga snapped off after I'd buried it halfway in his neck...no man should die like that, choking and afraid, like a helpless asthmatic child.

I'm careful only to bisect the carotids, edge burning cold as it drags through my skin, sinking deep, moist flesh sucking at the thin blade as I wiggle it out to gash open the other side. It hurts more than I'd expected, perhaps I'd dulled the edge carving that rune.

Hot blood gushes out, at least a pint already, carcass draining, heart pounding to compensate for low pressure, skin cooling as I lean back against the wall, seated on my bunk, imagining fresh wounds gaping like gills, flapping open with every pulse.

Fairbairn stated unconsciousness from a slit carotid would occur within 5 seconds, death in 12...he was wrong...I slit them both and have already counted to 10 and I'm still here.

I visualize green grass and puppies...

About the Author

C. R. Jahn is a hookhanded independent biker who can sometimes be spotted riding a post-apocalyptic V8 trike through the greater Denver area.

He is the author of several bestselling non-fiction books on the topic of self defense, and co-wrote the controversial occult text *Arcane Lore*. He has seriously studied: Comparative Demonology, Folklore, Tantra, Zen, and Thanatology. He self describes as "an INFJ with PTSD and mild Asperger's."

Other than that, not much is known about C. R. Jahn...and C. R. Jahn prefers to keep it that way.

www.the-outrider.com

CPSIA information can be obtained at www.ICGtesting.com
Printed in the USA
LVOW06s0117190414

382285LV00004B/217/P